"I thought I was to be asked to leave."

"We could never get on without you," Jareth murmured, turning to face her.

The words touched something in Chloe, a distant hope, a desire held at bay. It must have shone in her eyes as she raised her gaze to his. "You could not?"

He seemed to realize his error. His expression sobered.

She lowered her gaze, ashamed of what he might see in her eyes. The touch of his fingers along her chin made her catch her breath. They were warm and smooth, and tiny shivers of excitement shot forth like sparks from a flint to singe her cheek and sizzle down her neck.

"Sweet Lord, Chloe, are you never satisfied with anything? Do you always need to push me beyond comfort?" His words were harsh, but they were spoken in a tone that was almost a caress....

D1040314

Dear Reader,

Autumn is such a romantic season—fall colors, rustling leaves, big sweaters and, for many of you, the kids are back in school! So, as the leaves fall, snuggle up in a cozy chair and let us sweep you away to the romantic past!

Rising star Jacqueline Navin returns with her *fourth* Harlequin Historical novel since her publishing debut in March of 1998. Her latest, *Strathmere's Bride,* stays true to her passionate and emotional style. In this Regency-style historical tale, a duke who is now the single father of his two orphaned nieces intends to marry—quickly. He courts a lovely and proper woman, but is much more intrigued by the very *improper* governess running about with his nieces. Will he choose duty, or desire…?

Bestselling author Ruth Langan brings us the final book in THE O'NEIL SAGA, *Briana*. Set in England and Ireland, this is the tale of a feisty Irish noblewoman and the lonely, tormented landowner who first saves her life—and then succumbs to her charms! In *The Doctor's Wife* by the popular Cheryl St.John, scandalous secrets are revealed but love triumphs when a waitress "from the other side of the tracks" marries a young doctor in need of a mother for his baby girl. And don't miss *Branded Hearts* by Diana Hall, a Western chock-full of juicy surprises. Here, a young cowgirl bent on revenge must fight her feelings for her boss, an enigmatic cattle rancher.

Enjoy. And come back again next month for four more choices of the best in historical romance.

Sincerely,

Tracy Farrell
Senior Editor

P.S. We'd love to hear what you think about Harlequin Historicals! Drop us a line at:

Harlequin Historicals
300 E. 42nd Street, 6th Floor
New York, NY 10017

Strathmere's Bride

Jacqueline Navin

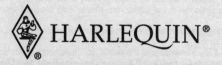

HARLEQUIN®

TORONTO • NEW YORK • LONDON
AMSTERDAM • PARIS • SYDNEY • HAMBURG
STOCKHOLM • ATHENS • TOKYO • MILAN • MADRID
PRAGUE • WARSAW • BUDAPEST • AUCKLAND

If you purchased this book without a cover you should be aware
that this book is stolen property. It was reported as "unsold and
destroyed" to the publisher, and neither the author nor the
publisher has received any payment for this "stripped book."

ISBN 0-373-29079-9

STRATHMERE'S BRIDE

Copyright © 1999 by Jacqueline Lepore Navin

All rights reserved. Except for use in any review, the reproduction or
utilization of this work in whole or in part in any form by any electronic,
mechanical or other means, now known or hereafter invented, including
xerography, photocopying and recording, or in any information storage
or retrieval system, is forbidden without the written permission of the
publisher, Harlequin Enterprises Limited, 225 Duncan Mill Road,
Don Mills, Ontario, Canada M3B 3K9.

All characters in this book have no existence outside the imagination of
the author and have no relation whatsoever to anyone bearing the same
name or names. They are not even distantly inspired by any individual
known or unknown to the author, and all incidents are pure invention.

This edition published by arrangement with Harlequin Books S.A.

® and TM are trademarks of the publisher. Trademarks indicated with
® are registered in the United States Patent and Trademark Office, the
Canadian Trade Marks Office and in other countries.

Visit us at www.romance.net

Printed in U.S.A.

JACQUELINE NAVIN

lives with her husband and three small children in Maryland, where she works in private practice as a psychologist. Writing has been her hobby since the sixth grade, and she has boxes full of incomplete manuscripts to prove it.

When asked, as she often is, how she finds time in her busy schedule to write, she replies that it is not a problem—thanks to the staunch support of her husband, who is not unused to doing the dinner dishes and tucking the kids into bed. However, finding time to do the laundry—that's the problem. Jacqueline would love to hear from readers. Please write to her at P.O. Box 1611, Bel Air, MD 21014.

This is Lindsey's book—my Chloe,
my very own little flibbertigibbet.
How well I know how trying they can be.
And how precious.

Chapter One

Northumberland, England, 1847

There was no doubt about it, Jareth Hunt, Duke of Strathmere, thought as he gazed out his study window at his two nieces and their governess frolicking on the grass. Chloe Pesserat was entirely unacceptable.

Narrowing his eyes, he shook his head in disapproval. The woman in question reclined prostrate on the blanket she had strewn on the closely clipped lawn, her head propped upon her two palms and one of her legs bent so that her foot—her shoeless foot!—turned lazy circles in the air. Miss Pesserat looked more as if she were in a bedroom than in a public place. Why, her entire stockinged leg was exposed. A very shapely one, with a finely tapered calf and slender ankle…

Inserting a forefinger inside the tightly knotted cravat, Jareth pulled hard, but he still had difficulty swallowing. The fire, he thought, glancing blamefully at the hearth. It blazed far too brightly for such a fine day as this. The weather was unseasonably warm, he noticed just now.

Unlatching the casement, he cracked the window to let in some fresh air. The high-pitched shouts of his eldest niece carried inside, making him wince. Rebeccah, who was five years of age, hooted and ran about, flapping her arms and chanting something unintelligible in a very loud, obnoxious voice.

He frowned at her ridiculous antics. She looked demented—completely unsuitable for the daughter of the late Duke of Strathmere. Yet, as unsightly as it was, he preferred Rebeccah's annoying behavior to the way three-year-old Sarah sat so silently, her tiny fingers clutching a withered flower left over from last summer.

Rebeccah cried, "And then what happened?"

"Then the prince carried off the evil dragon!" Miss Pesserat's voice held only a trace of a French accent, making it sound musical and lilting and undeniably enchanting.

"Hurrah!" exclaimed Rebeccah. "Kill the dragon!" She commenced with the leaping and shrieking once again.

"And then..." Miss Pesserat said in a provocative way, holding up a slender finger.

Rebeccah froze. "Yes?" she urged gleefully.

"He came back for the princess and..." She paused, and in chorus the two voices chimed, "They lived happily ever after!"

Rebeccah clapped and jumped in place. Miss Pesserat turned to Sarah and prodded her with a set of wiggling fingers, making the little girl smile.

But no laugh. Jareth's heart constricted as he watched his youngest niece, solemn little Sarah, who had uttered not one single sound since the accident that took her parents' lives three months ago.

Sheer bad luck, an error in the driver's judgment, a ripple in the fabric of destiny—something unexplainable had caused Jareth's elder brother's carriage to overturn on a hairpin curve and spill down a sharp, craggy ravine. The duke and duchess were killed. Blessedly, the children, who had been with them, had survived. But not unscarred. Rebeccah had been injured, but her physical recovery had been swift.

Oddly, Sarah had escaped with nary a scratch, except that she no longer possessed a loving mother, a devoted father or the ability to speak. It wasn't that she had any physical damage to her vocal cords. The once exuberant child had simply ceased talking. She made no sounds, in fact—not crying, not laughter, not the tiniest noise since the accident.

That terrible event had also left Jareth the seventh duke, riddled with grief and utterly miserable. Gone was the life he had led as a contented second son. His business, his friends, his much valued freedom were gone. All he had now was duty. Duty to the duchy and duty to his family, his nieces in particular. And one big headache in the bargain. Miss Chloe Pesserat.

Miss Pesserat scrambled to her feet, pausing to slip on a discarded slipper. As she balanced on one foot, she held out her slender arms in a delicate move that was reminiscent of the prima ballerinas Jareth had seen on the Paris stage. Miss Chloe, as the little girls called her, possessed an uncanny grace. It was evident in her smallest movement, making each motion extraordinarily…well, beautiful.

She now began a very *un*graceful chase of Rebeccah, claiming to be the dragon come back for revenge. Rebeccah squealed, declaring herself the prince and facing off against the evil monster. Sarah smiled, running when her sister warned her of the mortal danger she was in, but still in silence. Always in silence.

Jareth watched Rebeccah, who looked joyful at this moment. She seemed, as far as anyone could surmise, to have survived the loss of her parents without incident, except of course for the howling night terrors. Almost every night in the wee hours before dawn, Jareth was told, the five-year-old hovered in some netherworld between sleep and wakefulness, her thrashing and sobbing so alarming as to send normally affectionate servants scurrying away in tears. The only one who could quiet her, and not without effort, was Miss Chloe.

Jareth scowled, returning his regard to the young woman carrying on in the most indecorous manner, issuing sounds no human had any business making, skirts hitched up almost to her knees.

"Outrageous, isn't she?" a cultured voice asked from behind him.

Jareth nodded. Now the chit tumbled Rebeccah onto the ground. As they rolled about, they kicked up chunks of mud. Dark stains appeared on their skirts.

"Abominable," his mother said.

"Is there no way to dismiss her?" Jareth asked. Really, this was preposterous. Cavorting like village urchins!

"The doctor said absolutely not. Both girls' nerves are fragile. He is fearful of what would happen if they had to do without her. He believes they have transferred their affections to their Miss Chloe. Losing her, so quickly after the loss of...'' The dowager duchess faltered only a little, but to her son, who had never heard his mother's voice so much as quiver throughout all of this wretched tragedy, it was as startling as her dissolving into tears.

He remained perfectly rigid, knowing any sign that he had noticed her distress would be inappropriate. When she spoke again, her voice was restored. ''The loss of their parents, it might be devastating.''

''Has anyone spoken to her?''

''I have, on numerous occasions.'' A long, indrawn breath, then a protracted sigh. ''She refuses to heed my instruction and makes no secret of telling me so. She informed me that the children need joy in their lives, that propriety and convention need to be suspended during this period of time she referred to as 'mending.'''

Jareth snorted.

''My sentiments exactly, Strathmere.'' Strange how easily his mother altered his name, and with no sign that only a short time ago a different son went by that title, a son now dead. He was no longer Jareth. He was Strathmere, even to his mother. Everything was altered irrevocably, even that primal bond with the woman who bore him thirty-one years ago.

She continued, ''I was hopeful that you could be more forceful with her.''

''Certainly,'' he said with conviction. He observed that Miss Pesserat had swung Rebeccah onto her back and was galloping about like some kind of maniacal racehorse.

''Disgraceful.'' Just by the tone of his mother's

voice, Jareth could imagine her top lip curled in contempt.

At that moment, the object of their disapproval's eye caught his through the open window. She stopped, the wide smile freezing on her face for a moment, then wilting rapidly until it was gone. Oblivious to the change, Rebeccah urged her on.

She certainly looked normal enough. Unflinching under his regard, she was merely an unremarkable girl, perhaps a bit pretty, with gray-blue eyes of a strange quality, tilted-up nose and wide, mobile mouth. Her hair hung in dark strands about her face, almost completely out of the sloppy knot sagging on the back of her head.

Not beautiful, no. But something about her made a man look twice.

She dropped her skirts into place and reached around to catch Rebeccah as she straightened. The child slid safely to the ground, grumping her disappointment at the end of their game.

His mother whispered in his ear, "I know you only arrived yesterday, but I want you to see her as soon as possible. We have visitors coming later today, and it would be unthinkable for them to witness anything similar to what we've just seen. You remember the Rathfords? You met Lord and Lady Rathford, and their delightful daughter Helena, when last you visited."

"Yes," he answered curtly, never taking his gaze from the girl. Miss Pesserat, his late sister-in-law's cousin who had come all the way from France to care for Sarah and Rebeccah, was giving the girls orders in her charmingly accented voice as she balled up the blanket into a messy armful.

Rebeccah, it seemed, was having none of it. Miss Pesserat handled the recalcitrant child's protests with a firm tone and determined repetition of her request for cooperation. Eventually, Rebeccah stomped off toward the house.

For Sarah, Miss Pesserat only had to extend her hand and the little girl came up and took it. Jareth battled a fresh wash of pain as he considered how changed this little sprite was from the lively two-year-old he had met on his last visit, only seven months ago.

"Be firm," his mother urged. He heard the rustle of her dress as she headed toward the door. Before she left, she added in a stiff, grudging voice, "But do not be unkind. The children need her. God help us, *we* need her."

Miss Pesserat and the children disappeared around the corner, presumably to enter through the kitchens. His mother was gone. The soft click of the door told him he was alone.

Jareth Hunt let his head drop and felt the weariness lay claim to every inch of his body.

Chloe managed to settle the girls into their beds for a much needed nap, but it wasn't easy. She had to promise Rebeccah there would be her favorite biscuits on the tea tray when the child awoke, but that was not a problem. Cook always did little favors for Chloe. Cook was French, and though the two of them had never set eyes on each other before coming to Strathmere, Cook considered them related, as countrymen if not kinsmen.

Humming lightly, Chloe crossed to Sarah's bed. The child lay clutching her bear, the one with the

mottled fur, which had weathered too many hugs
from sticky hands. He was missing his left eye and
several seams had to be restitched on a regular basis.

Touching Sarah's white-blond hair, Chloe smiled.
"Good Samuel will guard your dreams."

Samuel was the bear's name. Much too solemn an
appellation for a fellow blessed with so much love,
Chloe had always thought, but it had been his name
before she arrived seven months ago to care for her
cousin Bethany's children, and so it stayed.

Under the tender ministrations of her soothing
voice and the lightest of touches as she stroked the
child's hair, Sarah was asleep in no time. Chloe crept
to Rebeccah's bed. The girl's mouth gaped open, and
she snored lightly. Dear, impulsive, bossy, demanding Rebeccah. Chloe's heart felt tight gazing at her.
In some ways, this child's scars were deeper than her
sister's. Chloe knew well the horrors the girl kept
buried within.

She closed her eyes. *Dearest Bethany, I shall look
after them. I shall see them out of the shadows. Send
your love to help me, cousin, and show me how.*

A young upstairs maid named Mary appeared at
the door. She nodded when Chloe laid a finger to her
lips. Silently Mary held up a letter.

"Thank you," Chloe whispered softly, coming to
take it. Mary followed Chloe as she exited the girls'
bedchamber and walked across the playroom to her
own small chamber.

The missive was from Papa. Chloe recognized the
handwriting immediately. How she loved his long,
chatty letters, full of news of her family. How she
missed them all. Oh, she longed for home, that lazy,
contented life in the Loire Valley, with everyone

around her she had known since birth and no one frowning at her in disapproval or thinking her daft just because she laughed out loud.

"And his grace wishes to see you in his study when you have finished with the girls," Mary added in a hushed tone.

Chloe's head snapped up. She had known it was only a matter of time before she was summoned before the new duke.

She had seen him on two occasions. The first time was yesterday when he arrived. He had not come to his brother's funeral, as he had been abroad and his last visit was a month before she herself had arrived at Strathmere. From her window, she had watched as he alighted from a stylish charcoal brougham. Lean, elegant, dressed impeccably in tailcoat and pants with a single, sharp crease, his snow-white shirt crisply pressed, he looked exactly as a duke should. Except for his dark chestnut hair. His hair surprised her a little, for it was left to curl loosely about his crown, not slicked back with Macassar oil as was the fashion. Of course, he kept it neatly trimmed, but there was something untamed about that hair. And, she had thought in her brief glimpse of him today through the library window—her second sighting— something soulful in the large, deep brown eyes.

She didn't dread the upcoming confrontation with him, but she didn't savor it, either. It was just that it was tiring to battle the mighty Hunt family's disapproval all the time just for the privilege of being herself.

Glancing at the letter in her hand, she felt a sharp pang of homesickness. Squaring her shoulders, she put the letter on her bedside table to be enjoyed later.

To Mary, she said, "Tell him I shall be down directly. I just want to tidy up."

Mary's gaze swept the length of Chloe's dress, then she giggled. Chloe sighed, looking down at herself. She was a mess. She always seemed to be untidy. She was never quite sure how that happened.

It took her only a few minutes to change her dress into a pretty muslin print and restyle her hair in a simple twist. Of course, the results were hardly impressive. She was not particularly talented with hair. Too impatient, she supposed.

Peering closer at the small pier glass, she saw her reflection was one of a pleasant-faced girl with good skin and clear, unusual eyes of blue, overlaid with wisps of pale, pale gray. Her father always said her eyes looked like a stormy sea. She liked that. Her nose was pretty, too, sort of small with a tiny slope at the tip. Her mouth was large, with wide full lips that had a tendency to break into an infectious smile.

A pleasant-faced girl, certainly, but not a true beauty, which pleased her just fine. Beauties, like her late cousin Bethany, had too much responsibility living up to everyone else's expectations or apologizing for their good looks. Bethany had spent enormous effort trying to convince everyone that even though she was beautiful, she was still a nice person.

With a last pat for her hair, she went down to the library. Pausing just outside the threshold of the room that was now the new duke's domain, she drew in a bracing breath. The dowager duchess wanted to dismiss her, that she already knew, and perhaps the duke agreed. The ironic thing was, she wanted to go, but she couldn't let that happen for two very good reasons. One's name was Rebeccah, and the other's was Sarah.

With a perfunctory knock on the door, she let herself in.

Chapter Two

Jareth turned to greet Miss Pesserat as she came into the room.

She looked much different than she had earlier, which was an improvement, for her hair was neater and her dress clean.

And then again, it was not an improvement. Her face was plain, devoid of expression, and that fascinating mobility he had seen when she was with the children was gone.

She sketched a neat curtsy for him. "Your grace wished to see me?"

"Yes. Please have a seat, Miss Pesserat."

"Thank you."

She sat, folding her hands on her lap, and waited. The picture of decorum.

Jareth pulled himself up straight, clasped his hands behind his back and began to speak. "Miss Pesserat, I believe you know why I have asked to see you today."

"Yes, of course. You disapprove of me, *non?*"

Jareth stopped. Chloe just stared back at him with

wide, innocent eyes. They were so *pale*. Haunting eyes. Eyes that could look clear through a person.

"Those are your words, not mine. I prefer to use my own, for they will convey my meaning more directly, so if you will be patient, please."

He was satisfied with the demure expression she donned. He continued, "Principally, I am distressed at your behavior. It has come to my attention that you are leading my nieces in daily activities that are filled with far too much play."

"Children should play."

"Of course, Miss Pesserat. Please do not think to twist my words to put me at the defense." Her lashes swept down, betraying her. Oh, Miss Pesserat knew exactly what she was doing. And she was very good at it. "Play is essential, but not the only thing that must be present in a child's life. Discipline, for example, must serve to balance."

"I quite agree, your grace."

"What I have observed since I have arrived home is a deplorable lack of discipline in the children. They are allowed to romp about most indecorously—"

She held up a slender hand in one of those gestures that seemed as light as air. "Pardon, your grace. I do not understand, *in-dec-roos-ly*."

"Like urchins in the streets of London, *mademoiselle*," he explained impatiently. "I observed them today gadding about in a most unseemly fashion out on the lawn. Their behavior would have disgraced this family should a visitor happened to have seen such screeching and laughter as was taking place."

"I am sorry we disturbed you." She looked up, as if troubled. "You dislike laughter?"

Jareth narrowed his eyes. "When appropriate, I do not, Miss Pesserat, disapprove of laughter, of course. However, hysterics are a different matter."

She smiled and nodded. Her smile lit up her face, transforming it and warming the room. "That is good, because the children need to laugh. It is joy that will chase their sadness away. They need to learn how to live again, your grace. To enjoy what life can give them." Frowning slightly, she asked, "Do you not agree that life is to be enjoyed?"

Despite her disconcerting remarks, Jareth countered without hesitation. "Yes, I do indeed. In its proper place, enjoyment is essential to a satisfactory existence. But there are other things that make for a complete life. Duty and responsibility, for example, and conducting yourself with dignity and self-respect. And all things in moderation, Miss Pesserat."

She wrinkled her nose. "You English put much stock in all of that *mod-a-ray-shon.*"

Was she mocking him? "Are you saying you think it useless to know how to hold oneself with dignity?"

Her spine stiffened visibly. "The French have dignity."

Now she had made it sound as if he were insulting her heritage. He sighed, shaking his head in exasperation. "If you wish to misunderstand me apurpose, I can do nothing to stop you, but I suggest you listen closely to my words to avoid unpleasantness. I believe I am being quite clear. We—my mother and I—would like you to alter the haphazard way in which you perform your duties. The children must be schooled in their manners and appropriate decorum befitting their station. You have an obligation to instruct them in these things, Miss Pesserat, as is your duty as governess.''

''I agree with you, I do.'' Chloe paused, seeming troubled. ''But not at this time, your grace. They are recovering from an unspeakable event—''

''More the reason to establish normal routines,'' he interjected forcefully, ''to help them recover and enjoy the security of a structured environment.''

''I disagree,'' she countered. Jareth couldn't help a grudging admiration at her courage, for as much as he did not appreciate it, he couldn't fault her for it. She was fighting for what she believed in, fighting for the sake of the children.

But she was, of course, wrong.

''They need love and joy,'' she insisted.

''In measure, Miss Pesserat, in measure.''

She stood in a breathtakingly fluid movement. ''No, in abundance, sir.''

He stared at her, donning the careful languid laziness those of his class cultivated to handle such vulgar outbursts of emotion. After a long pause, she sat back down. He said in a clipped, precise voice, ''If you have reined yourself under control, we can resume our conversation.''

''But there is nothing to discuss. You and I disagree. You are in charge, but I am the one with the children in my care. What precisely do you suggest we discuss?''

Surprisingly, she had summed the situation up quite succinctly. They were at an impasse.

However, before Jareth had ever dreamed he would inherit the dukedom from his brother, he had spent eleven years in the business world. He had started a shipping business with an adept young commoner, a man by the name of Colin Burke, who had won a sturdy vessel in a game of cards. Jareth's infusion of capital created Burke and Hunt Shipping. They started with one ship. The fleet grew over the years. Colin captained his own vessel and dealt with the local merchants in each port of call, but Jareth had been the one to move among his peers, culling investors and striking deals among the aristocracy.

He was a duke by birth, but a deal maker by trade. Why hadn't he thought of that before?

"We should discuss a compromise, Miss Pesserat," he said at last. "Since we both have differing views, as you so aptly put it, but both sincerely want what is best for my nieces, then I suppose we must find some way to meld our ideas together."

He could see she was suspicious. "A truce?"

"A compromise. Meeting halfway."

"I know what compromise means." She wasn't ready to give in. "What do you suggest?"

"A parceling of time, as it were." He sat down across from her and leaned forward, wanting to meet her eye-to-eye. When he had wanted to intimidate her, he took the advantage of having her seated and him standing, but now they were going to *compromise* and so should meet as equals. Or so it would appear.

"What I suggest, Miss Pesserat, is that the children's time be structured to include a substantial amount of time for play. This would have to be conducted within the confines of the nursery, however. Of course, there should be occasional outings, but these should proceed in an orderly fashion with an eye toward their education. Perhaps a stroll to the pond to observe the ducks and other aspects of nature.'' She was sitting perfectly still. He inclined his head forward and lowered his voice slightly, lending an illusion of conspiracy. ''During these times they will conduct themselves as ladies should, you understand. The kind of romping the children presently engage in should be kept to contained places where they may not be inadvertently observed. The walled garden beyond the kitchens, for example, is a lovely place.''

She remained quiet. This encouraged him. ''Also, I am told their manners at tea are atrocious. I should like to begin taking tea with them so as to help with their instruction in this regard.''

Chloe felt her eyes snap wide and a snorting sort of laugh escaped her before she could stop it. She brought her hand up quickly over her mouth. Visions of the duke seated at the tea table with the children, observing their antics—which were, she would agree, deplorable for gentle company but perfectly natural for children of their age—were decidedly funny.

The duke snapped his mouth shut and stared at her. She disliked that look. She had seen it before. It was how the dowager duchess always regarded her.

Coughing, she brought herself under control. ''I am sorry, your grace. Please continue.''

He waited a good minute or more before he spoke again. ''I wish to be more involved with my nieces, and I shall be. I will be overseeing their instruction and so I expect to see progress in the areas of self-discipline.'' He leaned back in his chair and laced his fingers together over his chest.

Chloe had had enough pretense. Politely, she said,

"But that is no compromise, your grace. It is what you have wanted all along."

He didn't move, didn't even blink.

Then he smiled. It wasn't a warm smile.

"Miss Pesserat," he began with studious patience. "I am going to see that my nieces are brought up as proper ladies of their station should be, with or without your cooperation."

Was he threatening her? "*Monsieur,* are you saying you will dismiss me if I do not agree?"

"If you think your position in this house, and in those children's lives, is utterly inalterable, I will tell you, Miss Pesserat, that I will not hesitate to terminate your employment here regardless of the dire warning of the doctor—of which I can only assume you are aware, since you seem uncannily sure of yourself. This I will do *if* I determine the damage to the children would be greater if you were to stay than to go."

A sick, heavy feeling pressed down on her chest, making her feel slightly ill. Chloe tried to determine whether or not he was bluffing.

Not that she cared a whit for the position. Or Strathmere or England for that matter. But the children...

That she could not have. It was a sacred trust her beloved cousin had given her. Bethany had brought her into her children's lives to help strike a balance between the constraints of the girls' societal position and the more simple pleasures life had to offer.

Friends since girlhood, Bethany had always said Chloe had a talent for living. Chloe hadn't understood what she meant, for the manner in which she approached life was completely natural to her. How-

ever, she had recognized the blatant appeal in her
cousin's letter and accepted the position. When she
arrived at Strathmere, she had seen immediately what
Bethany had feared—that her precious daughters
would miss out on all the *joie de vivre* and lead, if
it were up to the dowager duchess, a dreary existence
dominated by etiquette, restraint and, above all, *moderation.*

Chloe looked at Jareth with cool assessment.
"You would pitch the children into another loss so
soon after the death of their parents just so you might
have your way? Is it so important, then, to win?"

He was visibly taken aback, stunned to hear it put
that way. Recovering quickly, he countered, "I will
take whatever steps necessary to protect and guide
my nieces."

"You spent too many years at the bargaining table, your grace. Your mother loved to tell everyone
of your great success, so I know you were a very
good businessman. But this is not a cargo we are
speaking of, but little ones, precious to me."

"And to me," he added sharply.

She shook her head. "You do not even know
them. You were not here when they lost their mama
and papa. You do not hold Rebeccah in your arms
at night while she cries out. You say you know what
is best for them, but how can you know?"

He paled. "How can *you?*" he challenged, but his
voice lost its edge.

She gave him a little smile. "I do not know, your
grace. I only follow what is in my heart."

He stayed silent, watching her with those dark,
dark eyes. They were like pools of pitch. Something
passed over them, an indefinable emotion Chloe

didn't understand. She didn't have any hope of him comprehending what she was trying to accomplish with the children, and she certainly didn't expect to win his approval. But she would not be dismissed.

Drawing in a long breath, he said, in a steady, deep voice, "I will not argue with you, Miss Pesserat. I have a duty to my nieces that I shall see done to the best of my ability. You—" he paused "—shall make your own choices."

"Yes," she said quietly, standing. "You speak of duty as if only a duke could truly know its meaning. I have a duty as well, your grace."

With that, she strode to the door, bracing herself for some comment, some parting gibe he would throw out in order to have the last word. When it didn't come, she placed her hand on the doorknob and glanced back over her shoulder. The duke was watching her, body stiff, face inscrutable.

It was then it struck her that she had been wrong. He wasn't interested in "winning," as she had accused him. She saw the troubled look on his face and it wasn't anger. He truly cared about his nieces. He wanted what was best for them.

But he was, of course, wrong.

She turned back around and left, heading to her room.

It didn't matter what his motives were. Chloe loved her cousin's daughters with a fierce protectiveness, no less than if they had been her own. She would not allow the duke to destroy them, even if he did it with the best of intentions.

Chapter Three

In the drawing room, Helena Rathford arranged her skirts with a quick flick of her wrist, then gave a nod to her accompanist seated at the pianoforte. Her mother nodded back and struck the first chord.

Jareth watched the young woman, impressed with her grace, her self-possession, her lovely face. Hers was a commanding kind of beauty—strong, high cheekbones with slashing hollows underneath, thin lips of bright primrose, a fine nose and chin, all framed with silvery-blond hair. She closed her pale lashes over ice-blue eyes, drew in a breath and began to sing.

Her voice was magnificent. Jareth stood transfixed for a moment as Helena gave life to the notes. It appeared to be almost painful, as if she dragged the melody up from her soul to set it free into the air.

Something, the touch of her gaze perhaps, made him glance at his mother. She was looking back at him, a crafty, knowing smile just slightly twisting her lips. Her eyes slid away, but there was satisfaction in them, he saw.

Jareth was no idiot, which was what he would

have to have been to be oblivious to his mother's intentions with regard to Lady Helena Rathford. He glanced up, examining the woman his mother wanted him to marry. Beauty, breeding, accomplished in the arts, congenial and pleasant. His mother's discriminating taste had ferreted out a superior specimen of womanly excellence.

The music washed over him, and he let it take him with it as it built. His gaze drifted to the window. To the night, and to the stars, spilled across the sky like a thousand brilliant diamonds on black velvet. They were his great love, the stars. So beautiful, so mysterious. Complex, yet predictable, stable. Each season bringing its own patterns to study, to wonder about, yet an ever changing panorama.

Strange, but he felt so emotional just now. Perhaps it was Helena's impassioned song, perhaps it was being home after so long, perhaps grief. He didn't know. He only knew a bleak sadness was welling up inside him, hardening his throat and pricking the back of his eyes.

That was when he saw the movement. Down in the garden, a shadow flitting among the symmetrical boxwoods. Dark gray against the paler color of the night sky, it was the figure of a woman.

She moved out into the open. She must have heard the music, for she lifted her hands and Jareth knew her identity, for only one person in all his life had he ever witnessed to have such beauty in her movements.

Miss Pesserat swayed, then folded her arms about herself. The moon was fat and low behind her. She twirled, then pointed a toe. He could almost imagine her laugh when her head fell back and all that loose hair caught in the moonlight.

The ache within him eased.

Catching himself, he turned his attention back to Helena. Poised, so very lovely, her face bespoke of the anguish of her song, the gorgeous Italian words sung with fluency and expertly accented. Behind her, Lady Rathford beamed. So proud, her face flushed, eyes almost glazed over as she gazed upon her offspring. Curious, Jareth shot a glance to Lord Rathford. He was seated on a Chippendale chair by the fire, his chin on his chest. He was sleeping.

Jareth almost smiled at the contrast between the man's apathy and his wife's euphoria. During dinner, he had been witness to the many differences in them, almost polar opposites on every matter. Yet between them, they had produced this remarkable creature.

Regarding Helena once again, Jareth studied her, assessing her for the role for which his mother had brought her before him. She would make an exemplary duchess, and an acceptable wife and companion.

Yes, he decided. He could do much worse than Helena Rathford.

Chloe settled into her bed. The cup of tea she had set on her bedside table had cooled, but that didn't disturb her. She still found the drink soothing. She loved the English custom of drinking tea, and she loved their gardens, although she considered them much too severe in design. Everything exact and perfectly aligned. She wanted to plant a huge bush on the right, sprinkle some bulbs from Amsterdam off to the left, draw the eye to an asymmetrical configuration, but it wasn't her house. It wasn't her garden, although she always referred to it as such in her mind. She'd sometimes think, *I shall go down to my garden tonight, and walk in the darkness and dream of home.*

Except tonight her thoughts had been much closer to her present home than her past. She could not keep herself from thinking about the duke. For all of his impeccably tailored clothing and unwaveringly cool manner, she had thought she spied a sadness in his dark eyes, eyes that were almost pretty, with an absurd abundance of sooty lashes that would make any debutante weep with envy. But he had disappointed her in the end, hadn't he, caught just as much in the trappings of high convention as his myopic mother.

She sighed and sipped the tepid tea. She had almost forgotten her father's letter, with so much on her mind. With a smile, she sank down against the assemblage of pillows piled behind her. It was one of the few luxuries in which she indulged, this plethora of pillows.

She opened her letter. Papa's bold, spidery handwriting scrawled out the French words. Reading them was like music to her.

Dearest daughter,

It is my fondest wish this letter finds you well and happy. Your last letter was amusing, so I am to think you are faring better in England than I would have guessed. How I miss you. Last night, Madame Duvier asked about you and we laughed, recalling how you sneaked the lamb into your bedchamber when you were five years old, and I realized then that I miss your mischief, though I can hardly believe I'm saying so.

Madame Duvier loved to tell that story. The pretty widow had a talent for making people laugh, and her father had been mentioning her often in his letters of late. Perhaps he was hinting at something, seeing if Chloe approved. She resolved to include abundant praise for the woman in her next letter. Papa was so funny to worry. Hadn't she been prodding and pushing him for years since Mama had died to find someone to fill his life?

The rest of the letter included the usual gossip about her brother, who continued, against her father's good counsel, to pay court to a village girl everyone knew was fickle and false. Her sister, Gigi, was well, her baby growing rapidly and, according to Papa, petted and spoiled and utterly enchanting.

When Chloe was through, she read it again, then folded it and tucked it in her nightstand drawer. She would read it several more times before placing it with the others in the cloth-covered box under her bed.

She stretched out, feeling the familiar warm mixture of pleasure and pain in her breast. It was always like this after Papa's letters. She missed them all, her family, who were flawed, yes, and not grand like dukes or duchesses, but pleasant, simple folk.

That was what she missed most of all. Being loved.

She dreamed that night of swimming. Somehow, she could breathe when submerged, and it was exhilarating. Exploring delightful worlds, she kicked upward, beckoned by muffled screams.

The screams were real. Rebeccah, she realized, her feet swinging out from under the covers. Without a second thought, she rushed into the nursery next door.

"Do we call him Uncle Strathmere?" Rebeccah asked, frowning.

"No, *ma petite,* you simply address him as you've always done."

"He never smiles. I do not like him. I think he may be mean."

Chloe angled her head, setting a mobcap onto the child's dark curls.

They were dressing up in the old garments from a trunk pilfered from the attics, one of Rebeccah's favorite activities. She was currently garbed in a flowing empire gown, a fashionably flimsy piece from the previous generation, when bodices were dampened and nipples rouged. Now the once decadent garment sagged, sadly innocent on the thin coltishness of the little girl's body.

Turning to Sarah, Chloe dropped a huge bonnet made up in the fashion of the cavaliers, with one huge plume curling behind, on the tot's head. Rebeccah cried, "I want that one!"

"You have a fine bonnet," Chloe protested, adjusting the hat so that the three-year-old's eyes were no longer covered. "Sarah shall be your suitor."

"Oh, horrid!" Rebeccah cried in disgust. She ripped off the mobcap and flung herself down onto the floor with a flourish.

"Please yourself," Chloe said with a shrug.

"All right!" Rebeccah replied when she saw Chloe meant to leave her alone to sulk. Snatching up the mobcap again, she jammed it on her head. "But I'm ugly."

Chloe gave her a long, thoughtful stare. "Perhaps you are right, *chérie*. Let us find something that suits your fancy dress better, *oui?*"

When investigation of the trunks failed to reveal anything as dazzling as Sarah's hat, Rebeccah went into another sulk. "Everything is horrid," she complained. "First Uncle is mean, and now I have no beautiful hat."

"Your uncle is not mean," Chloe protested, although she could barely think of something positive to say about the man. He *was* rather dour. "Perhaps he has much on his mind. We must do our best to welcome him and help him. He has been away from Strathmere for a very long time."

The child folded her small arms across her chest. "He must not interfere with the nursery. You must tell him, Miss Chloe. Except, of course, for new toys. We simply have to have some new toys."

Chloe rolled her eyes.

The child continued. "I shall tell him everything is dreadfully old. Grandmama won't let us have any fun. He must tell Grandmama to stay away from us and to let—"

Without a word, Chloe placed her hand on Rebeccah's forehead and gave a gentle push. The little girl flopped backward, landing among the heap of dresses behind her, her legs flailing in the air.

Chloe turned to Sarah, who smiled. "What do you think of your uncle, Sarah?" The child merely gazed back. Chloe continued, unperturbed by Sarah's silence. "Ah, I agree. Much too serious. It is rather sad, I think, to mope about in such a manner all the day." As if to herself, she muttered, "Moderation. Humph." With a quick sigh, she reached out a hand and pulled the struggling Rebeccah to her feet. "Enough, Queen Rebeccah. You can think up orders for the new duke another time. Let—"

Chloe stopped, stunned into silence, for she looked up just then to find a tall male figure standing inside the doorway of the nursery.

Instantly, she was aware of the confusion around her, of the children's mussed appearance, of her own rumpled dress and hair all astraggle. She sat there, staring at him, the picture of decorum in stark contrast to her dishabille. He was, as was his custom, dressed in dark trousers that had been so crisply pressed the seam was as fine and straight as a saber's edge. His expertly tied cravat lay in soft folds against a shirt as white and pristine as a new sheet of bleached parchment. Steady eyes glittered at her without a hint of reaction to anything he might have heard.

He glanced around the room. She saw his nostrils flare, a sign of annoyance, she was certain. The toys had not yet been put away, and the watercolors were still out, curdling in their ceramic trays with caked brushes scattered over the children's masterpieces.

Chloe came to her feet. "Good morning, your grace."

Rebeccah sidled to Chloe's side, all show of bravery gone. Chloe's hand came to rest on the child's shoulder, hugging her against her hip protectively.

The duke looked simply…contemptuous. Clasping his hands behind his back, he walked a tight circle about the nursery, like a general inspecting barracks.

He paused over the colors bleeding into one another on the children's paintings, and moved on.

He sniffed. "The nursery is untidy, Miss Pesserat."

"We are playing," Chloe answered. "See? Dressing fancy." She gave him a small, ironic smile. "A kind of history lesson, *n'est-ce pas?*"

"Unacceptable," he shot back, and began to walk about again. "This room is a disgrace. The children must be taught to pick up after themselves. The servants are not to be used as an excuse for bad habits."

Chloe almost groaned when he picked up a smashed wooden figure. Rebeccah had demolished the thing during one of her tantrums, then thrown it aside. Chloe, intent on gaining control of the child, had forgotten to discard the ruined toy.

Without thinking, she stepped forward and took the piece from him. His long, sun-browned fingers released it, brushing hers for an instant. She was surprised how warm they were, for this was a cold man.

She glanced at him to find a satirical smile twisting his handsome mouth. "I quite agree. We do our cleaning before lunch. Would you like to stay and supervise?"

Jareth gave her a withering stare. "I have other duties." He spoke in a calculated tone meant to convey an order. "I have no doubts that the room will be put to rights, just as I instructed. I trust that from our last conversation we understand each other very well."

The arrogance of his words brought instant reaction. "There was no understanding, your grace. At least I was not brought to any further understanding of you. You may have had some enlightenment from my explanations of my philosophies, but I..." She tapped her fingertip against her bottom lip. It was an insolent gesture and she knew it. "No, I cannot say I understand anything about you."

His eyelids lowered in a lazy, dangerous look. "You are very clever, Miss Pesserat, and right to remind me of it. I was misled—falsely so, I admit— by your irresponsible behavior. It made me think you simple, but you are far from that."

He dare... "I am so glad you admit being wrong."

He took a step closer. "And you forget yourself. Allow me to remind you that you are the children's nurse, or governess if you will, in my employ. And whether or not you—"

He stopped, for a faint keening sounded in low and began to build. Chloe looked down to find Rebeccah whimpering and frantically pulling on Chloe's skirt. The child's distress instantly brought Chloe out of her single-minded rage.

Snapping her head up to face Jareth again, she said, "We are upsetting the children. May I suggest that you scold me later if you are still so inclined, when they are not present?"

His eyes flickered from the child to Chloe, his gaze dark and intense and so very, very hard. She sensed he was genuinely appalled at Rebeccah's distress.

"I shall take you up on that invitation," he drawled, "for this is not settled to my satisfaction. The conditions in the nursery—" he took in a sweeping glance as if to illustrate his point "—are unsatisfactory."

The pressure of Rebeccah against her thigh, the still, silent form of Sarah as she watched her uncle with mistrust in her eyes prompted Chloe into capitulation. "You have my pride at a disadvantage. I shall make an effort to please you in this manner, if only for the children's sake."

Jareth didn't move for a moment. Chloe thought perhaps he was shocked she had behaved so humbly. Then he did something very, very odd. His expression began to alter. A stricken look replaced the cold arrogance of just moments ago.

He squinted at her, blinked and looked horrified, though she could not fathom why. Without another word, he made for the door, stopping halfway because his foot hit Sarah's bear, which had fallen onto the floor at some point during their altercation. He stooped, retrieved it and rose, standing there for the space of a few seconds, just staring down at it. Then he turned slowly and held it out to Sarah. She regarded him solemnly for so long, Chloe feared she was going to refuse to take it.

Finally, she reached for the toy, and the duke smiled ever so slightly, stretching out long, elegant fingers to brush the slightest of caresses along her chubby jawline.

He dropped his hand, whirled to confront Chloe once again and said, "Please forgive my intrusion. It was unforgivable.... I didn't mean to upset the children."

He left, clicking the door shut behind him with care.

Rebeccah was in a mood after that. Chloe did her best to soothe her, knowing she was frightened by her uncle's visit, but her already challenged patience was stretched to its limit. Sarah, on the other hand, seemed strangely content. She kept staring at her bear as if to glean some insight from the flat, dark button eye.

Chapter Four

"Really, Strathmere, that is the third time I've spoken to you and you have neglected to answer," the duchess scolded. "And you look positively dreadful. You aren't coming down with the ague, are you?"

Jareth turned to his mother, attempting to compose his face in placid lines. "Yes. I am a bit out of sorts." His voice drifted into a soft, reflective tone. "Not quite myself..."

"See to it that you are not less than your best this afternoon. I have invited the Rathfords to tea. I do so enjoy Lady Rathford. Such an impeccably comported person. Lord Rathford can be crude, it is true, but no more so than is typical of the country gentleman." A slight, nearly imperceptible pause. "Of course, Helena is absolutely charming."

There was an awkward silence during which Jareth realized he was expected to respond. "She is exemplary," he said.

"Yes," his mother nearly crooned with satisfaction. Settling back in her chair, she fiddled with the fan on her lap.

Jareth felt a strange emotion curl like a wisp of smoke, tangy and elusive, then gone. He thought it was annoyance, at his mother no less, which was not something he was used to feeling. He had the greatest respect for his mother. She was the force behind the family, taking the helm of what she would often and proudly boast was one of the finest families in England. She had led them through disaster more than once, even when his father was alive.

She had only been vaguely interested in him growing up, much less exacting than she had been with Charles, which had meant there was room for a degree of fondness in their relationship. With Charles there had been no respite from the demands incumbent upon him as heir. His mother had been ruthless—a strange word to choose, but somehow it fit—and almost viciously vigilant.

Jareth felt a dawning dread. Now that critical eye was turned his way. His days of freedom were over.

Had it been like this for Charles? Had he felt this sense of suffocation, of generations of Hunts weighing down on him—the crushing burden of responsibility squeezing out his own essence?

Fanciful silliness, he thought with disgust, then discovered that his mother was talking to him again and he hadn't heard a word she had said.

"I am sorry, Mother," he apologized.

The woman narrowed her eyes at him. Never beautiful, Charlotte Harrington Hunt had always been what was referred to as a handsome woman. In her older years, that handsomeness had hardened, but her eyes were still bright and lively and the flawless bone structure had held up well.

"Is it that wretched Pesserat woman?" she demanded.

Jareth blinked, disconcerted with the non sequitur. "Pardon me?"

"I was told you visited the nursery the other morning. Was that Frenchwoman impertinent to you?"

He shook his head, but he could feel the frown lines deepening on his brow.

That Pesserat woman... Had she been impertinent? He had to allow her devotion to his nieces was fierce. And that there was an aura of capableness about her, there amid all her haphazard foolishness. But she was so...*disconcerting* was the word. Indeed, the woman was that in spades.

His mother was saying, "You must not be too lenient with the servants, Strathmere. You need to remember your station. It is a grand one, but it must be used properly, and wisely. As a boy, I did not think to instruct you as I did your brother. In this I failed you, I see, for tragedy is always a possibility, and one must be prepared. For my lack of foresight, and in allowing you to affiliate so many years with commoners, I regret bitterly the loose attitude I took with you."

Among the commoners to whom she was referring was his old partner, Colin Burke, and the reference stung. Although Colin was not a peer, his wealth was greater than the majority of titled families of England. The contempt in his mother's voice whenever she referred to his business partner—and the man who had been his closest friend—was somehow...violating.

"However, there is no sense dwelling on the past.

You are the duke now. Let the knowledge of that fact take root inside of you and blossom.''

The duke now. Yes, oh yes, how he knew it. As if for one second, for one blessed moment of peace, he could forget it.

His mother continued, ''Duty, Strathmere. Your duty to Rebeccah and Sarah is to show them a strong hand in their rearing. Never forget who you are. You are in command of this family.'' She wrung her hands and looked at him with pity in her eyes. ''Oh, my son, you were always such a gentle soul. Weeping for wounded pigeons and nursing baby rabbits unearthed in the garden, you were a sweet-hearted boy—but you must put all that behind you. You must change, alter your very character so that the easy authority of your title is second nature to you, as natural as all that you've known in your past used to be.''

Her words spun around in his head, draining away to a hollow echo. There were more, but try as he might to concentrate on them, they were lost to him, drowned out by the shameful realization that he was, God help him, terrified of what she was describing.

Because it was already happening. And he knew that it must.

For he was the Duke of Strathmere, now and evermore.

Helena Rathford made an even better impression—if that were possible—on Jareth that afternoon than she had the first evening of their acquaintance. Garbed in a day dress, she appeared refreshingly pretty with her soft blond ringlets bobbing about her face. The taut beauty of the previous meeting seemed more relaxed.

Lord Rathford sent his apologies at not being able to join them this afternoon. These were prettily pleaded by his wife, who deftly took herself off with the duchess to examine his mother's porcelain collection in order to leave Jareth and Helena alone.

He gave her a rueful glance, and she remarked, "I am afraid they are rather obvious."

Her directness he liked. It relaxed him, and it felt good after the tensions of the day. "Don't fault them too much."

"How kind you are," she said, as if she truly meant it. He laughed and gave his head a shake.

"Not at all, Lady Helena. I simply know there are many times when my behavior could warrant a little understanding, and so in the interest of reaping the benefit of like charity one day, I dispense it with generosity. Purely selfish, you see."

"Rather wise," she corrected, sounding like a schoolmistress. He chuckled and she smiled wanly.

Looking out of the window, Jareth frowned. "It is unfortunate the weather is disagreeable today. I believe a tour of the grounds is called for when a lady comes for tea."

"I adore gardens. I couldn't help but notice you have a lovely one. However, it does seem rather ominous." She ducked her head to peer up at the sky. Iron-gray and so thick with clouds it looked flat. It cast a weird glow on the late afternoon light.

"Rather lovely," Jareth commented, studying the unusual colors. "In a way."

"Good heavens, who is that?" Helena exclaimed.

"Do they mean to go out and about with rains coming?"

That, Jareth saw immediately, was the intrepid and apparently incredibly stupid Miss Pesserat, tromping across the front lawn with her two little charges in tow.

He was too angry to speak for a moment, then said simply, "Will you excuse me, please?"

It took several moments to locate Frederick, the butler. "See that Miss Pesserat is brought back here immediately," Jareth told the gaunt older man with thinning hair and a huge beak of a nose. "Tell her I wish to speak with her as soon as the Rathfords depart."

"Yes, your grace," Frederick said without expression. "I shall send a footman right away."

The weather worsened. A steady drizzle thickened into a downpour, making it untenable for the Rathfords to leave as planned. His mother asked them to stay to supper, and Lady Rathford agreed with a rapacious gleam in her eye she didn't bother to hide.

They were shown to a room where they might refresh themselves, and Jareth retired to his library. It was a dreary place, more so with the wet-streaked windows weeping tearily against the implacable sky. He called for a fire to be made up, then settled down to do some of the accounts.

Remembering that he hadn't been informed of Chloe and the children's return, he laid down the quill and summoned Frederick.

"No, sir, I have not seen her," the butler informed him.

"Send Mary to the nursery and see if they came in unnoticed."

Frederick went to search out the maid. Jareth crossed the room to stare out the window at the vicious skies. The wind had picked up.

What had made that fool think of taking the children out and about on a day like this? She didn't have the sense of—

He spied a movement. Peering closer, he saw indeed it was someone dashing across the lawn.

Damnation! Chloe Pesserat ran with Sarah on her hip, Rebeccah held by the hand and trailing along behind like the tail of a kite in a blizzard. They were headed for the rear of the house.

The exasperating woman meant to sneak them in through the kitchens and avoid detection. Anger moved him before any conscious thought registered in his brain. Storming out of the library, he strode with long, purposeful steps through the dining room, startling Cook as he burst into the largest of the kitchens—a long, cheery room where a huge fire blazed in the cooking hearth and aromas, spicy and delectable, assaulted him.

Cook looked up, her thick arms poised over a mound of dough. She stood behind the scrubbed oaken table that was sprinkled liberally with flour, and she wore some of it herself. "Your grace?"

He opened his mouth, but another sound preceded him. Giggles.

The door to the outside was located in a short hallway where the smaller kitchen rooms and assorted pantries were housed. It was from this direction the commotion was heard.

"Oh, you are a wet mouse, aren't you?" a gay voice exclaimed. He had no trouble identifying Miss

Pesserat from the definitive accent. "Come, come. To the fire."

"Have Cook fix up some chocolate to drink!" Rebeccah cried.

They came into view, the three of them stumbling under the weight of their soaked dresses and sodden cloaks. They were still laughing, talking over one another, excited and unruly.

"Bonne idée, chérie!" Chloe exclaimed. "And some pastries, *bien sûr*. I am starving!"

She stopped in midstride, frozen in an awkward position, her face going suddenly immobile. Rebeccah saw Jareth at the same time as her governess and made an immediate retreat behind Chloe's skirts. Only Sarah regarded him with a mild expression, as if he were merely a personage of passing interest.

The words, when he spoke them, were like an epithet. "Miss Pesserat."

Cook cut in, bustling up to the children and waving her arms. "Come along, then, *mes amours,* come to the fire in the little dining room."

Jareth looked at the woman askance, suspicious for a moment until he recalled her nationality was the same as Miss Pesserat's. For a space, he had almost thought the governess had infected the household so that they were all talking like her. The accent was, he had to admit, one of her more charming attributes. The only one he could think of.

Mostly, she seemed to have a knack for driving him straight to madness. Take this very moment, for example. She was standing there, still stuck in that ridiculous stance. Her hair was soaked, plastered to her head like a cap, and a very unflattering one at that. He took exactly four steps forward. Four slow, calculated steps. Up close, he could see the way her lashes were starred from the rain, making those steel-blue eyes more brilliant.

"What," he managed to utter through his clenched jaw, "did you imagine you were doing with my nieces in the midst of this storm?"

It was as if the words released her. She straightened.

"If you please," she began carefully, "we were out for a walk. I admit I mistook the weather. I am terribly inept at such things, I confess it, but the sky in England is so often gloomy, we would be closeted in the house forever if we didn't take a risk now and then."

It would have been ridiculously easy to anger, for her words had the ring of sauciness in them, except her look was so sincere. Fat rivulets skittered from her drenched hair down her nose and she didn't even bother to wipe them away.

"Miss Pesserat," he said at last. "I fail to comprehend what is so woefully mysterious about a sky filled with clouds. If your judgment is so profoundly impaired, perhaps I had best reassess your capabilities."

"Capabilities?"

"Yes, you know the word. Your vocabulary is quite accomplished when you are speaking, I noticed, yet when you wish to defer a comment you do not like, you plead ignorance of a word. Charmingly demure, and effective, I must imagine, on the more unsuspecting."

She pulled herself up in a stance that was nearly military. Absurd, utterly, and it should have annoyed him—that and the defiant way her pointy little chin jutted out at him. Strangely, though, he found himself wrestling with the most insistent urge to *smile,* of all things.

"Yes, I understand your English very well, but there are a few words that confuse me from time to time. You must allow for that at least, your grace. In this instance, it was not that I did not know the word, but was taking exception to your questioning my *capabilities.*"

"What would you have me do?" he demanded hotly. "You run the children about in the most unseemly and unmannerly ways—"

"I most certainly do not!"

"Miss Pesserat—"

"I cannot see why you are so disturbed. It is merely water. It will not melt us, like sugar candy."

With each breath, his temper seemed to expand. "That is not the point—"

"You would think a little thing like rainfall were a foreign phenomenon in England. Yet, I have never seen such a place as this, miserable always from wretched weather."

"A very entertaining opinion—"

"Really, it is quite—"

"Do not interrupt me again, young miss!" This he thundered, his fist raised with his index finger pointing to the ceiling. In the silence afterward, he was aware of two sensations stealing over his person. One was mortification—damn this imp to tempt him into a most disreputable show of temper—and the other, inexplicably, was a deep sense of…pleasure. It had felt good to shout for once. So much for moderation.

He looked at his erect finger, astonished. His father

had always performed the gesture when scolding one of his sons. When had he developed such a like habit? It was an impossible question to answer, for never, *never,* had he been as incensed as he was at this moment.

"I am sorry," she said.

He heard the sound of the door behind him opening, then a murmured, "Oh, dear," before the door shut again, leaving them once again alone. One of the servants.

"I do not mean to disrespect you," Chloe continued.

He forced himself to relax his stance. "And yet you do. You do it constantly, Miss Pesserat, and without much effort, it seems."

She issued the most forlorn sigh he had ever heard. "It does seems inevitable."

"You need only make more of an effort to conform."

Her eyes flashed. "Can you not make a similar effort?"

"I," he answered simply, "am the duke."

Unimpressed, she countered, "*That* does not make you infallible."

Oh, Lord, she was at it again! "It does make me lord and master here and I will be obeyed—and without question, if you please."

He immediately regretted adding the last, since it gave her a clear opening for one of her clever little quips: *no, it does not please.* But she surprised him. Instead, she tipped her head to the side and asked, "Why did you leave the nursery so abruptly the other day?"

He blinked in surprise. "Pardon me?"

"In the nursery, when you were angry. You suddenly seemed to lose your anger and you left so abruptly."

"What the devil…?" He pushed his hand through his hair while letting out a long breath. "Why do you wish to know that at a time like this?"

"Because, you see, it seemed as if you regretted getting angry when you saw how upset the children became. In fact, you seemed rather surprised to find yourself in such a state. The look on your face led me to believe that, anyway. And I thought you might be feeling the same way now. I don't wish you to regret what the heat of your anger makes you say."

"It is very kind of you to be solicitous of my sensibilities." He had meant it to be sarcastic, but instead the words sounded gentle in his own ears.

One of those irritating droplets was meandering down her prettily flushed cheek. He reached for his handkerchief and handed it to her. She stared at it. "Oh, for pity's sake," he muttered, and snatched the thing back and pressed it to the moisture. "Your hair is leaking."

She touched her head self-consciously. "Oh, bother."

It was such an inane thing to say, he did smile then. He almost wanted to laugh, as if the contention between them were suddenly all mere silliness. "You'll be fortunate if you don't come down with the deadly ague."

"It is only rain," she said diffidently.

"Come by the fire, or you'll chill."

She appeared surprised at his solicitousness. Frankly, so was he. "Thank you, your grace."

He led the way to the brick hearth with its iron

doors and large, open flame. Pulling up a seat, he fetched a square of linen and held it out to her.

Chloe sat down and began to dab the towel about her face and head. Jareth stood behind her, watching her movements, which were like the exacting motions of a dance. How did she always manage to make even the most ordinary actions seem beautiful? What Helena did with her voice, Miss Pesserat did with her body—

He shook his head as if to rid himself of the wayward thought. It seemed somehow disloyal to liken Lady Helena's great gift with a girl's artless grace. And how ungentlemanly to be reflecting at all on his nieces' governess's body.

His voice sounded harsh when next he spoke. "Do not take the children out of doors again without my permission," he said, and was about to turn away when he heard her say, "No."

He stopped, cocking his head. "Can I have heard you correctly?"

She remained with her back to him, ramrod straight and staring into the fire. "It is not right to keep the little ones confined. I do not agree to it."

"Perhaps you misunderstand. I meant that they will go on outings with my permission only."

"Why not under your supervision?" She turned so her face was in profile. She had the most extraordinary scooped nose, he noticed. The backlighting from the fire made her pose a perfect cameo. "It would be lovely if you were to spend time with the children. They need their family with them."

"Do you find fault with my stewardship of the children?"

"Only in that you favor an approach reminiscent

of one of the posh princes of the East—full control and no responsibility.''

His temper was rising again, and quickly. "Why, Miss Pesserat, you are most insulting.''

She stood and whirled on him, her face flushed—though from the proximity of the fire or her rage, he did not know—and her eyes were positively brilliant. "I hate when you call me that. My name is Chloe. Could you not manage that bit of informality, or will it choke you to speak it?''

He felt as if the wind had been knocked out of him. Just as swiftly as it rose, his irritation receded. "Miss Chloe. See, there. I did not burst into a ball of fire.''

She paused, not trusting him it seemed, before she smiled, one of her wide, true smiles. He watched the slow way it crept across her face, taking that generous mouth into an upward curl and showing even, white teeth. "And you are jesting. However, this time it is not at my expense. You surprise me, your grace.''

"How rewarding. I endeavor to never be boring.''

Why did everything he said to this woman end up sounding...unpleasant?

Surprisingly, however, she wasn't deflated. "You can never be that, your grace. Oh...'' She let the word die and again that smile appeared. "For all your faults, never, never that.''

Absurd, the flash that skittered through him. What difference did it make what this country maid thought of him? Still, the compliment warmed him.

It was a compliment—wasn't it?

"At least,'' he said to cover his disconcerted

thoughts, "promise me you will not take any more strolls through violent spring storms."

"Oh, la!" she sang, flipping her hand in the air in a fluid gesture. "The children had fun. Did you never do such things when you were a boy? Walk in the rain? Catch raindrops on your tongue?"

The words fell over him like a pall, pressing on his chest, his shoulders. Unwittingly, she had brought to mind the two things that left him weak with grief—the past and his lost freedom.

Why had he tarried so long with the silly girl, anyhow? "The matter, Miss Chloe, is settled. No more outings in the rain. If you do not abide by this, I will be forced to take broader action to ensure my wishes are being observed."

The smile disappeared, and she bowed her head. Her drenched hair hung stiffly in pointed strands. "You have made yourself very clear, your grace."

He trusted her not to lie to him outright, but he knew she would not flinch from a lie of omission. "Tell me you will obey."

After a mutinous pause, she said, "I will obey." She raised her head, her face blank and plain. When she had smiled, it had been transformed, almost pretty. Yes, actually, quite lovely, in a way that was so very different from Lady Helena's pristine beauty. Chloe Pesserat was meant to laugh, to run, to do everything in extreme. Wholly opposite to Helena, whose attraction was her—

The thought struck him and it was accurate, but he still couldn't resist an inward cringe. The word he had found to describe Helena was *moderation.*

The same sense of disquiet followed him out of the kitchens as it had the last time he had conversed with Chloe, in the nursery. He wondered if such a reaction were unavoidable with the capricious imp that held his nieces' sanity in her slender, sensuously expressive hands.

Chapter Five

Chloe prowled in her chamber that night, her thoughts tumbling one another in an agitated rush.

How could she have thought there was wisdom and pain in the duke's cold eyes? He was completely intolerable—scolding her like a wayward child herself, questioning her competence! The blundering, self-important, conceited…bore! She had thought there was a trace of humanity behind his supreme dukeness, but she had been mistaken, clearly.

As the anger drained out of her, exhaustion descended. Cook, having heard of her disquiet, sent up a steaming teapot and a generous supply of short-bread, which was one of Chloe's favorites. She curled up with a novel pilfered from the dowager duchess's stash in the library, but soon dozed with it open on her lap.

Rebeccah's fitful cries woke her sometime after the hour of three. Chloe came to her feet before the last vestiges of her dream had cleared her head and moved with swiftness to the child's bedside.

In a firm, soft voice, she said, "Hush, Rebeccah,

it is Miss Chloe here now with you. Everything is fine, *ma petite*. Hush, now.''

She wrapped her arms about the wailing child and pulled her in tight against her breast. Rebeccah always resisted this at first. She grabbed fistfuls of Chloe's nightrail in her little hands, pulling and punching, but the efforts soon grew weak. Her muffled cries subsided until at last she was at rest.

Gently, Chloe laid her back in her bed. She looked at the small face—the pert nose, the thick fan of lashes against the rose-kissed cheeks, the pouty mouth hanging agape with the unselfconscious ease of childhood slumber. She was not the easiest child with which to contend, but Chloe loved her with a fierceness that made her soul ache. Needing to touch, she smoothed a hand over the limbs that were just now losing their babyish roundness as Rebeccah passed from infancy to childhood.

Chloe spoke in a whisper as the child's peace deepened. ''Sleep, *chérie,* and dream of happy lands where knights ride in gleaming armor and ladies dance among perfect roses and all the dragons are slain, asleep forever. Dream of laughter and of those who love you, *ma petite*. Dream of good things, and love. Dream of love.''

Rebeccah inhaled a trembling breath, releasing it slowly as she nestled deeper under the coverlet. Chloe smiled, reflecting that it was infrequent that Rebeccah stayed put for longer than a moment or two. A time like this—just the stillness of it—was precious.

Suddenly, Chloe became aware of the fact that she wasn't alone. Her gaze lifted to find the duke standing in the doorway.

He was dressed in dark trousers, still crisp somehow despite the wilting weather and the late hour. His coat was off, however, and he stood in his shirtsleeves—a deplorable breach of propriety, but Chloe barely noted it, for it mattered not at all to her. She only thought it odd because it was so out of character for him.

His hair was disheveled, and taken with the discarded tailcoat, signified he had been restless, perhaps bedeviled by irksome thoughts about a particular employee of his who was fond of storms and refused to bend to his indomitable will....

"You have been there for all this time?" she asked, amazed she hadn't been aware of him before.

He gave a brief nod. "I was awake and roaming about. I heard her cries," he said in a rough whisper. He stepped into the room, just two steps, and inclined his head to his niece. "Will...will she be all right now?"

"She shall sleep until morning," Chloe reassured him.

"Every night this happens? That is what I was told."

"Yes, your grace."

She bowed her head, not wanting to look at him as he stood gazing down at Rebeccah. She had spent the evening building him into an ogre. He seemed all too human just now, with his shirtsleeves and all. And that concerned expression on his face was disconcerting.

"Is it always this...severe?"

"Tonight was not severe," she said, coming to her feet. "It is much the same each night."

"You are the only one who can quiet her, I am told."

She didn't answer. It seemed a rather rhetorical question.

"I watched you tonight, and I must admit you are very adept."

Looking at him at last, she saw his eyes were steady and serious. They were dark in the shadowed room, lit only by a magnificent moon spilling in through the large double window. "Only hours ago you questioned my competence," she reminded him.

"Your judgment, Miss Chloe, but not your skill. That you are kind beyond measure, and uncannily in accord with the moods and needs of my nieces, I cannot argue."

It was as near a retraction as she was likely to get. Moving to the window, she reached up for the drape, thinking to close it against the abundant moonlight. A sharp hiss from behind her made her stop in mid-reach and look over her shoulder to the duke.

He stood in the midst of a flourish of light from the swollen moon, his face fully visible, his eyes narrowed to slits and focused directly on her. Puzzled, she said, "What is it?"

His voice was like gravel. "Miss Chloe—Miss Pesserat. You are…your attire, *mademoiselle!*"

With a start, she remembered that she was in her nightrail.

"*Mon Dieu,* it is my nightdress. My bedroom is through that door, and I was sleeping." She added tartly, "It is my habit at this hour."

The shadows took him as he retreated backward, as if he didn't trust her enough to turn his back on her. "This is most unseemly. My apologies." From the darkness, she heard the sounds of the door opening and closing.

Chloe shook her head, bemused by his peculiar behavior. He was a strange man, she already knew, but this really was the oddest thing....

Then she realized how much light was pouring through the window, and she had been framed in it, arm extended, and dressed only in her nightgown of modest enough design and not at all risqué. But when backlit, it would become—

Completely transparent.

The drive to Rathford Manor took just under an hour, making the Rathford family Strathmere's closest neighbors. But even the short interval seemed endless with the dowager duchess seated across from Jareth, her sturdy scowl firmly in place and her occasional exclamations centered completely on the unacceptable qualities of their governess.

"I wish you would speak to the physicians again and see what they can tell us as to when the woman can be dismissed. We cannot be expected to withstand her haphazard—and, yes, dangerous at times—attentions to the girls."

Jareth looked out the window. His mother's diatribe was only a distant annoyance.

"They could have been brought down with all manner of mortal illness from her abominable behavior, not to mention the humiliation of it all. Lady Rathford was kind, of course, as any woman of breeding can be expected to be, but what she must think! I tell you, it is simply horrible to have to live with that Pesserat woman."

Distractedly, he said, "It was only a mild spring rain. And no harm was done."

There was a momentary silence, then the duchess exclaimed in a tight, high voice, "What did you say? You dare defend such irresponsible behavior as that?"

Blinking, Jareth snapped to attention. "Pardon me? What was it I said to upset you, Mother?"

"No harm was done? Only a spring rain?" The woman sounded as if the words were choking her.

"Mother, please calm yourself. You will work yourself into a state, and you wouldn't wish for the Rathfords to see you with your face all red. They would fear for your health." It was the right thing to say, for the duchess immediately and with visible effort brought herself under control.

Closing her eyes, she took several deep breaths. When she opened them again, she leveled an icy stare at her son. "Now, kindly explain what you meant by that absurd remark."

"Only that Miss Chloe caused no harm to the children. I'll grant you," he added, holding a hand against her prepared objections, "that she is irresponsible, and I have told her she may not take the children out without my permission. I believe that should settle the matter."

His mother looked pleased as they fell into an uneasy silence.

"Strathmere?" she said suddenly.

"Yes, Mother."

"When did you begin addressing Miss Pesserat as 'Miss Chloe'?"

Jareth didn't answer, and to his great relief, his mother did not pursue the subject.

They arrived at the Rathford mansion, a beautiful Palladian masterpiece. Disappointingly, Lord Rathford was not in attendance, so Jareth took refreshment with the ladies in the grand salon, which showed the Rathfords' affluence to its fullest advantage. Looking about, Jareth felt a wave of distaste for the gaudy Florentine pilasters and gold leafing all about, regular fare for the grand Georgian era that had just passed. For his own tastes he preferred the subtle distinction of aged wood rubbed with lemon oil until the patina shone. He also liked sturdy chairs, something of some substance upon which to sit rather than these delicate things with spindly legs and carved backs that dug into the flesh.

They seemed to suit Helena, however. Back rigid, she perched on the Sheridan chair as effortlessly elegant as a Madonna. Her cap of cleverly arranged ringlets caught the sun. It was a beautiful shade of blonde, so pale. She sat in rapt attention to her mother, who was speaking on some subject Jareth could hardly muster any interest in until he heard his name.

"…the music room. Go ahead, Helena. Show the duke the pianoforte used by Mozart himself."

Of course, he should have known. Lady Rathford had been bragging.

Helena looked at him with that soft gaze of hers. "Would you like to see it, your grace?" He thought he detected a silent apology for her mother's conceit.

Jareth felt a pang of resentment at being moved around like a helpless pawn, done so expertly by these matrons, but squelched it as unimportant.

"That would be entirely enjoyable," he replied with a bow.

Helena led the way. The music room was on the second floor, a grand chamber with pointed vaults crisscrossing the painted ceiling, where cherubs frolicked in naked abandon. The classical technique was stunning. Jareth stopped to admire it from the doorway.

"Absolutely lovely."

"Are you a patron of the architectural sciences, your grace?"

"Only an admirer."

He wandered about, eyeing the treasures ensconced within the magnificent room.

Helena walked behind him. "Do you enjoy music?"

"Listening only. I have no talent. I see your family has a love for it, do they not?"

"Yes, we do favor music."

Jareth waved his hand at the pianoforte. "Do you play?"

"Of course," she answered, and sat down dutifully. "What would you like to hear?"

"Something airy, nothing dark. My thoughts are gloomy enough today."

"I believe I have something," she said. Her long, elegant fingers closed over the keys. He watched as they moved up and down the keyboard, coaxing from the instrument a lilting, playful melody that made him smile.

She didn't smile, however. The same pained look came over her face as he had seen when she sang. It distorted the careful beauty. Closing her eyes, she tilted her head down and to one side as she played, brows drawn in concentration, then occasionally shooting upward as though she were surprised by a particularly sprightly part of the piece.

As with her song, the music was powerful. It ended abruptly, and she bowed her head, seeming to need a moment to collect herself before the serene expression was back in place and she raised her eyes to his.

What lay beyond that composed expression? He experienced a dismal sinking disappointment as he recognized he would never sample it. It was too tightly controlled, too remote—as far away from his reach as the stars he so loved to view. Yes. The same unapproachable beauty was in Helena.

"That was breathtaking," he said, and the words sounded like such an ineffectual way to describe what she had just given him.

She rose, a polite, controlled smile in place. "Do you have any hobbies, your grace?"

He hesitated. Her eyes were on him, expectant. "Yes, actually, I do. The science of astronomy is my hobby."

"You watch the stars." He detected no real interest.

"Yes. The constellations, all the heavenly bodies and celestial phenomenon. It is fascinating, how they ever change, but like seasons return again and again in their predictable patterns. And then there are always new discoveries. The other day I read in one of the papers written by an eminent astronomer that there is to be a comet visible soon in the northwest sky. I have ordered a special telescope for the occasion so as not to miss it."

"How interesting. I understand seamen often navigate with only a perfunctory glance at the night sky, so skilled are they in predicting direction.''

It wasn't an unpleasant comment. Yet it showed how absolutely she had missed the point, the wonder and fascination of the night sky, not simply its utility. Yes, the skill of a seasoned navigator was impressive, but that wasn't what made the heavens fill him with an aching sense of wonder and whet his hunger for discovery.

''Yes, it is true,'' he answered, and smiled blandly.

When eventually they rejoined his mother and Lady Rathford, he received a sharp look from the dowager duchess coupled with a slight incline of her head. Approval. It failed to have any impact on him.

The afternoon progressed with a game of whist. Helena was an excellent player, but somehow managed to lose. He was not enthusiastic about cards as a rule, but he enjoyed watching how expertly Helena played each hand and then threw away her lead without seeming to at all.

She was a very accomplished girl, indeed. He caught his mother's thinned lips, as if an unborn smile were being held at bay. She thought she was being subtle. If she had jumped up in the air and clicked her heels she couldn't have been more obvious.

On the way home, his mother pleaded one of her migraines and lapsed into silence, for which Jareth was exceedingly grateful. It gave him the time he needed. To think.

It was already dark when they pulled up to Strathmere, the lights in the windows like poor imitations of the sparkling display of the star-strewn sky. He angled his gaze upward.

Tonight he would spend in the sweet air of the garden, reading the stars and trying to convince himself that the path he was on was the right one.

Or maybe he would just lose himself in the wonder of the heavens and leave the rest of it to be contemplated later.

Chapter Six

"Your grace, may I speak with you?"

Jareth looked up from his ledgers to see Miss Pesserat standing in the doorway, leaning inward in an inquisitive pose. With her hair neatly pulled back off her face, she looked rather...appealing, Jareth noted. Her skin almost glowed, perfect skin with a natural blush to her cheeks that lent her a fresh-faced, innocent quality. Remarkable, he thought as he sat back, surveying her openly. Her dress was even clean and relatively free of wrinkles.

"Come in, Miss Pesserat." He paused, smiling at his slip. "Miss Chloe, I meant to say."

"*Merci.* I shall not keep you. I merely wished to ask your permission to take the children on an outing."

That broadened his smile. This was a good sign. Apparently, he was being quite effective in establishing his authority regarding the activities of his nieces.

Chloe stepped forward and laid a carefully lettered document before him. "See, here I have a schedule prepared for each day of the week. It is important for children to have exercise regularly, do you not agree?'' Before he could even formulate an answer, she made one of those sweeping, fluid gestures that never failed to astonish him with their pure artistry. ''When I was a child, we walked everywhere, every day was a different adventure. It builds the lungs. Too much indoors...'' She paused, frowning meaningfully at him. The way her bottom lip stuck out was almost adorable. ''It stifles the brain. Not enough air.''

Jareth held his hands up as if in surrender. ''Your point is taken, Miss Chloe, and though it is at odds with conventional medical wisdom, it happens to coincide with my views, as well. As a child, I too loved the out-of-doors. I would not dream of cheating my nieces out of such enjoyment. Now, let me see here, on Tuesday you have written you would like to take the girls on a walk to the pond. What educational benefit were you planning to achieve with this excursion?''

Chloe looked startled. ''Why, to see the ducks.''

''Excellent. A study of nature, the local wildlife in particular.'' He took a quill out of its ink pot and made a mark next to that activity. Pen poised over the next item, he lifted his face expectantly. ''What is the purpose of Wednesday's trip?''

''Ah, *pardon*, what was Wednesday's trip?''

''The walk into the eastern woods.''

''Oh, well...that was... *Mon Dieu*, I cannot quite recall.'' At his reaction of displeasure she hurriedly said, ''Yes, now I remember. We are to look for small animals and see if we can find where they live.''

Jareth was even more pleased with that activity.

"Wise, Miss Chloe. You challenge the children to think, to see beyond a cute fluffy tail or huge, limpid eyes. They must learn of the living habits of the creatures we share the land with."

He made another check and perused the rest of the proposed activities. "I think on Thursday, you shall remain indoors. Mother and I are traveling to Rathford Manor again, and I would prefer you not leave the house. Perhaps your planned activity to study the fauna of the area can be postponed."

Chloe smiled sweetly. *"Certainement."*

She looked positively angelic, and he wasn't too humble to feel a puff of satisfaction.

Returning the smile, he handed back her schedule. "With that small alteration, I can give my approval."

"Merci, your grace."

She whirled to take her leave, and if it hadn't been for the quick curtsy she dropped, he might have never suspected. But when she left, he paused, pen pressed against his bottom lip as he thought over his sudden misgivings.

Dismissing his doubts, he went to work on the documents before him. There wasn't a need to question her motives just because she had seen sense in the end—she, Miss Chloe, the flibbertigibbet who usually made no sense at all....

Sometime later, he realized how foolish he had been to think it would be so easy. Miss Chloe and the two girls marched across the front lawn, Miss Chloe calling out commands as the children high-stepped in time. The last thing he heard was her exclaiming something about a herd of elephants ahead of them, and the trio went screaming down the hill and disappeared.

Presumably, he thought wearily, to the duck pond.

In the garden that night, the air was wonderfully cool. Jareth liked it thus. He had removed his jacket and turned up his shirtsleeves clear to his elbows.

This garden, this place that had been his nightly refuge as a child and now as a man, brought him the peace of mind he needed so badly.

He fiddled with the calibrations of the large telescope he had dragged out with him. In his youth, when the desire to study star patterns began to become an obsession, he would spend many a night out here, gazing upward and marveling at this particularly magnificent wonder of creation.

Adjusting the angle of the delicate instrument, Jareth bent over and peered in the lens.

A shadow crossed the verdant path, blocking the moonlight.

"Good evening."

The voice was so unexpected he started, straightening to face this intruder. Chloe smiled at him. He was surprised to note it was a warm smile, full of genuine greeting. A fleeting thought passed through his mind that not even his own mother looked happy to see him anymore. Her features were always strained in lines of concern, and she seemed, whenever in his company, more relieved that he was finally present to air her assorted worries than pleased to be sharing his company.

"Hello, Miss Chloe."

"What are you doing?" Without waiting for his answer, she sidled around to stand beside him, her eyes never leaving the strange contraption he had set up before him. "What is this?" she asked in wonder. She touched a black knob.

"Please," he said, taking her slim fingers in his and guiding them away. He was surprised she didn't snatch her hand back, at least not right away. Her skin was cool, the contact pleasant. Then he remembered how unseemly it was to have skin-on-skin contact with any woman. He was not, nor was she, wearing any gloves.

He released his grip.

Her heavily lashed lids slid over her eyes and she glanced away. "I am sorry, I am intruding. I shall leave you," she said, and had already turned to go when Jareth heard somebody say, "Wait."

It was a heartbeat or two before he realized he had been the one to speak.

She looked at him and blinked those wide, stormy-blue eyes at him. "Yes?"

He held out a hand to her in invitation. "I did not mean to frighten you away."

Ah, she was predictable. Her chin came up and she said, "I am not frightened."

In a conciliatory tone, he said, "Come and take a look."

She hesitated a moment—perhaps she *was* a little frightened—before coming to stand before him. "Your grace?"

In the moonlight the gray-blue of her eyes gleamed pale. They were wide with genuine interest and a touch of apprehension.

Pointing to the viewing lens, he said, "Look through there."

She struggled to focus through the awkward angle. "What is that?" she asked.

"What does it look like to you?"

"A dragon," she replied.

Puzzled, he said, "What?" She straightened, and he stepped up to have a look for himself.

"How do you see a dragon? That is Piscis Austrinus. The heavens do have a dragon, but Draco is farther north, on the other side of Polaris."

Turning, he was just in time to catch her shrug. "You asked me what I see. I only can say what it looks like to me. A dragon."

He let out a sigh. "You do see the strangest things, don't you, Miss Chloe?"

Her smile was brilliant. *"Merci beaucoup!"*

Shaking his head, he chuckled. "And you always mystify me."

"It is good not to be predictable, *oui?* Surprise makes life fun. But too much, it can disturb. We need to know the same things are always there for us. To depend on. Otherwise we grow anxious and our moods grow poor."

"This is a side of you I never thought to see. You are quite the philosopher."

"Do you think so, your grace? They are just my thoughts, you see." She shot him a mischievous glance. "I do have thoughts."

"I never doubted it. It is just that they rarely agree with my own."

"Ah," she said, nodding wisely. "It is true. But which one of us is in the right? Is it always you? Is it always me? I think neither, though we are both too stubborn to admit any such thing."

"Why, you amaze me again."

"And another wonder to speak of is the fact that we have something in common, eh? You come to the garden to enjoy the night.'' She swept her arm skyward like any prima ballerina. "And I, to walk the garden paths. It is where I gather thoughts.''

"So this is where you get all those ridiculous ideas.''

A wry smile and the slightest of giggles were his reward. "Among other sources.''

She tilted her head back to view with her naked eye what his telescope had just given her a glimpse of. "Without the tube it just looks like a blur of light. I think I like it better like this. It leaves more to the imagination, *n'est-ce pas?* One looks at the stars and sees the patterns and dreams of heroes and deeds of magic and bravery and perilous quests, of fortunes and wars and all other manner of glories to be won.''

Jareth angled a glance above him. The majesty of the clear night had always inspired him, and Miss Chloe's poetic statement caught fire to the tendrils of his imagination, filling him with heady vision. "It is a fabulous stage, upon which countless dramas are played,'' he agreed.

"See, there.'' Chloe pointed excitedly. "Does that not look like a snake?''

"That is Lacerta.''

"It does not matter what some ancient man named it or what tradition holds it to be, but what your imagination can conjure. I see a snake.''

"Do you always disapprove of tradition?''

"No,'' she answered, squinting at the sky. "Do you always adhere to it?''

"No.'' Looking upward, he was disturbed to note that the pattern of stars she had indicated did indeed appear to resemble a snake.

"And there,'' she cried, pointing in the direction

of Pegasus, "it is a woman leaning over as if working in a garden."

"Impossible. I see no such thing."

"Yes, there. The form of her hunched over, the drape of her skirt."

Jareth angled a look at her skeptically. "You are making this up."

"*Non!* It is true. It is a story, you see. The woman is working in the garden. She is a poor woman, scratching out a meager life from the earth."

Jareth looked up at the heavens, his features full of doubt.

Chloe continued, "Her young man is gone, and she is grieving her loss."

"How can you tell that from the stars?" he demanded. "I don't even see the woman and you can see all that?"

"*Bien sûr,*" she exclaimed. "Do you not see her tears?"

"This is ridiculous," Jareth murmured.

"And so the snake comes upon her and bites her in her foot and she dies."

"How utterly morbid."

"No, it is romantic!"

"You call that romantic?"

"Have you never read the great tragic loves—Arthur and Guinevere, Tristan and Isolde?"

"Horrible stories. But they do teach a good lesson. Guinevere betrayed Arthur, and so she was condemned to death. Likewise, Tristan—"

"*Non, non, et non.* Guinevere was saved from the fire by Lancelot!"

"Ah, yes, now I remember. But didn't she go to

a convent and pine the rest of her days for her fatal error in judgment?''

Chloe crossed her arms over her chest and shook her head stubbornly. ''No, again. They lived happily.'' She steadied her gaze at him meaningfully. ''In *France*.''

''Miss Chloe, you contradict yourself. At one moment you are arguing the attraction of doomed lovers, and the next you are saying that they didn't really find disaster in the end.''

She shrugged a bit sullenly, completely unconcerned that she wasn't making any sense. ''Sometimes the whole romance is the ill-fated aspect. Like Romeo and Juliet.''

''Italians are rash and hotheaded.''

''It teaches a moral,'' she corrected patiently. ''That to judge another because of their name, or nationality, or social rank, is wrong. Did you never read Capulet's speech at the end?''

''Kindly explain the moral of your tale of the weeping lady. No, no. Allow me. Never garden without proper shoes.''

Chloe laughed, a loud, gusty, infectious laugh that spread out over the night, a sweet and utterly tangible thing. He smiled. She looked so radiant, her head thrown back, her straight white teeth flashing in the moonlight, and that wide, full-lipped smile stretching her mouth in a way that was captivating.

He laughed, too. He hadn't meant the comment to be comical. He had—he was not proud to admit in retrospect—intended to be a bit snide, but it really was funny.

''*Eh, bien, monsieur.* I believe we shall leave the mythmaking to Homer and his friends.''

"It would be a relief, I assure you."

"You did not like my story?" Her mouth puffed into a delectable little *moue*.

Jareth felt a tightening low in his gut at the sight of it. "*Mademoiselle,* you have too much imagination. It is pickling your brain."

"Yes, yes, it is true." She reached out and touched her fingers to the telescope in a gentle sweep that was almost erotic, more so for its casual innocence. "But you are not so lacking in it yourself as you would wish others to believe, I think."

He pretended to be offended. "I'll have you know that astronomy is a science."

"Science and art, sometimes they are the same." She turned, then hesitated, twisting her head so that perfectly pointed chin was directly over a slim shoulder. "And any scientist worth anything is a dreamer. If not so, we would make no progress. How is one to have vision if one cannot dream?"

He didn't answer. She smiled at him and went on her way, leaving him to ponder that thought.

In the silence, he stared at the telescope. He angled a doubtful eye at the heavens and squinted. Did she really see a woman with the soft folds of her skirt outlined in stars?

After ten minutes, he gave up, reasoning that the little minx had made up the whole thing to devil him. But when he hoisted the telescope onto his shoulder and carried it back into the house, he was still chuckling.

Chapter Seven

"So what did your papa say?" Mary asked.

"Hmm?" Chloe was watching the clouds, her mind lost in other matters. Namely, that it was Thursday, and an outing with the children had not been "approved." She thought that perhaps she was being a bit absurd to worry so. Surely, the duke wouldn't mind them stepping into the small walled yard off the kitchen—he himself had suggested it once as a play area.

Except he had also said that Thursday they were to remain indoors. It had been his expressly stated wish.

Command.

She tossed the thought off with a flick of her hair. "Papa? Oh, his letter, *oui.* He has a new love, I think. He is letting me know little by little to see if I object."

"Do you? Who is it?"

"A widow who lives in our village. I like her, and I want Papa to have someone to love." She paused, considering this. "*Non.* He will never love like he did Mama. That was a beautiful love, the kind that comes only once in a life."

"My mother and da fight every day. But still, I think they love each other," Mary said. "What was it like to have parents who were so happy all the time?"

Chloe looked surprised. "I didn't say they were happy all the time. I know they were not always in agreement. When they fought, there were large arguments with yelling and stomping and banging, but afterward there were hugs and tears and kisses and so much joy. They loved each other, and so when they were unhappy, they found their way back together."

"Oh," Mary said with a protracted sigh. "So beautiful. Do you think…?" Her question trailed off as her hands wrung the starched apron on her lap.

She didn't say it, but Chloe knew what she was about to ask. She had asked herself the same question countless times. *Is such a love possible for me?*

It was what every girl asked herself, yearned for, hoped for. Papa told her there would be such a love for her. Someday. He told her to wait and listen to her heart, and she would know it when it came. Of course, he had been dismally inept at describing "it." He said it was peaceful and restless and hungry and completely satisfying all at the same time. Then he had colored a deep, ruddy red and pressed his lips together, patting her hand and refusing to say more.

Similarly, the conversation with Mary dwindled into silence. After a while, Mary said, "I completely forgot! I heard something very interesting the other day. About the duke."

Chloe clamped an iron will over the instinctive reaction of rabid interest. "The duke?"

As if cued by the confidential tones of the adults' voices, Rebeccah's head came up. She and Sarah were digging in a dirt pit. They had constructed a fairly decent tower and were working on its twin. Sarah's little tongue jutted out from between her lips as she concentrated on piling up shovelfuls of earth, but Rebeccah looked like a rabbit who sensed a hunter nearby—alert and all ears.

"Come," Chloe said, tugging Mary toward the hedgerow bordering the kitchen garden, where they would not be heard.

Mary cast a worried glance behind them at the two children covered in filth. "Aren't you concerned the duke will be angry when he sees them like that?"

"The duke and his mother are visiting friends. We have hours before they are due to return." Waving her hand airily in the air, Chloe spoke with confidence. "The children shall have their baths and be safe in the nursery before the carriage even turns up the drive. Now, tell me what is your huge secret?"

Mary darted a glance at the children. Rebeccah had gone back to her digging. "It is wrong to gossip, I know."

"Gossip? We never gossip."

Mary was vexed. "But I should not carry tales."

"Well, is it unkind?"

Mary thought for a moment. "Not at all."

"Good, then it is not gossip. So, tell me."

This satisfied Mary, who sat forward eagerly. "I was talking to one of the grooms and he said old Jarvis was once head groom and he knew the duke and his brother from when they were boys. He was telling him—my friend, that is—that he remembers the duke as a delightful lad, and everyone loved him.''

Chloe scowled. ''Why is that such a huge secret? The duke was once human. Surprising, *oui,* but hardly something to shock.''

Mary shook her head. ''No, no. That is not the amazing thing. Jarvis said that once the duke—the old duke, Charles, that is, the elder brother—well, they were out on the lake in a boat and the boat capsized and Master Jareth—the duke, the new duke, I mean—''

''I know who you mean! Now, what happened?''

''Master Jareth saved his brother and Jarvis came upon them on the bank, sopping wet and bawling like a pair of babes, and Charles—the duke—was saying how he wished Master Jareth hadn't done it. He kept saying, 'Why didn't you just let me drown? I hate it.' ''

Chloe's eyes opened as wide as they could go. ''Why was he saying that?''

''Jarvis told my…*the groom* that Charles hated being duke. His mother always kept him inside, studying his lessons and talking with the solicitors, and he and Master Jareth, they loved to be outdoors. Master Jareth—I mean the duke—was even allowed to play with the village children on occasion, though no one ever forgot who he was for a moment. The two brothers were as close as two boys ever could be. They looked out for one another, but it was the younger son protecting the elder. The more experienced brother sheltering the poor young duke, who was put on such a tight rein.''

The words were true, Chloe recognized that in an

instant. The something unnamable she had known about Jareth Hunt, Duke of Strathmere, was the boy he had been, still inside him somewhere, staring out of those large, soulful eyes with all the sadness of the world. The boy who had frolicked with village children and saved a brother who would, at that time, rather have died because the burden of being duke was too unbearable.

Poor Charles, to feel such despair so young. "How horrifying he wished to die," Chloe said, surprised to find tears of sympathy for the youth she had known as a man. Charles had been a good husband to her cousin, a good father, a good son and a good duke. He had seemed, all the times that she had seen him, as if it were all part of his nature, as easy as breathing, to wield the power and serve the obligation that came with his station. Who would have guessed at what cost such competence had been gained?

"Jarvis told us…that is, told the groom who told me—"

"Wait one moment, Mary," Chloe said with a delicate lift of her brows. "Why do you seem determined to hide from me that you have a man?"

Mary stared back, horrified. "I…" Her shoulders sagged. "You won't tell, will you?"

"Of course I shall not if you forbid it, but I cannot understand why you should wish to keep it a secret."

Mary wrung her work-roughened hands as she fretted. "The duke saw us, you see, down by the stables. That is how Jarvis came to tell us the tale. You see, my man, Daniel, he was one of the village boys who used to play with his grace, and we got to talking about him after he…well, he *saw* us."

"He saw you?" Chloe repeated. "Saw you what? What were you doing?" Horrified at the possibilities, she held her breath.

"It was a stupid thing to do. I don't know what got into us, but we were…well, we were very…um, *close*. Do you know what I mean?" Her color deepened to an alarming crimson. "We were…*kissing*."

Chloe closed her eyes and sighed impatiently. "*Oui, oui,* you were kissing. Now go on, what did he do?"

"He was very angry. He threatened to dismiss us if he ever saw us doing such a thing and…"

Mary's voice trailed off as her eyes took on a distant glaze. Her mouth fell open and began to work, as if she were desperately attempting to communicate but found herself unable. Instead, she lifted a trembling hand to point at the gate. Chloe turned, knowing the impossible was somehow true. Knowing he would be standing there.

And, of course, he was. Equally predictable, he was frowning severely.

Chloe stood. "Go, Mary," she said under her breath. Louder, she said, "Thank you, Mary. Go directly to Cook with my answer that, yes, we shall be late to tea as the children need to wash."

His coal eyes flickered to the children, and he visibly winced at the dirt-smudged pair. Mary scampered off, and Chloe stood alone against the duke.

"Miss Chloe—" he began, grinding out the words through gritted teeth.

"Yes, I know." She sighed fatalistically. "I shall tidy up the children and meet you in the library directly for my dressing-down."

* * *

He was waiting, standing in front of the hearth and staring at the portrait over the mantel. It was of some long-ago Hunt, Chloe had no idea whom. He looked quite serious, with a long, angular face and a straight mouth set in a sober expression that was most severe. Although the present duke was far more handsome than his ancestor, was younger and possessed softer features, Chloe would wager a month's wages the man with his back to her wore a look on his face that matched the dour visage in the painting.

Jareth turned, and she saw she was correct. She blew out a long breath and mentally braced herself.

His tone was quiet. "Please have a seat, Miss Chloe."

"Yes, your grace."

If ever there was a time to play the docile servant, it was now. She sat and clasped her hands on her lap, but her back was so straight it didn't touch the carved back of the chair at all. Her breath hitched, catching in her throat. She made herself look up, not down at the nervous fingers squeezing one another among the folds of her dress.

His dark eyes were on her, inscrutable, intense. She met his gaze head-on, though it took everything in her to do it.

"About today—" She bit off her explanation when he held up a well-manicured hand. The long, tapered fingers were sun-browned, she noticed in a moment of surreal awareness, and very strong look-ing. Hands used to hard work, not the hands of a duke.

When he spoke, his voice was so controlled and quiet, she had to strain to hear it. "Did I perhaps not make myself clear when we last spoke regarding the children's outings?''

''No.''

He gave a slight incline of his head. ''Did I not indicate to you that I wished the children to stay indoors today?''

''Yes, you did, your grace.''

''And is there any time, any time whatsoever, when I would approve the children—'' his jaw worked as he visibly struggled with the next words ''—wallowing in the *dirt?*''

She tried a weak smile that turned into something more akin to a grimace. ''No.'' To her horror, her voice squeaked.

''Thank you, Miss Chloe, for I feared that perhaps my sanity was failing me. I knew I had specified in clear language what my wishes were regarding Rebeecah and Sarah's excursions out-of-doors—*what* they were to be, *when* and *how* they were to be conducted. I was even given to understand you were in compliance with these wishes.''

She knew she should sit quietly and wait him out, but she couldn't help herself. ''Your grace, if I may—''

''No!'' he thundered, his eyes blazing as he brought his left hand slashing through the air. Chloe sat back with a little squeak.

He seemed no less surprised than she. He angled his head down and away from her, peering intently at some point on the Aubusson carpet to his left, or perhaps beyond it, until he could speak again. ''No, Miss Chloe, you may not.''

''I only wished to apologize.''

He gave her a hard stare. ''And should I expect

you mean that, or is this another of your convenient shows of capitulation meant to appease me, which, I have learned, are as sincere as crocodile tears?''

"I am no liar, *monsieur.*" It was said with dignity.

"I am glad to know it. I would like to hear an explanation."

"What do you wish me to explain?"

"I want to know *why* you disregarded my wishes and took the children outside and allowed them to roll in filth like common waifs in the streets of London?"

Her mouth opened and the words spilled out before her brain even registered the impulse. "Did you never enjoy the play of children less noble than yourself?"

It was unconscionable, really, to use the snippet of gossip Mary had related so relentlessly against him, but the way it stymied him brought a thrill to her heart, and it drowned out the pangs of her conscience.

When he was silent, she asked again, "Did you never play as the commoners do? Or was it always lofty pursuits? Geometry and finance and classical literature?"

"I fail to understand," he said at last, "how this *questioning of me* relates to your giving me an explanation. Please address the topic, Miss Chloe, and avoid straying into one of your delightful tangents, which always seem to conveniently divert attention from the matter at hand."

He was lending no quarter. "I merely wished to know if you could understand the intention behind what I admit was my disobedience. I did go deliberately against your wishes. I regret that. I have no real explanation except that I think having the children indoors all day in such fine weather as this, with winter fast approaching, is criminal. I believe they need diversion, especially at this time in their lives."

"And I have stated that they need stringent routine, to bring structure and security to this particularly difficult time."

"With all respect, your grace, I do not know how you would be aware of what Rebeccah and Sarah need. You know them not at all."

"This is a conversation we have had before. They are children. And they are the children of a duke. They need instruction and discipline. That is final, *mademoiselle*."

Quietly, wearily, she said, "No, your grace, they do not."

"I trust I am in a better position to determine what my nieces' needs are than you."

"No, your grace, you are not. I know them. You do not. I am very sorry for the message. It gives me no pleasure to tell you that you have no idea what is best for those two little girls. It is a harsh truth, but there it is."

"And I suppose you are well versed in child rearing. What philosophies do you espouse, Miss Chloe, that advocate thorough soaking in storms and then allowing children to grovel in muck?"

"Water dries, sir. And dirt is washed off. Within moments, *voilà*, one is 'good as new.' But the heart, that is what matters, not so much the skin. If building castles in the dirt brings the children joy, what harm is there in it? Would you have them tied to their nursery, allowed out like animals to be exercised when their owner deems?"

"*Mademoiselle,* please do not insult me."

"Then what philosophies do you, your grace, espouse?" She was becoming impassioned, her resolution to remain calm and unflustered giving way under the pressure of the emotions building inside her. "Do you believe children should be kept on a tight rein as your brother was, never allowed..."

She stopped when she saw his face, not understanding at first what she had said. When she realized, she pressed her hand over her mouth.

His tone was flat. "I believe that is all for today, Miss Chloe. You are relieved of your duties with the children until further notice."

As intense as her regret was a moment ago, it faded quickly in the face of her righteous anger. "If you will dismiss me, do it now. It is what your mother has wished from the start. She tried to get Charles to do it, but Bethany wouldn't allow it. Now she has your ear, and she will use it to get her way. I wonder if these are your thoughts at all, or merely her bidding."

His eyes widened for a moment before he turned away sharply, presenting his profile. "That is all, Miss Chloe. I have dismissed you."

"Then I am to leave?"

His head snapped around to her. "I did not mean for you to leave for good. Believe me, when I send you packing, you will know it."

"Then you intend me to go! Why wait?"

He took a step toward her. It was almost threatening, and some insane instinct made her take a step forward, too, until they were only inches apart.

She had to tip her head up at him, but she met his glare head-on.

"You ought to tread very carefully here, Miss Chloe."

"Why, sir? Why? To keep this precious job? Do you think I need it so much, or that I even *want* it? My father can well afford me to return home. Do not forget, your grace, that my bloodlines are blue enough that my first cousin was deemed worthy to be the Duchess of Strathmere. And I come from no line of paupers, I assure you. So, why should I take care when I wish for nothing more than for you to do the very thing that you want so desperately to do?" She bared her teeth in a flash of a smile. "We are both trapped, *non?* I wish to leave, but cannot. You wish to send me away, but you cannot do it. The children, your grace. We think of them and can do nothing of what we wish."

His breath was fanning her cheek. He was panting a little, and his breath was warm, almost as real as a touch. It distracted her. As she watched him, his eyes moved over her face, losing their intensity, and something began to grow, to come alive in the air between them. Within moments, it filled her nerves with leaden tensions, but she had no name for the dense atmosphere that arose suddenly between them.

"How right you are," he said, and there was a distant, whimsical quality to the words. "Trapped. The two of us, in our separate prisons. How aptly put."

Insanity reigned, registering the absurd notion that there was raw pain behind that statement. It raged, making Chloe want to reach out her hands and touch His Perfectness, who sometimes let her see that he wasn't so perfect, so all knowing, so heartless.

God, what was this feeling stealing her mind from

her? Her chest burned, her arms ached with the effort to keep them still and off the duke's exalted person.

"Please leave me, Miss Chloe. I will be visiting the nursery for afternoon tea tomorrow. I will expect to see you there."

"Then I am not relieved of my duties, your grace?"

He closed his eyes and shook his head once. "A rash statement. You saw through it immediately, did you not? No. I am not sending you away from the children. It would be detrimental to them to toy with separating them from you. And I have seen, first-hand, how irreplaceable you are. Much to my regret."

He was referring to the night he had come to the nursery while she was quieting Rebeccah. Remembering how he had seen her in such a state of dishabille, she blushed and turned away.

"But do not mistake me, Miss Chloe. Push me too far, and I will do it. Not for the thrill of power, not for the need to prevail, not for spite. Understand that it will cause me great anguish, but I will not allow you to damage those girls with inappropriate behaviors."

"I understand," she said sincerely. "And I am sorry, your grace. I truly am." The strange tension of earlier had dissipated, leaving her feeling empty. "I do not think what I did was wrong. However, I apologize for disobeying you. It shall not happen again."

He didn't say anything. The silence stretched on, and she felt awkward. Then, she remembered she had been dismissed some time ago. "Very well, then, good day."

She turned toward the door, took a few steps, then stopped. "I am particularly sorry for the unforgivable thing I said regarding your brother. That was very wrong of me. I do not know why I did it, but it hurt you and I deeply regret that."

She didn't look at him; she didn't dare. She waited a few heartbeats before continuing on her way, almost running up to her room before the tears fell.

Ridiculous to let the disastrous interview disturb her so. She never cried—at least almost never. She had cried when her mother died, and she cried when that terrible accident took the lives of Bethany and Charles. Grief was something she could understand. What she couldn't fathom, as she threw herself on the counterpane once she reached her little room off the nursery, was why she was crying now.

Chapter Eight

He came to tea the next day, just as he promised he would.

It was a horribly awkward affair, filled with gaping silences and strained nerves as the two adults and two children poured tea, stirred in sugar and passed the scones, cucumber sandwiches and biscuits. Rebeccah was clearly afraid of the duke, watching him with wide eyes. She refused to eat or drink any of her sugared tea with generous quantities of cream stirred into it. Sarah, on the other hand, had no such qualms. She stuffed biscuits in her mouth with aplomb and grinned at her uncle, crumbs spattering all over the chair, the table, the floor and her chest. Chloe tried to swipe them away as inconspicuously as she could, but the duke caught her and she gave up, knowing she was not getting anything past his eagle eye.

She was still aching from yesterday. It was strange, the weak, helpless sensation that weighed on her heart. There was no hope of ever making the duke understand what she felt, and felt so strongly, was best for the children. And the truth was abysmally clear. It was only a matter of time—assuredly not a very long time—until she would be asked to leave.

She tried to ignore the melancholy pulling at her insides as she nibbled with flagging enthusiasm on a strawberry tartlet while her tea cooled in the china cup.

"Miss Chloe," Rebeccah whispered with a furtive glance at her uncle. Chloe was sympathetic to her awe. The duke did, indeed, look large and alien seated at their plain wooden table and chairs in the corner of the nursery.

"Hmm? Yes, Rebeccah?"

She looked as if she hardly dared give voice to her request. "May I have a cucumber sandwich, please?"

"*Certainement, ma petite.* Your grace, would you please pass the sandwiches?"

Jareth grabbed the platter and held it out to the child. She shrank back as if it were a plate of fire. Beside her, Sarah munched, oblivious to the swelling tensions.

"Take the plate from your uncle, Rebeccah," Chloe said in a reassuring voice. When Rebeccah looked at her, her eyes filled with fright, Chloe nodded and prompted, "Go ahead. It is all right, *chérie.*"

Her little hands trembled visibly as she held them out to receive the platter. To Chloe's great relief, she set it down gently and placed several wedges of sandwich on her plate.

"*Très bien,*" Chloe said.

Sarah looked at the duke and smiled, reaching a chubby hand toward the sandwiches. Smoothly,

Chloe picked up one and placed it in her grasp to keep her from rummaging among the neat pile.

Searching wildly for some—any!—topic of conversation to relieve her growing anxiety that the children would do something unmannerly to anger the duke, Chloe struck on an inspiration. "Why do you not tell us of your adventures at sea, your grace? I was given to believe you were in the shipping business. You must have sailed the seas to all manner of exotic destinations."

"I was in the shipping business, but I did not sail often."

That was all he said. In the silence, he picked up his cup and sipped. His dark eyes seemed fastened to Sarah.

"But you did go to America, did you not?"

"Yes, once or twice."

She wanted to take the teapot and tap him on the crown of his head for his meager effort. "I am certain the children would love to hear your tales of that fascinating country."

"It is always busy, everyone is much too loud, uncouth, and it is dirty."

Silence. He still stared at Sarah as she began searching on the floor for a lost piece of bread. Chloe quickly intervened. "No, no, *chérie,* here is a new one."

Sarah was happy with the replacement. Rebeccah munched silently on her sandwiches, her eyes round and alert. Her prolonged quietness was disturbing.

"Your grace, did you ever meet any of the famed Red Indians while in the American country? I hear they dress in buckskin—whatever that is—and run about constantly, whooping loudly."

"Buckskin is a leather made from deer hide," he explained, lifting his cup to his mouth. "They do whip themselves into a frenzy before battle by issuing eerie war cries, I have heard it said. I never met one myself." His expression bespoke of no interest in the topic as he sampled a sugared lemon peel.

"Oh."

It was no use trying to engage him in any sort of conversation that would involve the children and therefore allay their fears, at least Rebeccah's fears. Oddly, Sarah was quite comfortable in the man's company, though he did nothing but stare at her in a fashion that was so intense, it was almost rude.

She was about to surrender to silence when a tiny voice asked, "Did you ever see any pirates when you were at sea?"

Rebeccah had spoken. Chloe glanced anxiously at the duke, hoping against hope that he would not brush off this inquiry as he had the others, that he would understand how vital it was that he respond to the girl's question with some measure of positivity.

She was sorely disappointed.

"There are no pirates, or at least very few these days. Do not believe in those ridiculous stories—"

"Surely, your grace, you have encountered a brigand or two in your travels," Chloe said, trying to give him the hint.

Jareth shook his head and frowned. "I assure you, Miss Chloe, I have never had any such unfortunate altercations. However, had I the occasion to make one such fellow's unfortunate acquaintance, I should not think I would deem it suitable entertainment for children's stories."

She could have killed him. Rebeccah stayed perfectly still in her chair, eyes downcast. Chloe wanted desperately to reach out a hand to the small shoulders so stiff with apprehension. "What a shame, *monsieur,* for the children would be so happy to hear such tales as those."

His gaze drifted once again to his youngest niece as he took another sip of his tea.

Chloe resigned herself. It was an utterly disastrous afternoon.

Sarah wriggled off her chair and took up Old Samuel the bear, stuffing him into a toy perambulator and wheeling him about the nursery. The stiff silence of the remaining three at the table was punctuated with crashing and banging as Sarah worked busily.

"May I be excused?" Rebeccah said.

Chloe would have answered, forgetting it was the duke's place, but she was saved that embarrassment by Jareth's quick reply in the affirmative. The child nearly scurried away, grabbing a picture book and curling up in the window seat with her back to them.

He looked after her only a moment, then switched his attention to the younger, who was fussing importantly with her miniature pram.

"Why do you keep looking at her?" Chloe asked.

He blinked and lifted his eyes to hers for a moment before they wandered off, focusing on some faraway point beyond the window. Her question he obviously had chosen to ignore.

"Well," Chloe declared, rising. "This was *très amusant.* Please make your visits more frequent. The children enjoyed it so. And I have rarely been treated to such delightful companionship."

She immediately regretted her jest; it seemed

cruel, but she was frustrated with his insensitive abstraction.

He didn't react to her sarcasm. He didn't even seem to hear her. He appeared to be lost somewhere within himself.

Without word or comment, he stood, folding his napkin and placing it on his plate with as much care as they had been in the formal dining hall. "On Monday, Lord and Lady Rathford and their daughter, Lady Helena, are coming to dine. I would like to present the children to them. Please prepare my nieces for the meeting. If there are any expenses involved, see the housekeeper, Mrs.—Mrs.—"

"Hennicot."

"Mrs. Hennicot, yes."

"Very well, your grace."

As soon as he was gone, Chloe went to sit by Rebeccah, avoiding several collisions with the manic perambulator driver on the way.

"What are you reading?" she asked the child gently.

A pause. Then, "King Arthur."

"One of my favorites." Chloe smiled gently. "I was speaking to the duke the other evening, and he was saying how well he liked King Arthur."

Ah, a spark of interest. "He did?"

"Actually, I know a great secret about him."

The spark surged into a tentative flame. "I can keep a secret!"

"I believe the duke is shy, and that is why he did not talk much to you today. He has no more idea what to say to you than you do to him."

She was clearly disappointed. "Was that the secret?"

"No, *ma petite amour.* He is shy, *c'est sûr,* but he is not so when you are talking about the stars. You know, the night lights that wink and twinkle in the sky."

"Why?" she asked, quite skeptical.

"It is his hidden passion—to watch the stars. That is the secret. Not many know of it. I am trusting you with the secret, but you must be worthy."

"Oh," Rebeccah said with a wise nod. "I will be."

Chloe laughed a little. "So, what I was thinking was that if perhaps you and I work very hard to learn some of the constellations in the sky, the next time your uncle comes to tea, we would have something we could talk about and it would be a more pleasant time."

"Oh! Do you think it will work to please him? A very fine idea, Miss Chloe," Rebeccah declared with as much arrogance as would make her grandmother proud. "Let us begin right away."

Chloe ruffled her hair. "So you have decided to like this uncle?"

Rebeccah shrugged. "He is strange, but maybe he could be nice. If *Grand-mère* does not make him grumpy."

As Chloe perused the shelves for a book to help her teach the constellations, she thought that the child had spoken a profound truth in that last statement, indeed.

"I have invited your cousin Gerald to come for a visit," the dowager duchess said over deviled lamb's kidneys the following morning.

Jareth replied, "Did you? That should be delightful."

"Yes, I am quite fond of the rascal. It shall be good to see him."

"Indeed."

"He said in his letter he should arrive within the week."

"I hope you have his old room prepared for him."

"Mrs. Hennicot will see to it, of course."

Jareth rose and came to brush a kiss against her cool, papery cheek. "I am looking forward to Gerald coming."

"Yes, he was always a good friend to you boys."

They both stopped. Jareth swallowed, even this offhand reference to his brother putting a painful lump in his throat. "He was at that," he replied gamely, and exited into the hall, thinking to head straight for the library, then reconsidering.

He felt restless. Perhaps a ride would be the thing. Pulling aside a footman, he sent him to the stables to tell a groom to saddle his gelding, then headed upstairs to change out of his morning coat and into his riding breeches.

When he was ready, the horse was waiting for him in the semicircular driveway in the front of the house. He mounted and kicked the beast into action, taking off at a breakneck speed across the front lawn and heading directly toward the woods.

He slowed, giving the horse his head as they entered the tangled paths of the copse. The sounds of summer were gone. A growing chill brought a leaden silence to this part of the country. He opened his cravat and let the cool air twine into the collar of his shirt. He shivered when it touched his sweat-drenched back.

In front of him, a deer appeared. A doe, a young one.

He stopped, staring. The doe seemed to stare back. Stock-still, they faced off. Then she looked away, apparently unconcerned at his presence. The touch of the brisk wind traced cold fingers along his flesh, and he was filled with a trembling awe.

"Hello, girl," he said. His voice did not frighten her. Her nose quivered in the air, then her head dipped down to nuzzle the brown grass.

"You aren't afraid of me, but you aren't curious about me, either."

She ate for a while, lifted her head and took a few steps to a new patch, then nibbled some more.

Jareth relaxed. He had played in these woods as a boy, ridden in them when on holiday from school as a youth, but he had never known a deer to be so casually accepting of human company.

Sliding off the horse, he flung the reins over a sapling and sat down on a rock, pulling his knee up under one arm.

The quiet and the doe worked their magical spell on him.

"Do you want to know something?" he said at last.

The doe didn't stop her meal. She didn't react at all to his question. He answered anyway. "I am a fraud."

Her head came up, ears cocked forward, listening. It took only a moment for her to leap three times, then she was gone. He heard the fading sounds of her passage in the woods before all was silent again.

He let out a great sigh and came to his feet, grabbing the gelding and swinging into the saddle.

What do you know? he thought as he wove his way through the dying bracken, *She doesn't like frauds.*

Chloe was cutting paper dolls for the girls when Jareth came again to the nursery. He stood inside the door, appearing tall and out of place in the room full of miniatures. As soon as Chloe saw him, she stood, the trimmings from her project falling like a colorful rain onto the carpet.

"Please continue with what you were doing," he said, entering. His hands he had clasped behind his back, like a general perusing his troops.

Chloe's mind raced. What had she done lately that would merit a visit? Could she think of any transgression, however minor, that would explain his presence here? Nothing came to mind, but that didn't comfort her.

She sat down, deliberately feigning a casual attitude for Rebeccah's benefit. The little girl's body had gone stiff the moment the duke's presence was noticed. Chloe began to cut again. "Perhaps we shall fashion her a ball gown?"

Rebeccah didn't reply. Chloe began to cut.

"What exactly is that?" the duke asked.

Chloe nodded to Rebeccah. "*Chérie,* show your uncle the paper dolls we have made."

The child obeyed, but appeared as if she were offering a sacrifice before a fickle god. He took up the proffered piece, considering it with a frown of thoughtfulness creasing his brow as he sank into a nearby chair.

"These are shockingly good," Jareth said, holding the paper figure up and turning it about. "You made these yourself? You must have some talent at sketching, Miss Chloe."

"It is a hobby, but not only good for recreation. It is an excellent method of acclimating the girls to proper dress requirements for the various social occasions they will be expected to attend when they are older." She hoped she sounded convincing.

He shrugged, picking up the riding habit she had sketched quickly and cut out for the doll. "Quite amazing. Of course, this sort of talent is always incomprehensible to those of us who cannot draw a straight line."

She smiled and returned to her task. "Did you have a particular reason for visiting us today, your grace?"

"Ah, yes." He sat back in his chair and smiled in turn at each of the three faces peering intently in his direction. "I recalled something I thought the children would be interested in. Something about *pirates*."

There was a leaden silence after this grand announcement. As it stretched on, the pleasure evident on his handsome features waned. "I was given to understand you liked pirate stories."

Coming out of her shock, Chloe said in a rush, "Oh, we do. That is, the children adore them. Do not be afraid they will become frightened. I can attest to the fact that they are quite bloodthirsty. Go ahead."

"Well," he said with anticipation, "I was thinking about our talk last time, and realized that I had indeed met a buccaneer, a man of questionable reputation who was later tried and hanged for his crimes."

"What happened?" Rebeccah demanded. Bless her curiosity, for it forced her to overcome her awe.

"I was on the docks one day, overseeing the loading of a particularly valuable shipment of home furnishings."

Chloe exclaimed, "Oh, my goodness, did he steal them right out from under your chin?"

Jareth bit his cheeks. "I believe the expression would be 'my nose.' And no, he did not. He walked past me, brushing against my shoulder and not apologizing for it. Rather, he looked accusingly at me and seemed to consider for a moment whether or not to take exception to my rudeness at having been standing in a spot through which he wished to walk. When he went on his way, the fellow I was standing with, my partner, Mr. Burke, said, 'Do you know who that was?' and I answered I did not. He told me then that the fellow was a well-known privateer whose thin disguise of legality was known by all to be false. His reputation was fierce, and only a few short months after our altercation, he was caught and tried, whereupon he was found guilty and sentenced to hang."

Dead silence. It stretched onward, yawning into discomfort as Chloe struggled to find some suitable reply.

Unfortunately, Rebeccah beat her to it. Even worse, she was honest. "That was it? He brushed up against you on a dock?" Her disappointment was palpable.

Chloe shot him an apologetic smile and interjected her person in between the two of them. "I told you they were bloodthirsty. Nothing short of someone losing their head will satisfy them.''

He was disappointed his grand tale had not been more of a success. Chloe almost felt sorry for him. He was lost when it came to all of this business with the children, but she so appreciated his trying.

''Speaking of boats,'' she said, casting her young charge a leading look, ''Rebeccah has been learning a bit about them.''

''Ships,'' he corrected in a flat voice.

''Pardon me?''

''Not boats. Ships.''

''Ah, *très bien*. Yes, ships. We learned, your grace, that *ships* maneuver using the stars as guides.'' She looked to Rebeccah and widened her eyes.

''It is called navigation,'' Jareth explained.

''The con-sell-a-shun called ass-a minor is the Big Dipper,'' Rebeccah blurted.

Chloe let out her breath in relief.

Jareth looked down at his niece, puzzled. ''Pardon me?''

Panic and confusion marred her hopeful face. Chloe laid a reassuring hand on her shoulder. ''It is Ursa Major, *ma petite*. Is it not wonderful, your grace, that she has learned so quickly? She wanted to know all about the things that you like, so I showed her some books on the stars. *Immédiatement*, she loved it, too.''

His eyebrows came down, but his look was more one of guardedness than displeasure. Then she saw his Adam's apple bob with a hard swallow and she knew it was pure emotion on his face, as if he was touched that the children would wish to please him.

Or perhaps he just couldn't fathom that she would want to.

"It's the Big Dipper," Rebeccah repeated with a wide-eyed stare of earnestness. "It looks like a giant spoon in the sky."

Jareth nodded solemnly. "I have seen it. And it does look exactly so. Have you ever viewed it through a telescope?"

Rebeccah was unflustered by the question. "A telescope is an in-stru-ment used to see stars," she recited, flicking a quick glance at Chloe, who beamed back at her with pride.

"Just so," Jareth agreed. "And I have one—several, actually. Would you like to see it sometime?"

"But it has to be dark outside. I go to bed when it is dark outside."

"Yes, it is best to use it at night. Perhaps some evening when you have behaved particularly well and are deserving of a reward, and *if* Miss Chloe feels it is acceptable to part from your bedtime routine, I could show you one of my telescopes. We could look for Ursa Major."

Her head bobbed enthusiastically. "Yes, I would like to see it. Very much, thank you."

She was so solemn, her small features relaxing for the first time in the presence of her uncle, that Chloe felt a pang of joy threaten to bubble up from somewhere inside her chest. She pressed her hand over the aching spot and blinked back the tears welling in her eyes. Rebeccah looked to her and broke into a large, brilliant smile. "Did you hear that, Miss Chloe?"

"I did, indeed," she answered. "Now go and gather up the paper dolls for me."

Usually, such a request would be met with an argument, but Rebeccah's good mood buoyed her contentious nature. "Yes, Miss Chloe," she cried gaily, and skipped off.

Chloe looked to Jareth, her smile trembling with emotion. "Thank you, so much."

He seemed genuinely surprised. "What did I do, Miss Chloe?"

"Your kindness to Rebeccah. She needs so much. The attention you just showed her, well, it meant a great deal to her."

"But it was such a small thing," he said dismissively. "Rather, I should be thanking you. I take it you encouraged her fledgling interest."

He stood smiling at her, a smile that warmed his eyes. They were a soft, deep brown, fathomless and beautiful with the heavy fringe of black lashes surrounding them. She felt warm, all of the sudden, and acutely self-conscious.

A small voice inside her—her conscience, she supposed—argued this was bad. Bad to be aware of the duke as a man, bad to be noticing how beautiful were his eyes, bad to be having these giddy tremors shooting through her nerves like tiny jolts of lightning within her body. She was not naive about men and women. Her mother had not believed in the impractical sheltering of female children and had argued that ignorance was dangerous, as many girls were unprepared for the feelings that developed when they became attracted to a man, and it often led to trouble.

Not that Mama had been wrong, but no amount of discussion on the topic prepared Chloe for the actuality. Feelings were…so…very…*powerful*.

If he felt it, as well, he gave no indication. After

a moment, he said, "Thank you, Miss Chloe, I have had a lovely time."

"Thank you, your grace," she managed to reply, though her throat felt dry and her voice sounded so faint and wispy, surely he would notice and know her shameful thoughts.

He didn't appear to. He paused to stare down at Sarah, who had sat so calmly during the entire exchange. A slight frown creased his forehead, and she wondered what it was that troubled him when he looked at the girl.

He seemed to shake himself out of whatever it was and cross to the door without another word or glance. When he was gone, Chloe wandered to the window. The gardens lay below. She stared at them, but didn't see them.

Pressing her hands to her cheeks, she felt their heat against her palms. She wondered if she had been blushing and if, God forbid, he had noticed.

"Miss Chloe, can we fashion some gloves for the doll?" Rebeccah asked, once again absorbed in the day's project.

"Yes, *chérie,* I am coming."

Chapter Nine

Lady Rathford had him in her sights. Jareth felt rather like a specimen on a glass slide being inspected with microscopic fervor. His natural instinct was to stare back at her with a touch of his irritation heating his gaze, but impassive was the ultimate in blue-blooded deportment.

He was getting better at it, he felt. Stilling his restlessness—how he longed to be out-of-doors, preferably near the sea!—he sat with his legs crossed and hands dangling over the carved armrests of the upholstered chair, beautifully at ease, though with everything in him he craved a yawn.

Helena was reciting a poem, a sonnet by someone or other. Probably Shakespeare. Her voice was dulcet, well modulated and expressive. Jareth needed to yawn so badly, his eyes watered.

"To this urn let those repair
That are either true or fair;
For these dead birds sigh a prayer."

Jareth's mother clasped her hands together and made a small gasping sound. "Oh, my dear, that was so very lovely. Oh, Portia—'' this she addressed to Lady Rathford ''—your daughter's accomplishments are legion! How well you have done with her.''

Lady Rathford's spine appeared to elongate several inches, and she dipped her head down in an acknowledgment of the compliment. ''You are kind to say so, your grace.''

''And now we have a presentation for you, as well,'' the duchess said, her anxiety betrayed by the quick glance she shot to Jareth and the slight waver in her voice only he would notice. To the butler, she said, ''Summon my granddaughters, Frederick.''

The servant bowed and exited. Jareth sat up, knowing the same apprehension his mother felt. It would not do to have Sarah drop onto her hindquarters and pull off her shoes and socks to play with her feet, or for Rebeccah to take the cream from one of the tarts and smear it all over the furniture. Either was liable to happen. The children were, despite their favorable impression last time he saw them, woefully undisciplined.

''I cannot take all the credit for Helena's accomplishments,'' Lady Rathford was saying with inflated pride. ''She had an excellent tutor. The woman was very stern, exacting at all times, and so Helena always performed her best. Miss Clavermore was in full agreement with our philosophies. A perfectionist at every turn, she never allowed Helena's efforts to flag, not for one moment.''

Jareth felt a hardness in the pit of his stomach at her words. He looked at Helena with pity in his heart, but she was stone-faced with only the slightest trace of a smile on her exquisite mouth.

Of course, one must always look pleasant, even in repose.

"Miss Chloe, Lady Rebeccah and Lady Sarah," Frederick announced. Lady Rathford fell blessedly silent. Jareth braced himself and turned.

Before him stood two young ladies, dressed as miniature princesses in stiff crinolines and with satin bows cinching their waists, and a very docile-looking young woman with her hair neatly pulled back in a tight, unflattering chignon. But Miss Chloe's eyes sparkled, almost dancing with pleasure as she came into the room, her two charges in hand. She paused in front of him, kicking her foot behind her and dropping into a respectable curtsy. To his amazement, the girls did the same.

"Your grace," she murmured.

The transformation was fascinating. She still moved like a dancer, she still buzzed with a vitality that was both intangible and undeniable, but to all intents and purposes, she was blamelessly comported. Good heavens, she was nearly unrecognizable!

When the children were presented to the Rathfords, each stepped forward and smiled at Lady Rathford and Helena in turn. Rebeccah even gifted Lady Helena with a painting she had done herself, explaining that it was of flowers and she hoped that Lady Helena liked flowers.

Helena smiled and told the child she did indeed love flowers and would treasure the painting.

Altogether a rewarding exchange, Jareth noted with satisfaction. Chloe hovered in the corner, clearly the puppeteer. The girls looked to her for signals, which she gave with little nods and almost imperceptible hand movements. Jareth saw she had cleverly positioned herself behind his mother, so the duchess remained ignorant of the machinations, taking full pride in her granddaughters' exemplary behavior.

"Why, your grace, your family is charming," Lady Rathford declared. "What a pleasure to see children so well behaved."

Jareth's mother glowed. "They are darlings."

Lady Rathford addressed Rebeccah. "Do you enjoy music, child?"

"I like to sing. We sing songs in the nursery. Would you like to hear one?"

The older woman seemed to find this delightful. "I would indeed."

Rebeccah, who apparently thrived on having an audience attend her, performed several children's rhymes.

From the corner of his eye, Jareth saw Chloe silently clap her hands twice as if to applaud Rebeccah's efforts.

"Wonderful," Lady Rathford declared. "What other things do you like to do, my dear?"

"I like to dig in the dirt," Rebeccah proclaimed.

The room went silent.

Lady Rathford blinked rapidly, her right hand coming up to toy with the frothy lace at her throat. "Pardon me?"

Chloe stepped out of the shadows. "She said she likes to sing in church."

Lady Rathford was immensely relieved, although how she could have believed such a feeble excuse, Jareth couldn't fathom. "Oh! Oh dear! Of course.

Would you like to share one of your favorite songs—''

''I believe we should have our next song from Helena,'' Jareth interjected. ''The children have yet to hear her wonderful voice, and it would be such a treat for them.''

It was exactly the correct diversion. Far more interested in her own daughter's talents, Lady Rathford quickly agreed with the idea. Helena complied with a soft hymn that kept the children spellbound. When she was finished, Chloe suggested that perhaps the children had stayed long enough, and the duchess readily assented.

Far later, after the Rathfords had taken their leave amid a flurry of compliments, when Jareth and his mother were sitting in the drawing room, Jareth said, ''The children did quite well today.''

''Yes.'' The duchess sounded distinctly relieved. ''I hardly dared hope it would go so well.''

''Miss Chloe did a fine job preparing them, did she not?''

His mother gave him a look he remembered well. It used to cow him when he was a boy. As a man, it gave him pause, and he wondered what he had said to win such blistering disapproval.

''Perhaps in the future she will counsel them to dispense with the merits of mucking around in the dirt.'' The words were spit with vituperative emphasis.

Jareth countered, ''Yet it was Miss Chloe who eased the situation.''

The duchess's eyes narrowed. ''Are you defending her, Strathmere?''

Jareth made a harsh sound, meant to be a short

laugh. "Hardly." Yet his mind was betraying him, dwelling on how her presence had filled the room with energy. Even with the distance she kept, he felt her, sensed her intensity, her desire to please, her desperation that the children shine. And they had. She had made it happen against all odds.

His mother didn't answer. They fell into silence until he took his leave and retired to his chamber.

In her little room off the nursery, Chloe fingered the paper doll she had made that day.

She had a flair, that she knew, for drawing. The doll was a good facsimile. So was the gown she wore. Chloe had bared the shoulders, capping them in a swath that draped softly with large rosettes at the neckline. In pale mint-green—colored by borrowing Rebeccah's water paints—it was befitting any debutante.

The kind of dress Lady Helena would wear, Chloe thought. Unhooking the paper dress, she placed the pieces in the wooden box where Rebeccah had determined the treasures would be held for safekeeping.

Rising, Chloe brought it back into the nursery and returned to her room. She paced a bit, arms wrapped around herself to ward off the chill.

Lady Helena Rathford was the perfect mate for the duke. Beautiful, poised, accomplished, she was everything Chloe was not.

What an idiot she had been to even think of the duke for a moment as anything other than what he was—the man who employed her. No more. Never more. He was worlds above her, his life was beyond hers. All this she understood and accepted. What she couldn't reconcile was the new experience of wanting it to be different.

Sighing, she laced her fingers through her thick brown hair and lifted it, then let it fall in a silky cascade. She wasn't making any sense, not even to herself. It was as if she saw the duke as two people. The *real* duke, trapped inside, was the one with the soft eyes, the haunted features, the awkward pauses and unsure silences, as if something were within, tugging at him, fighting the *other,* who was, as she thought of him, The Duke. Capital letters, no other explanation needed.

Lady Helena was perfect for The Duke. But oh, what a dismal trap for the real man.

There were ghosts in the garden that night. Jareth watched them. Even the lure of the clear night—a star-filled sky and a waning moon—could not distract him.

They were mere memories, but somehow alive and real in the darkness around him, so real he could almost touch them. He could hear them, he could see them. The images filled his head, his internal vision, and took him back…

Himself. And Charles. How many years ago? In this garden that had been his refuge and where Charles would run whenever his tutor allowed him any time to himself.

A great sadness welled up inside Jareth. As a boy, he hadn't understood the import of the events around him, but as a man full grown, a man now in the position of duke and with all of the responsibility that had, at that long-ago time, rested on Charles's boyishly slight shoulders, he knew better how it had been for his eldest brother, and he felt Charles's grief.

It was his own now.

As Jareth was now finding out, the yoke of the dukedom was unavoidable.

The garden, shrouded in the welcome press of night, came back to him as the shades of memory faded away, into the past again.

Emotion left him trembling a bit. His hand sought the back of the wrought-iron bench he knew to be about somewhere. There, he found it and sank down.

A few deep breaths to clear his head, his heart, and he looked up. The lights at the back of the house were yellow squares, a mocking symmetry that the garden mimicked with its carefully laid-out paths and clipped hedges. The drawing room was still occupied. Its gas lamps still burned. Upstairs, in the nursery—oh, he could remember looking out those windows on rainy afternoons down upon his garden—a weak light burned.

He thought of Chloe. It was strange, but he wanted to see her—a dull yearning. If she would walk past the window just now, it would be enough.

Why this would occur to him didn't bear examination. He just sat with the wanting for a while. He gave up after an hour, feeling a bit of a lingering ache as he headed inside.

It was a lonely night.

Chapter Ten

Gerald arrived, and with him the first hard blows of winter. He made his entrance at Strathmere with profuse exclamations over the harshness of the clime, shaking the cold rain off his greatcoat and stamping his muddy boots.

The duchess hurried him into the library, although a cozy fire was already dancing a lively jig in the fireplace in the parlor. She argued that it would be much cozier. At first Jareth was puzzled by this breach of convention until he saw the mud flaking off Gerald's soles onto the old worn carpet. The carpet in the parlor was a plush Persian, purchased only last year, but the library one was old and in need of replacement anyway. Jareth chuckled at his mother's cleverness as he poured out a generous snifter full of brandy for his cousin.

"Everyone is heading to Italy and France," Gerald grumbled as he inched his chair closer to the fire. "What I'm doing here in the north of England at this time of year, I haven't the slightest idea."

The duchess smiled, not lifting her eyes from her crochet. "It is because you are so selfless. You think of how we have missed you, and deny yourself the pleasures with which others consume themselves.''

A bland smile graced Gerald's ruddy face. ''Aunt Charlotte, you are too flattering. However, I regret to disabuse you of the notion of my virtue. It is completely selfish of me to come and visit with my favorite aunt.'' His watery blue eyes slipped to Jareth, who was standing by the window. ''And cousin.''

Jareth turned to him and answered with a small nod.

Gerald had changed. His body was loose and thickened considerably with the years, and his face held the telltale look of a man too fond of drink. Red, large-pored skin, a bulbous nose, the tiny veins visible all gave away his penchant for spirits. His languid ennui bespoke of the dissolute life-style to which he must have become accustomed in London. He had run with the affluent young bucks, that much Jareth knew from his frequent visits to town. He used to arrange to have dinner with his cousin, but they had drifted apart and the points of common interest became harder to find. The dinners became less and less frequent, which was a relief—for both of them, Jareth suspected.

But his mother's perceptions were anchored in the past, in a time when they had all been companions. She smiled at her nephew now. ''We do so love your visits. Do we not, Strathmere?''

''That we do,'' Jareth agreed without much enthusiasm.

''Strathmere. Seems odd to call you that. It must take some getting used to, eh?'' Gerald swirled his brandy about in its snifter, studying it absently.

Jareth looked at him sharply, but Gerald refused to meet his eye. He kept staring into his glass.

After a moment, Jareth answered. "It grows on you."

"On me? Not on me, dear cousin. *You* are the duke. I am merely a poor relation."

"Of course he is the duke," the duchess interjected smoothly. Her brow was slightly creased in confusion. "And you, sirrah, are a most *treasured* relation. You are being so silly, Gerald."

He lowered his face to his glass. "Yes, Aunt, I am indeed."

She laughed as if to indicate that all was settled satisfactorily. "Tell us what you have been doing in London all this time. You naughty boy, you never write."

Jareth couldn't keep his peace. "When I saw you last, you were busy at the various gaming halls in the city. Are you still at it?"

"What?" the duchess gasped. "Surely not. Gerald?"

"Fell in with bad company, Auntie, I confess it. Played too much, too hard and for far too much money. The wages of sin." He paused, tucking his thick chin into his chest. "It is not easy for a man like me—with limited means—to keep up with his betters."

Jareth raised a brow. "Trouble?"

Gerald squinted at him. "I don't suppose you'd understand. You never went in for gambling, did you?"

"My dear fellow, I gambled very heavily in my past. My entire quarterly allowance, as a matter of fact. Sunk every dime into a business with one ship my partner had won in a card game and knew how to sail, but that was about it. Neither one of us was educated in commerce.'' He felt the swell of pride building inside him. How exciting it had been to build Burke and Hunt Shipping from nothing into a small empire. "So, yes, I am familiar with the art of putting one's life-style on the line.''

"It is not the same thing.'' Gerald threw back his brandy and wiped his hand crudely across his mouth. "It is a pestilence inside me. I can't stop thinking about it. It rules me, makes me sick, yet I crave it.''

"Oh, surely you exaggerate!'' the duchess declared, her tone indicating that the messy little confession was to be dropped.

Jareth felt a stab of pity as he watched his cousin. Gerald gave a single, silent laugh and rose to fill his glass again. "Of course I am. I acquired a taste for the dramatic in London, Auntie. Comes from rubbing elbows with all those court dandies and their gossiping ladies.''

The duchess sniffed. "Well, it is not amusing, Gerald. Really, to discuss something so *common*. Do remember yourself in the future.''

A new voice cut into the tensions of the room, just a small gasp, a barely breathed, "Oh!'' Recognizing it, Jareth snapped his head up to see it was indeed Chloe, looking apologetic and a bit frightened, standing in the doorway.

"Excusez-moi,'' she declared, backing up. "I came for something to read to the children. I did not know anyone was in here.''

Jareth made to move forward—not even giving it any thought—when his mother's voice sounded sharply. "My dear, your manners are atrocious! Have you never been taught to knock before entering a room?''

Chloe kept her chin up, yet managed not to look defiant. ''The fire was laid in the parlor earlier. I merely assumed you would be entertaining your guest there. I see I was mistaken. I apologize for disturbing you.''

''No,'' Jareth said, finding his voice. ''It is no imposition. What book were you looking for?''

''It is not important. I shall come back later.''

''I shall get it for you now if you like.'' He tried his most winning smile. ''It will save you a trip.''

''I...'' She was indecisive. ''It was one of the astronomy books you told Rebeccah she could see. May I borrow it to read to her?''

''Yes, yes, of course. I believe I have one that would be suitable for your purposes.''

He went to the shelf and began to search for the volume. She was trying so hard to bring the children and him together, fueling their interest in his hobbies.

''Still stargazing, Jareth?'' Gerald threw out the question.

His mother's voice behind him sounded almost shrill. ''You knew about that?''

''Certainly. Jareth can be a damnable boor when he gets talking about the equilibrium and solace and other such phenomenon.''

''That is absurd,'' Jareth replied as his eyes scanned titles. ''Those terms have nothing to do with astronomy.''

''Oh, whatever,'' Gerald sighed.

''I hope you are not boring Lady Helena with talk of such trivialities,'' the duchess said. ''You cannot expect a lady of such quality of breeding to be tolerant of unconventional interests.''

He found it. That first volume that had sparked his interest as a boy. Cradling the well-worn leather in his palm, he turned to Chloe, locking eyes with her stormy ones. He had a strange thought. It occurred to him just then that a man could get lost in those eyes. They held such pity, such understanding, and something within him surged to life.

He held out the book, taking a step forward. She held out her hand, moving toward him. Her eyes wouldn't let him go.

Without shifting his gaze, he said to his mother, ''What would you have me say in conversation instead, then? Regale the fascinating details of the new lace from Brussels? Perhaps the merits of curling tongs used on dampened hair versus dry?''

Chloe touched the book, taking its weight from him. Somewhere else in the room, in the universe, his mother huffed, ''Oh, really!''

''Start with that one,'' Jareth said softly.

It was she who broke eye contact, glancing to his mother. He watched her narrowed gaze, the almost imperceptible hardening of her features.

She was angry at his mother on his behalf.

It made him smile, genuinely pleased. She said, ''Thank you, your grace. I regret to have disturbed you.''

''It was a pleasure,'' he replied. And he meant it.

She turned, leaving quickly. He was aware of a wish to follow, envying her the ability to quit this room.

In the ensuing silence, Gerald's voice sounded large and loud. ''*Who* was that?''

His mother didn't answer, so Jareth turned to face his cousin. "Miss Chloe, my nieces' governess."

Gerald was sharp, at least sharp enough to be watching Jareth closely. "That accent…is she French?"

"Yes."

He curled his lip. "Never trust a frog."

"Gerald!" the duchess scolded, but it was a half-hearted reprimand.

"Chloe Pesserat is my late sister-in-law's relative. Her cousin. She came to tend the children several months before Bethany and Charles were killed and has been gracious enough to remain in order to avoid undo trauma to the children."

"Pretty thing," Gerald said. "Moves like a dancer." His grin was lascivious, meant to convey to Jareth just how appealing he found the French governess. Jareth sensed immediately that he was being baited.

"Do you think so?" he replied with a barely stifled yawn. He shoved his hands into his pockets to hide the white-knuckled fists from his cousin's too observant glances. "I always thought her rather plain."

"And plenty of trouble," his mother added. "We are planning to get rid of her just as soon as Jareth— as soon as the situation is resolved."

Jareth could scarcely believe his mother's blunder. Two, in fact. First, his name. Second, the "situation" that needed to be "resolved" was his unmarried state. How uncouth of her to mention her master plan so baldly. So, Chloe would stay on until Helena came to live at Strathmere after their wedding and then the responsibility of his nieces would be handled, naturally, by his new wife.

The new Duchess of Strathmere.

It was hard to pinpoint exactly why the plan didn't appeal to him. It made sense. Indeed, he was convinced of Helena's competence and had no doubts she would do an excellent job with the girls.

But she couldn't heal them. That he knew. This his mother didn't care about. He did. However, mindful of Gerald's perked ears, he kept his opinion to himself.

"Do you still like to hunt, Jareth?" Gerald asked.

"It was Charles who loved it, not I," Jareth replied without rancor.

"Ah, yes, I recall that now. Well, do you hunt at all? With the weather turning now, it is the most excellent season for deer. That is the only thing I missed about the country—"

"No."

"Pardon me?"

"No deer are to be hunted in my parks."

His mother scoffed. "Surely, dear, you don't mean to say—"

"I mean," he began, his voice lowering with sternness, "that no deer are to be killed on Strathmere lands. *My* lands. I am well within my rights to make such a rule. Is that clear?"

Silence. His mother's face was pure shock, something he had never seen before. It was the sight of it that brought on the realization of how coarsely he had just behaved.

Gerald murmured some excuse, quickly drained the remainder of his glass and placed it on a teakwood table before exiting the room quickly.

The duchess looked away with a sharp twist of her head, her face as stony as any statue's.

Regret washed over him. Taking a step forward, he placed a hand on his mother's thin shoulder. It felt bony and slight. She didn't recoil, didn't react at all to his touch.

"Forgive me," he murmured.

"I have given Gerald his old room," she said. "Do ask Mrs. Hennicot to check and see if he is comfortable."

And so Jareth knew his request was in vain. The transgression was already forgotten, but would never, never be forgiven.

Gerald took to quail shooting instead. Jareth accompanied him a few times, but, as he told his cousin in the library, the hunt was not one of his interests. The immense paperwork associated with overseeing the duchy provided an adequate excuse to avoid further outings, and a very real one. Visits from solicitors began in earnest now that more than a few months had passed since his brother's death and they thought, he supposed, that his mourning had lessened, at least enough for him to transact business.

He thought often of the past. At times, he longed to go back. He missed his old life. He wanted it again, wanted to be the man he once was.

Colin Burke corresponded regularly, and Jareth always looked forward to his letters, despite the fact that they were somewhat painful to read. Through them, Jareth was kept abreast of the happenings at Burke and Hunt Shipping. In addition, there was the matter of a young redhead of insurpassable beauty by the name of Serena Cameron, whom Jareth had met and liked very much. She was keeping his friend heavily occupied, it seemed. Between the lines of Colin's terse mention of her, Jareth recognized a burgeoning affection that didn't surprise him at all.

He had his own courtship, however, which he saw to dutifully. Helena visited, and he and his mother dined at Rathford Manor as often as possible.

As for Chloe, she was much in his thoughts. He saw her with the children sometimes and at night in the garden. He would be working in the library in the evenings, hunched over his desk, when he would get the urge to stretch his legs. Going to the window, he would wait. Wrapped in a great cloak and moving in those gorgeous, sweeping motions that were hers alone, she would come.

A strange, urgent longing began to grow within him as the days wore on. It seemed the more he steeped in his isolation, the stronger the need grew.

But what exactly that need was, he couldn't say.

Restless, he roamed the house, wishing the weather were pleasant enough to ride. He needed exercise, he needed the outdoors. The roiling confusion of his thoughts consumed him.

It wasn't until he was on the threshold of the nursery that he realized where he was. His mind had wandered while his feet had moved, bringing him here, of all places. But he found it was a pleasant discovery. The door was slightly ajar and he pushed it in.

She was alone, seated at the window seat. Head turned to look at the unhindered gray of this bleak winter's day, she didn't appear to have heard him enter. On her lap was a sheaf of papers, held in one limp hand while her other rested upon it.

"Miss Chloe?" he said softly.

She turned, but didn't rise. Her eyes matched the sky behind her. Her hair was in its usual state of disarray, but for once he could make no complaint. The tousled look suited her. If all those carefully groomed young ladies of London could see Chloe now, like this, this wild, natural beauty would be all the rage within the week.

"Good afternoon, your grace." Her voice was quiet and seemed a bit flat. "If you are looking to find the children, they are asleep. Tempers were short today, so I insisted on them taking a nap."

He took another step forward. "Is anything amiss? You seem distraught. Is it bad news?" He swept a hand toward the letter.

"*Pardon?* Oh, no, no. There is nothing bad from home. A new letter just arrived, filled with nothing but good news."

He sat with her on the window seat, turned so he faced her. His back rested against the worn paneling and his shoulder brushed the gauzy white voile curtains. "You look disturbed just the same."

She was quiet for a moment, turning back to the window. "It brings on a melancholy, sometimes. I miss him so."

There was an unpleasant pang somewhere inside his chest. "Him?"

"*Mon père.* Papa."

"Your father—you miss your father?"

"Of course. And he hates being separated from me, as well. His letters are always loving, saying how he longs to see me again. He is not lonely, however. He has found a new lady love."

"And that does not please you?"

"Oh, no, *monsieur,* it is not that at all. I am very

relieved to see him going on with his life, but it is sad not to be there with him, to share in his happiness."

"Ah," he said as if he understood. But he didn't. He himself had never known that kind of closeness with his kin. "What else do you miss from home?" He paused, then asked, "Where exactly is your home, Miss Chloe?"

"It is a small village called Saint-Remy in the Loire Valley. It is an enchanted place. So green, with large open hills that look like a painting. All the time, people are friendly and will help you."

"Has your family always lived there?"

"My father's family has. My mother was, as you know, English, but she loved it there. She never regretted leaving England, not one day. It is a simple life, a good life." She sighed, lost in fond remembrance.

He glanced out at the denuded garden below. "You must long for home. Perhaps one day you shall return."

Her eyes snapped to his. "Perhaps."

She must have thought he was hinting at her being dismissed in the future. "A week or two holiday should take the edge off your missing them," he said by way of clarification.

Visibly relaxing, she shook her head. "I cannot leave the girls just now. If nothing else, who would be with Rebeccah at night when she begins to cry out?"

"Yes, of course." They fell silent. He was struck with an idea. "Perhaps your father shall come to visit."

She looked at him suddenly with an amazed look

on her face. "You are kind to worry over my homesickness."

"I am not a complete ogre, Miss Chloe, despite what you may think of me."

"I do not think you are an ogre." Her voice lacked the edge of conviction.

He angled his head a little to the side, as if considering her. "You may have cause to. I have been harsh, though with reason, I will staunchly maintain. However, I have not been completely honest with you."

"Oh?"

"I...well, I must confess it, Miss Chloe—I had a recent memory of myself and my brother playing in the dirt, and at an older age than the girls."

Her look of concern changed into one of delight. "How horrid. And you weren't flayed for it?"

"Not in the least. But that is not the worst of it, Miss Chloe. No...not by far."

"Pray, do tell, your grace. Confession is good for the soul, they say. Bring it out, and by the telling you may find some relief for your troubled conscience."

"True enough. If you believe you can bear what I am about to tell you, I will go ahead."

Her lips trembled, warding off a delighted smile. "Please do. I have braced myself."

"It was fun. Playing in the dirt, I mean. It used to make me deliriously happy. Charles, too."

She shook her head as if in disappointment. "Now, that is difficult to imagine. The duke huddled in a dirt pile?"

"We would play soldiers. It was bliss."

"Ah, your secret shall remain safe." She cast him a glance full of mischief. "For a price."

"Now I shall regret my honesty."

"Not too steep a price, I promise."

"Then tell me what it is."

"Hmm." She rubbed her chin, deep in thought. "You must tell the children an honest-to-goodness pirate story."

"But I know no pirate stories!"

"Then you must make one up."

"I am no good at telling stories," he complained.

She nodded solemnly. "Yes, your grace. I had noticed."

"You must help me."

"Very well. Shall we seal our bargain with a handshake? A gentleman's agreement?"

"It shall be so, Miss Chloe," he said, and held out his hand for hers. The touch of her skin as her fingers slid into his was like a jolt to his nerves. Her smile wavered—he thought he saw it, but then the moment was gone and he wondered if he had imagined her falter.

"A deal," she pronounced.

"Yes."

He didn't want to let go. And, surprisingly, she didn't pull away. Not at first. They gazed at each other for a moment, then she seemed to gather herself mentally and her hand slipped out of his.

What the devil had he been playing at? he wondered. Angry at himself, he came to his feet. "Thank you." He felt a bit disoriented, not certain in which direction lay the door.

"Your grace, before you go...I have a question. Something that has been troubling me."

He paused. "Yes?"

"I hope this doesn't distress you. I fear it may. I do not wish to say anything that—"

"Miss Chloe, simply ask!"

"I only want to know—why do you keep staring at her? At Sarah? Is it because she cannot talk? Does it disturb you?"

Jareth smiled and shook his head. "You really are a trial, do you know that? Come, allow me to show you something."

He held his hand out and she came to him, brushing so close as she passed him that he could smell her clean scent. No perfumes, but soft and sweet, like wildflowers on a moist spring night. He inhaled greedily as she walked with him into the children's sleeping quarters, located on the opposite side of the nursery from her room.

From the doorway, he pointed to the blond child lying like a slumbering cherub in her bed. "See her?" he asked.

"Certainement."

"Do you not notice it?"

"What?"

"The resemblance. She looks so like Charles. I remember him well, especially what he looked like as a child. Perhaps the resemblance is stronger when he was younger, but she is his image."

Chloe looked up at him then. She must have caught something in his expression as he gazed down at his brother's youngest child, for she said, "How difficult it must be for you with him gone."

He would have answered that, yes, indeed it was, but his voice didn't function properly, and no sound came forth when he opened his mouth. He shut it and simply nodded.

Then she did the unthinkable. But, of course, Chloe, who cared nothing for convention and everything for humanity, would go beyond the bounds of propriety without a qualm. And do it in such a guileless, natural way that it was impossible to take offense.

She laid a hand on his arm. With empathy filling her eyes, she touched him in a way a woman has no business touching a man, not a man who is not her husband. Her fingers curled against the cloth of his coat, the soft pressure hot under the layers of lawn and wool.

"You must not turn away from the memories. I know it is not seemly to you English to dwell on the emotions you hold in your heart, but grief is like a wound—it must breathe and hurt to expel the poisons. If not, it only festers and grows worse."

"Miss Chloe, I hardly think it appropriate for you to be advising me," he said, but didn't take his arm out from under her touch. He couldn't. It was as if his body had lost the capacity to move. Or perhaps he simply didn't want to.

"Oh, your grace, you are correct, I know this. I am no one, and you are a duke."

"Do not say that," he said fiercely, surprising them both.

Her lips were so full, so facile. Each passing emotion played on them—a frown, a *moue* of confusion, a hint of a smile that entranced with the breathtaking suspense of whether she would grace the world with one of those fabulous smiles that stretched the generous mouth wide and lit up her face to impossible fascination.

Dear God, he thought as he stared down at her, eyes fastened to that decadent mouth. He wanted desperately to kiss her.

Chapter Eleven

Chloe shivered at the way he was looking at her.

She felt suddenly self-conscious, aware of every aspect of his body, and hers.

"What is it I should not say?" she asked.

"That you are no one. I thought the French had dispensed with all this ridiculousness about titles and peerage. You emulate the Americans and their republic, where all are equal, don't you?"

"Is that what you believe, that men are equal to one another, even here in England?"

"Being a duke doesn't make me better," he said with feeling. "It means more is expected of me. Certain things."

She bowed her head and laughed. "Why do you persist in that ridiculous idea? The only thing expected of you is what you expect of yourself."

"Miss…Chloe. It is not so simple."

She looked up at him. His square jaw was set, betraying his tension. She reached up and laid a slender hand against it, feeling the power, the hardness there.

It was incredibly stupid. It went against everything

she knew of this man, to think he wouldn't recoil from such boldness, such unseemly familiarity.

But he did not. He only closed his eyes for a moment and turned his face into her hand, grazing his rough-skinned cheek against her palm.

When he opened his eyes, she knew she was lost. Lost now, lost forever. His hands she felt on her, demanding and not at all gentle, slipping over her shoulders. She saw his lips part, his head angle to one side, and she stepped forward, just one step, in answer to the silent invitation, but it was a step that bridged leagues. Her breasts brushed up against his chest. His head bent lower, his mouth just before hers. Her eyes drifted closed.

In her mind, she refused to heed the alarmed voice inside her head that protested, telling her this was disaster, because all she could do was feel. His whole body was only inches from hers, held taut with leashed masculine power. She wanted him so intensely that it was an actual ache, and when his lips touched hers, she answered hungrily.

It was not a gentle kiss. It was greedy, illicit, frantic. Almost as if they both knew they would come to their senses and had only these precious moments of abandon to indulge their desire, so they gave themselves over to it with fervor.

He wrapped her up in his arms, tight and secure, and she pressed closer, savoring the forbidden feel of his whole body up against hers, the scent of his shaving soap and *him* filling her, making her dizzy.

Yielding to a slight shift in the pressure from his lips, she opened her mouth and felt the bold invasion of his tongue. Her stomach dropped to her knees, her heart melted into a puddle, and electric jolts of pleasure thrummed through every nerve.

Her brain ceased to function and she was spinning away, sinking, floating, some undeniable sensation that was deliriously joyous and exciting and—

He broke contact, pulling her away as he raised his head and gulped in air. Dazed, she curled her hands about the collar of his tailcoat, seeking stability, needing strength.

"Dear God," he muttered and shoved her away. He turned his back on her and walked toward the door, stopping in the middle of the room, not looking at her and thrusting his hand furiously into his tousled hair.

He stayed like that, back to her, head bent as he collected himself. It felt as if each second took an hour to pass, yet even with this slowed perception, her mind was having a difficult time comprehending what was happening. Her heart did, though, for it immediately began to burn with an exquisite blend of loss and humiliation.

She waited for what came next. He was rather predictable. There would be a polite apology, she supposed. The promise it would never happen again. The rebuke, the rejection.

"Do not dare tell me that was a mistake!" she blurted.

To her utter amazement, he shook his head and began to laugh. After a moment, he glanced back at her over his shoulder.

With his hair disheveled from his frustrated maulings and his brown eyes warmed by his laughter, he was devastating. "Do you never quit, *mademoiselle?*"

She smiled, relieved. Her spirits tweaked to the challenge. "The war between the French and the English is centuries old, *monsieur*. What gives you cause to think it shall be put to rest now?"

He returned to her, gently touching her chin as if toying with the idea of kissing her again. "It *was* a mistake, Chloe. You and I know it. I don't want it to be that way, I will admit that. And bless you for your erstwhile honesty, I can see clearly in your eyes that you don't, either. But there it is."

Her eyes misted. What a fool he was!

His hand dropped and he said in a different voice, *The Duke's* voice, "I do not see why this should disturb the professional relationship we have established. It was, after all, only a kiss."

She heard him leave. She didn't see it, for her eyes saw nothing.

Only a kiss.

Her body still trembled and her heart was beating so quickly she was panting from it. Her lips burned. Her hands burned. Everywhere he had touched her was on fire.

Only a kiss?

"Strathmere, you are too quiet tonight."

His mother's voice cut into his thoughts, rousing him from his deep contemplation of the utterly despicable nature of his character.

"It is rude to our guests," the duchess continued starchly.

Jareth looked up and mustered a smile for Helena. "Forgive me," was all he said.

She came to stand by his side, looking with him in the direction of the garden. "Perhaps the burdens of your new position wear on you. It must get tiresome.''

Pretty words, spoken in that velveteen voice that should have, by rights, banished his miserable mindset, but they sounded hollow somehow.

Ah, it was his mood tonight, he told himself, and said, ''All I need is to hear your voice, and I know it will bring me out of this dreadful ill humor. Would you sing for me, please?''

Helena flashed a glimpse of a smile. With her turned-up nose, she looked a bit mischievous. It was the only unconventional thing about her.

''If it would ease you tonight, your grace,'' she said with a humble incline of her head. To her mother, who was deep in conversation with his, she said, ''Mama, will you accompany me, please? The duke has asked me to sing.''

Lady Rathford immediately leaped to her feet with as much alacrity as if a full regiment of redcoats had filed into the room. ''Oh, of course, your grace!'' She hurried to the pianoforte.

Jareth's mother was no less pleased, folding her hands on her lap and giving her son a nod of approval. ''Gerald!'' she called sharply. ''Please attend! Lady Helena is to sing.''

Gerald had been huddled with Lord Rathford all evening, both having discovered a kindred spirit in their similar love of hunting. They had been talking by themselves for more than an hour.

Obediently, Gerald nodded to his aunt, but Lord Rathford, who had been implicated in the admonishment to Gerald, chose to ignore the directive until his wife hissed a loud, ''Christopher!'' Rolling his eyes, he flounced back in his chair and crossed his arms over his chest in an elaborate pout.

"Sing the aria from *La Traviata,* darling," the duchess requested.

"Very well, your grace," Helena answered, and bowed her head.

The song was magic.

Jareth let it pour into him, her passion touching all the raw places inside himself. He watched her, so beautiful and so brilliant.

He liked Helena, very much. Of her accomplishments, he was in awe. She was a kind person, if a bit bland.

She was a good woman. He could not ask for better in a wife. He must stop thinking her wan and spiritless just because she didn't act like a hoyden and say startlingly intuitive things.... Didn't she have such passion, such sensitivity that her voice could stir a jaded heart?

The tension began to ease in him. It had been there since that abominable loss of control in the nursery.... He had been foolish, putting too much stock in a moment's aberration. After all, he had said it himself. It was only a kiss.

The aria built, and with it his sense of well-being. It nearly eclipsed the earlier unrest that had him so undone until his gaze wandered to the garden once again.

She was there.

Chloe.

He closed his eyes and swallowed hard as he realized he had been waiting for her all night.

The children were excited to be visiting the stable, mostly because Rebeccah was besotted by all manner of felines and one of the resident cats had just had a litter of kittens. Sarah emulated anything and everything her elder sister did, so she was equally jubilant as the three of them headed toward the barn.

"Now, you cannot pick them up," Rebeccah was saying in a bossy voice to her little sister, "because the mama cat might not like it and she'll scratch your eyes out."

"Rebeccah," Chloe warned without breaking stride. Such moments of intimidation were expected with Rebeccah.

"It's true," Rebeccah retorted, needing to have the last word. Chloe looked at Sarah, saw that she seemed not the least bit intimidated by Rebeccah's dire warnings, and let the matter go.

Rebeccah resumed the lecture. "You must wait until I hold the kittens first. Each one, because I have to make certain that it is safe. You are littler, you see, and if the mama cat got angry, me being bigger, I could push her away. So wait until I give you a kitten and don't grab."

Chloe looked at the smaller child again, observed her unperturbed expression and smiled. For all of Rebeccah's lordly imperiousness, Sarah would most likely do as she pleased. Never had Chloe seen such an implacable child.

As they drew closer to the stable, the girls' excitement built and they broke into a run. They disappeared into the open doorway, Rebeccah shouting directions to Sarah, trying desperately to take command.

How like her grandmother she was!

A short shriek sounded from inside the barn,

bringing Chloe instantly to attention. Breaking into a run, she almost collided in the doorway with a figure hurrying out.

"Oh, my dear, excuse me—Chloe!"

It was her friend, Mary, flushed and panting and looking exceedingly distressed…and decidedly guilty. Another figure came up from behind the pretty maid. Chloe recognized him as one of the grooms.

Chloe said quickly, "Where are the children?"

Mary's mouth worked but nothing came forth. The groom stepped up and said respectfully, "They came in at full tilt, miss, and startled Miss Mary here. No harm done. It was Mary you heard give a shout, out of surprise, you see. The children paid it no mind and went on back into the stalls. I told them where the new kittens were."

Mary finally recovered herself, bobbing her head once. It was such a childish gesture, done so emphatically it knocked her mobcap askew.

Or had it already been crooked?

Understanding dawned as Chloe took in Mary's embarrassment, her reddened lips and slightly mussed appearance. Mary was a good girl, of that Chloe was certain, but she also knew the dangers of a man whose charms could seduce a woman into that realm beyond thought or care for the consequences.

"Well, thank you, then," she said to the man. "What is your name?"

"Daniel," the groom replied, touching his forelock and offering a jaunty grin. Oh, yes, this one had it in him to turn a girl's head for sure.

"Well, thank you, Daniel. Can you possibly direct me in the same—"

A loud shriek interrupted her, and for the second time, Chloe was struck with mortal fear on behalf of her charges. Daniel was quicker to respond, however, and he had already spun about and was racing into the barn before Chloe unglued her feet.

She followed him down the narrow corridor, lined on both sides with stalls. She could see the girls up ahead, clutching each other as a beautiful chestnut mare leaned out of her berth, sniffing the tiny intruders with interest.

Rebeccah shrieked again. Little Sarah had her eyes and mouth squeezed shut against the terror of the horse's curiosity.

Daniel skidded to a stop and chuckled. Chloe raced past him, collapsing to her knees in front of her charges.

"You ladies are afraid of Jess?" Daniel said, going directly to the horse and giving her a gentle nudge back into her stall, then shutting the upper half of the door to prevent her from returning, inquisitive thing that she was. "She's just an old mare, can't do you any harm."

"Shh," Chloe coaxed, peeling Sarah from her sister and taking both quaking children into her arms.

"I—I—I d-don't l-like horses-s," Rebeccah stammered before dissolving into loud, wailing tears.

Mary arrived. "What was it? What happened?"

Daniel explained, "Jess was poking her head out to see if these young ladies had brought her a treat, and they kind of got a bit scared, 's all."

"Oh, the poor dears," Mary exclaimed. "Well, of course they did, the horse being so very large to them, being so tiny themselves."

But Chloe knew it was not only the relative size

of the horse that had frightened the girls. Since the accident, they had been terrified of any kind of carriage or coach—anything, in fact, to do with horses.

Not for the first time, she wondered what those moments of catastrophic horror had been like for them. Worse, she *should* have known to avoid this, but her brain was in a fog these days, too consumed with her own worries.

She led them outdoors and continued to rock them until Sarah began to relax and Rebeccah's hysterics resolved into hiccups. Mary and Daniel stood by awkwardly, evidently feeling responsible in part for the fright the girls had received.

In the end, it was Daniel who succeeded in calming them. He fetched one wriggling, tiny kitten from its mother and brought it out to them. The tuft of fur was so new its eyes were still shut, and the girls were instantly transfixed.

Eventually, they were persuaded to come into the barn again after repeated reassurances that Jess and all the other horses were secured in their stalls. Chloe applauded their courage, and they made it to the mother cat's bed, where six newborn kittens dispelled the last of the children's apprehensions.

Rebeccah was so delighted with their boon she could hardly contain herself. "Can we bring one to live in the nursery? Please, Miss Chloe? Please?"

Hunkering down next to her, Chloe couldn't help but be charmed herself by their adorableness. "Perhaps. We shall have to ask your grandmother."

Rebeccah stuck out her bottom lip. "She would never say yes. She never allows us to have any fun."

Chloe looked at Mary with a roll of her eyes, in complete sympathy with the sentiment. Mary had to turn away and cover her mouth to stifle her giggles. Daniel was beside her in an instant, and Chloe did not miss the solicitous arm that went around her shoulders.

She sighed. She was happy for Mary. But envious. It wasn't a very attractive quality to admit, but there it was. Looking at what could never exist for her did indeed hurt.

After Mary left to return to her duties, Daniel said, "I'll be in the tack room, miss, if you need me. Remember, all the horses are either closed up or out in the pasture, so there's nothing to frighten the little ladies when you leave."

"Thank you, Daniel, you've been very helpful."

He smiled and seemed uncertain, as if there was more to say but he was uncomfortable saying it. "Miss…er, about Miss Mary. I would appreciate it, as perhaps one good deed in return for another, if you wouldn't mention to anyone she was here. You know she's a good worker, but if others learned of it, they might think she was shirking."

Oh yes, Chloe agreed, not to mention that someone could forbid the blossoming romance out of pure perverse meanness. And Chloe knew exactly who that someone was. "*Certainement,* Daniel. Mary is my good friend. I shall be happy to keep this to myself."

He showed off his handsome smile. "Thank you, miss."

Chloe returned to sparring with Rebeccah as that one insisted on exclusive domain over the animals. Sarah merely ignored her sister and gently cradled each tiny baby she could get her chubby hands on. As for the mother cat, she merely purred and blinked wisely, as if she were nothing but amused at this human fawning over her offspring.

As they sat among the straw, the children haggling over the kittens, Chloe was appalled when a masculine voice sounded above her.

"What have we here?"

It wasn't the duke, she knew. She would recognize that voice immediately. Looking up, she spied a ruddy, slightly portly man standing in the stall doorway.

She had seen him before, in the library when she had unintentionally invaded a private family gathering. He was Gerald, she had heard the gossip among the servants. No one liked him, except the dowager duchess, who seemed to dote on him despite his rather obvious shortcomings.

"We are looking at the kittens," Chloe explained, coming to her feet.

He looked down at the tangle of excited children and squirming animals with disinterest. "Yes, how charming." Lifting his watery eyes back up to Chloe, he said, "I am afraid we haven't been properly introduced, although I know you are my cousins' governess, Miss Chloe."

"*Oui.*"

His smile deepened, becoming more ingratiating. "I am the duke's cousin, Gerald Hunt."

"Pleased to meet you, sir. Have you met Rebeccah and Sarah?"

"No, I have not. But they are too fascinated by their pets to bother with an old boring relative like myself." He took a step forward, bringing him far too close for Chloe's comfort level. His eyes flittered over her face, down to her bosom. "How are you enjoying Strathmere? Quite a place, isn't it? You are French, aren't you? What part of France do you come from?''

Not certain which one of these inquiries to address first, Chloe took a step backward. ''I am from a village near Blois, and I find my duties at Strathmere most enjoyable.''

''Yes, children are delightful, aren't they? So, how do you find my cousin? Dour, isn't he? Not like I remember him. Dear Auntie Charlotte has her claws too deeply in him. Going to smother out the fun in him like she did to poor Charles—''

''Sir!'' she exclaimed, his last comments igniting her temper. ''The children!''

Whether or not Rebeccah had heard him, or understood if she had, Chloe couldn't tell. She did seem unnaturally still, and Chloe suspected she had heard the reference to her father. She kept her head bent for a moment, then looked up through her lashes and said, ''Miss Chloe, can you ask *Grand-mère* for us if we can have a kitten?''

Chloe opened her mouth to answer in the negative—knowing that should she approach the duchess with the idea, the woman would almost certainly deny the request out of hand—when Gerald hunkered down next to the child.

''How about if I do it for you, precious? Your *Grand-mère* could never resist me, the foolish woman.''

Rebeccah looked at him steadily, completely uncharmed by his efforts. ''Thank you,'' she answered.

Pleased with himself, Gerald glanced back up at Chloe, grinning winningly.

Chloe gave him a bland smile in lieu of her thanks.

Chapter Twelve

In the thick darkness of a moonless night, Chloe exited the house by the pantry door, pausing to gather her woolen cloak more closely about her shoulders. The sun had set on a clear sky, but it now felt moist all of a sudden. Glancing upward, she saw that only a few stars shone. These seemed to be dimmed, as if a thin haze obscured their brilliance.

She stepped away from the gas lamp installed by the back door and let the darkness swallow her. The garden seemed preternaturally still, caught in the thick soup of a gathering fog and the threat of an oncoming storm.

It made her shiver, the way one does when, as the saying goes, someone walks over one's grave.

A sound slowed her steps. She waited, stopping to listen for it again. After a moment, she decided it must have been some nocturnal animal—probably a sprightly field mouse about his nightly duties—and continued on her way.

Jareth let out a long breath as he stood, hands on hips, gazing disgustedly up at the sky. Beside him was his newest telescope. It had arrived this very morning and, anxious to try it, he had brought it out to the garden, only to find the cloud cover gathering at a discouraging rate. Having dim hopes it might clear, he set the instrument up anyway. He really just wanted to see its design, revel in its superlative newness and the promise of the wonders that would be within his view with this, the newest and most powerful tool of science.

The sound of footfalls behind him caught his attention. He had purposefully, and with admirable restraint, stayed away from the area of the garden where Chloe usually took her strolls, although he doubted even that indomitable soul would venture out on a miserable night such as this. Apparently, he had been wrong, but Chloe ever surprised him, he reflected.

The fog played tricks sometimes, throwing off perception and muting noises so one's judgment could never be trusted, but it sounded as if someone were approaching along the path from the back of the house.

He shrugged off the notion after a while when nothing materialized and no further footfalls came. He set about to unfasten the lens to keep it safe for transporting the telescope indoors. He slipped it in his pocket and hunkered down to disassemble the tripod upon which the casing stood.

There! The sound again. He knew he was not mistaken this time. Straightening, he turned, just as a large presence appeared in front of him. It was shrouded in the fog, but still distinguishable as the figure of a man dressed in dark clothing.

"Gerald?"

The blow caught him completely unawares. It struck him on the side of the head and felled him to his knees.

He stayed crouched until his brain could clear. Another blow, this one a kick, hit him in the ribs and he collapsed onto the ground.

He couldn't see, though he could sense the threatening presence hovering over him. His reflexes kicked in and he sprang forward, ignoring the pain, and wrapped his arms about the man's knees, toppling him to the lawn.

"Blimey!" the man yelled.

Jareth crawled upward, capturing a beefy fist in his two hands. The fingers were like sausages, curled like a claw as he bent them backward, the dull sheen of worn silver circling one of them. He pressed on, ignoring the cry of pain, until he heard the snap of the wrist. The man roared and brought his other fist down on Jareth's head and the world went blank.

It had been a mistake to venture out tonight, Chloe concluded, retracing her steps back to the house. The darkness seemed to tighten around her, and sound took on eerie, even threatening proportion.

There were strange noises just a moment ago, like someone behind her. She had even thought she had heard the sounds of a struggle close by. Quickening her steps, she heard a male voice swear. Twice. Then a scuffle, a grunt, a thump.

She wanted to run, but her legs seemed frozen. She listened, her heartbeat thundering in her ears. Footfalls receding told her someone was running away.

Suddenly desperate for the safety of the house, she took three long strides before her toes jammed up against an obstruction on the path. She pitched forward. It was not to the ground she fell, but upon a person. Peering closely, she found that person, upon whom she now lay, was the duke. His eyes were closed and he seemed to be unconscious.

"Your grace! Your grace!" Grasping his broad shoulders, she shook him. He groaned, rolled his head from side to side, and then his eyes opened to slits for a moment before he winced and shut them again.

She cradled his face in her hands, shaking it back and forth. "Jareth, wake up, *s'il vous plaît.*"

When he spoke, his voice was scratchy. "Either I've died and am at this moment reaping my just rewards, or I am dreaming, for I am under the distinct impression that Miss Chloe Pesserat is lying atop my person."

Relief and anger mingled, and stiffened Chloe's spine. "I was going to ask if you were well, but it is obvious that thick skull of yours is impenetrable."

He opened his eyes and smiled. "As delightful as this interlude is, I must ask if you would mind rising. I suffered a few blows and am, at this present time, unfortunately too uncomfortable to enjoy this...proximity."

Chloe dug her elbows into his chest and heaved herself back onto her heels. Jareth hitched in a short, pained breath at this inconsideration, but said nothing.

"Are you well enough to stand?" Chloe asked grudgingly, still angry but concerned, as well.

"Yes, yes." He moved slowly, however, coming first to his knees and pausing, testing his strength before standing.

Pity displaced her annoyance enough for her to offer, "Here, lean on me."

"No, I am fine." He stepped away as if scalded when her fingers brushed his arm.

He was again *The Duke,* and he needed nothing from her.

He looked back at her, seeming penitent at his rash behavior. "It bruises a man's pride, I suppose, to be found lying helplessly on the ground by the woman…by a woman."

The sting of a rabid blush still singed her ears, but she smiled. "We should hurry inside. Whoever struck you may return."

"Yes," he agreed. He stepped slowly, careful with his abused body. When they had gone into the empty parlor by way of the French doors, Chloe offered to call for someone to help him.

"I just need to sit," Jareth said. He eased back into a chair, choosing one wit the thickest cushions. "Could you light a taper? They are over by the table by the…yes, there. In the drawer to the right you will find…good."

The scant light seemed thin and weak in the gloom, but it was better than the dark. Chloe lit a second candle and a third, and the gentle glow softened the room.

"I had best not be bleeding," he said, touching his fingers to the wound on the side of his head. "My mother will be inconsolable if I stain her furniture."

"Let me see," she said, peering closely at his face. After a moment, she pronounced him sound. "No blood. Do you think anything is broken?"

"Nothing but bruises, I believe. It was a brutal assault, but brief."

"Why would someone attack you?" she asked.

He shrugged. "I have no idea. A thief, I should think. I shall have someone summon the sheriff, but tomorrow will be soon enough. No doubt the cur who attacked me is halfway to York by the midnight."

"A thief? Do you really believe that was who it was?"

"What else? No doubt skulking about in hopes of finding a way inside. I am sure the fellow never thought to encounter anyone out there on a night such as this. No one sane would, you know." He gave her a rueful smile, as if acknowledging their twin perversities in daring the outing.

She wasn't all that ready to believe his neat little explanation. What's more, she wasn't certain he did, either.

But what else could it have been? "I suppose so."

"There," he said with a nod. They looked at each other for a moment until he glanced away, tucking his chin down into his chest, but not down far enough to hide the smile toying with the corners of his mouth.

"What are you laughing at?" she asked, feeling defensive.

"Nothing. Not a thing, Miss Chloe. Perhaps you should summon a footman or something if you cannot locate Frederick."

"I will summon whoever you wish, *after* you tell me what is so funny."

"It is nothing, truly. I…I am just tired." He tried to look innocent, but she was having none of it.

She was not about to allow him to get away with that. "Your grace—"

"You called me Jareth in the garden."

The words took her aback. She stopped and swallowed. "Oh. Did I? I suppose I did. I didn't realize what I was saying, I was so overcome at the time."

"Do not apologize, please," he said. His tone was distant, thoughtful. "It has been months since I heard my name spoken. Can you imagine that?"

The fact of this sobered her. "No. I cannot." Realizing she had gotten diverted, she started. "And do not change the subject. You are laughing at me because I fell on you, aren't you?"

He held his hands up in front of him as if to ward her off. "Admittedly it was rather amusing, yes, to awaken to find you…"

"Enough! You insult me by intimating that you were either having a nightmare or had expired and found yourself in…well, Hades, and now you laugh at me. I was terrified, I shall have you know. How awful of you to make sport of me."

"No less frightened than I, I can assure you, if it does not lessen your opinion of me for me to admit it. As for my first words upon awakening to find the two of us in such an interesting position—think on my exact words, *mademoiselle*." He paused, giving her a meaningful look. "I chose them with care."

Chloe considered this, thawing when she recalled that he had, indeed, said only that he had thought himself either dreaming or reaping his just rewards. He had said nothing about either alternative being pleasant or unpleasant.

So, was he hinting that finding her atop him had been more of a heavenly than a hellish discovery?

The rational part of her brain began to refute this, backing away from it as gingerly as one would a bear reared up on its hind legs with its claws displayed.

But her heart would not be stayed. It pounded against her ribs, swelling with the promise that he…

What? Wanted her?

Even if he did, she was worldly enough to know exactly what it was he wanted. She herself had seen the woman who would be his bride, and soon. If he wanted her, Chloe, at all—if this belief were not a mere delusion of her own desperate desire—it was certainly with no intentions of honor.

How pathetic that even in light of this, the possibility that he wanted her at all made her stomach tighten with excitement.

"I shall go fetch that footman now," she said, and turned on her heel.

Unfortunately, the footman she selected felt the need to summon Frederick, the butler, who in turn felt it his duty to send a maid upstairs to inform the dowager duchess of the night's events. She came rushing downstairs in a state of barely controlled panic, demanding to have the doctor and the sheriff fetched, and exhibiting other varieties of hysterics.

Chloe was rather surprised Jareth handled her fuss with a firm hand, insisting he was fine and needed no physician and that the matter could wait until the morrow to be reported to the authorities. Disgruntled, the duchess subsided for a moment until she remembered Chloe. "What were you doing out-of-doors?" she snapped.

"I walk in the evenings sometimes."

"Cease such activities at once. It is obviously unsafe, and you must not encourage the criminal element by irresponsible behavior."

Jareth cut in, his voice sharp. "I hardly think Miss

Chloe's behavior is at issue here, Mother. She has done nothing wrong.''

The duchess glared at Chloe, as if to communicate that she wasn't at all certain this was true. ''Calm yourself, Strathmere. You have had a trying evening. Your judgment, therefore, can hardly be sound in regard to this matter.''

''I was attacked in the garden, it is true, but the evening did not even begin to be trying until just now.''

Chloe's jaw dropped; the duchess's tightened. Without another word, the older woman swept toward the door in a dramatic and elaborate exit. In the wake of it, there was a protracted silence.

''Well,'' Jareth said at last, slapping his thighs and speaking to the room at large. ''That did not go well. Perhaps I should go ahead and retire before something really catastrophic happens.'' To Chloe, he confided, ''It has not been a good day.''

He rose very slowly, muttered the word, ''Stiff,'' as a sort of explanation for his labored movements, and made his way to the door.

The following morning, the sheriff was summoned and Chloe was asked to give her version of the events. This she did calmly, her demeanor betraying none of the pulse-quickening excitement she felt when recalling certain details. The sheriff was a pleasant man who stuck to business and nodded thoughtfully as she told her story.

''Thieves,'' he pronounced. ''The duke agrees. Let me ask you, Miss Pesserat, did you see anything about the man that might aid us in identifying him?''

''No, *monsieur*.''

"No type of jewelry or anything of that sort?"

"Nothing," Chloe replied with a shrug.

Pushing his liver-spotted face closer, the sheriff asked, "A ring? Did you see a ring?"

"I did not."

"Then I must thank you for your cooperation, Miss Pesserat." He seemed pleased with her, smiling with approval. "You have held up well considering the circumstances. Most ladies, well, I imagine they would have fainted dead away, and where would the poor duke be then, I ask you?"

Chloe winced at the implication that since she was of good, sturdy stock, that of the commoner and not a lady of substantive breeding, she was not delicate enough to be subject to the vapors. Not that she wished to be silly, but the indirect insult rankled.

As she exited the room, Chloe tried to calm herself. Her father had always taught her to keep one's temper, one had only to breathe deeply and seek to focus one's attention on another matter.

In her case, another matter sought her. On her way to the stairs, she was waylaid by Gerald.

"Ho, Miss Pesserat!" he called, trotting up behind her. Chloe turned. "Ah, I see the good sheriff is busy gathering clues. Picked your brain, has he?"

"He merely asked me to relate the facts," she replied. She didn't particularly like Gerald, but after her initial aversion she had come to view him as harmless. He was no threat. Indeed, he had made it a point to be friendly, which was a welcome change from the rancor with which she had met at Strathmere thus far.

"Any theories on who the culprit could be?" he inquired.

"A thief, it is believed."

He nodded sagely. "The rascals are everywhere."

"If you will excuse me, I am already late."

"One more moment, if you please. I wanted to tell you that I have spoken to my aunt on behalf of the children with regard to the matter of the kitten." Puffing up his chest, he pronounced, "It was not easy, but I have gotten her to agree."

Chloe was truly delighted with this news. "Really? *Mon Dieu,* but this is wonderful. The children shall be so happy. Thank you, sir."

"I thought perhaps we could go together, the four of us, to pick out the new pet. What do you say?"

"Oh, *monsieur,* the kittens are too young to be separated from their mother just yet. It will be several weeks before one can be taken."

He was visibly disappointed. "Drat. I was rather fond of my good deed and am impatient to see its reward. I hate to be kept waiting."

Chloe giggled. "The children shall find it impossible, as well. No doubt they will pester me a thousand times a day with wanting to know if it is time yet to bring it home."

"I was under the impression that the little one doesn't speak."

"Sarah. Yes, it is true, but she makes her will known in other ways. Strongly."

"Ah, I see."

A new voice cut in. "What do you see, Gerald?"

They turned to find Jareth standing only a few feet from them. He had his arms crossed over his chest, and his expression looked as if he had just caught them pilfering wine from the cellars.

"We were speaking about the children," Gerald explained.

"I was not aware that you were interested in the children."

He pinned his cousin with his icy stare. His dark eyes had gone cold and hard and his angular face set in stern lines. She felt a tremor of response snake up her spine, touching off a slow burn in the pit of her stomach. For all his severity, he looked so handsome just now, she felt the strength drain out of her knees.

Gerald merely chuckled, as if Jareth's comment pleased him somehow, and excused himself.

"I see you are up and about, your grace," Chloe said. "Your injuries do not trouble you?"

"I have many troubles, *mademoiselle,* but other than a little stiffness and some bruising, my physical health is not one of them."

"Excellent."

"What were you and my cousin talking about?"

"He has received your mother's permission for the children to keep a pet kitten."

Jareth snorted. "He was always able to charm her. I believe he could procure her permission for his horse to be stabled in the front parlor if he put his mind to it." He peered more closely at her. "See to it he doesn't turn your head with his idle ways."

Chloe drew herself into a rigid posture. *"Certainement."*

He nodded, apparently satisfied, and waved his hand at her. "You may go."

Oh, how she wanted to slap his smug face when he was like this, *The Duke,* through and through. She did not, of course, nor did she say anything to the imperious dismissal. However, she did allow a touch of insolence to color her movements as she turned and headed up the stairs.

Jareth watched her go, his mood darkening, if that were possible. The swing of her hips was deliberate, he was sure, but not to entice. It was meant to convey insouciance.

The minx should straighten her manners if she were wise, because he was not in a mood to be trifled with. After being set upon last night, he had had a fitful night's sleep, his mind besieged with all manner of images of that infernally irritating woman stretched out on top of him and conversing with him as easily as if they had been seated at dinner. Then this morning, immediately after his meeting with the sheriff, he had been informed that one of his servants had behaved in a manner unbecoming to her position, and he had had to dismiss her.

But by far, coming upon Gerald and Chloe was the most distressing thing yet. This puzzled him, for while he was not fond of Gerald, he could certainly find no fault in his showing kindness to Chloe. Except that Gerald often delighted in stirring up trouble.

With a bit of surprise, Jareth realized he was jealous of Gerald. Gerald still had his freedom. Freedom to come to Strathmere if he wished, or to winter in Rome or Florence or the south of France. Freedom to while away his days hunting in the forests, his greatest love.

Freedom to pursue an upper servant, for example, an enchanting, exasperating, invigorating sprite with a French accent and a smile to light up the heavens more beautifully than any constellation.

Chapter Thirteen

As soon as she stepped into the nursery, Chloe was set upon by a tearful, trembling Mary.

"Chloe, I need to speak with you," the maid said in a rush, looking over to where the children played with a plump servant who was just barely out of childhood herself.

"Of course. Bette, would you mind staying a bit longer?" Chloe asked.

"No, miss. I enjoy the children. They're a pleasant break from my chores."

"Thank you." She pulled her distraught Mary along with her into her bedroom and shut the door.

"Oh, Chloe, he sacked me!" Mary sobbed. "Someone must have told him I was in the stables. He warned me to stay away from there, stay away from Daniel, but I couldn't! I love Daniel. How can I keep away from him? My heart breaks when a day goes by without seeing him."

Chloe was horrified. "Of course you should not be forbidden to see your love. What did the duke say?"

"He called me in this morning. He was terribly

angry. He said he knew I disobeyed him, and he dismissed me then and there.''

"But who told him you were seeing Daniel?"

"I don't know." Her face held a question, and Chloe reacted.

"You do not think that I told him about the other day when I saw you in the stables, do you?"

"No, no! I do not know what to think."

"It must be someone who is jealous of you. Another servant, perhaps, who wants Daniel for herself and so would like you gone?"

Mary paused and sniffed. "Oh, what difference does it make? I shall be in disgrace to return home after being dismissed, and how will I ever find another position?"

Chloe grabbed her hands and gave them a reassuring squeeze. "There is no disgrace, Mary. Never let him do that to you. Never let him take away your love. It is a wonderful thing."

"Why would he do this?" Mary wailed, collapsing into sobs.

Chloe sighed. "I have no answers for you. The duke is a man whose soul is dying. He is good, I believe—a part of him is good. But that part is losing the battle. Perhaps because he can't have love in his life, he wants to destroy it in others."

Mary was so amazed, she stopped crying. "How do you know him so well?"

Chloe fetched a handkerchief from her pocket and handed it to her. "I know nothing about him. Nothing at all."

Jareth was speaking to his mother—in fact he was in the middle of a sentence—when the pocket doors to the front parlor were thrown open.

Mouth still open, he turned to find Chloe standing in the doorway.

The bottom fell out of his heart. She looked magnificent. A deep blush stained her cheeks, her hair was in wild disarray about her face. Like Diana fresh from the hunt.

Dumbfounded, everyone in the room was silent.

"May I speak with you, your grace?" she said. Her voice had an edge.

He shut his mouth and frowned.

"Strathmere," his mother hissed. A little reminder not to be led about by this slip of a thing. He didn't even look at the duchess when he said, "It's all right, Mother. I shall speak to Miss Chloe in the hall." He tried to sound threatening. "After all, I know the matter must be of strident urgency to necessitate such a startling interruption."

Chloe's chin came up. "It is, I assure you."

His mother's glare of displeasure burned into his back as he stepped outside. "Shall we?" he asked Chloe, leading her across the hallway and into the library.

The heavy oak door had just clicked shut when she was upon him.

"How dare you!"

"Pardon me?" he asked, his voice lowering to convey his ire. "Do keep your head, Miss Chloe. You have a tendency to forget to whom you are talking."

"A man with a bloated sense of his own self-importance, that is who! I cannot believe you have done this terrible thing."

"I should ask what terrible thing I've done, but you see, I hardly care."

"Yes," she snapped with a wry twist of her mouth. "That is precisely what is wrong in this household. You do not care about anything or anyone save yourself and your whims."

"Miss Chloe," he began, struggling with the urge to shout, "if anyone else spoke to me in this manner, I would dismiss them without another word."

"Ah, your answer to all your problems with your staff. Dismiss people if they displease you. My goodness, I think you will be toasting your own bread in the morning and making your own bed if you keep it up at this rate."

"Is that what this is all about? You are angry because I dismissed a maid?"

"That maid has a name. It is Mary Curran. She also has a life beyond fetching your slippers and wiping the dust from your fine furniture. She has a family who depends on her income to make ends meet. She has a mother and a father who are proud of her, or were before you sent her home in disgrace. She had plans and dreams for her life, and yes, *monsieur,* it is true that she has a love. A nice gentleman, one of your grooms, a man named Daniel. Why this offends you so greatly, I cannot imagine, but it seems perfectly natural that a young woman and a young man would be attracted to each other, and therefore seek each other's company in their free moments."

"I need not explain myself to you," he said with a flick of his wrist, and began to walk away. She stepped in front of him to block his path.

"No, you need no one, do you, your grace? You are completely self-contained, secure in the smug knowledge that you are superior in every way to we simple folk of the lower classes. Why, you even have the right to dictate our lives.''

''I cannot have my servants sneaking off on trysts when they should be about their appointed duties! Or do you suggest I create Strathmere as a love nest, a pretty retreat for servants who wish to spend time with their beloveds?''

''Why do you mock love?'' she demanded. ''Is it because you have had so little of it in your life?''

He looked appalled. ''You don't know what you are saying. I never lacked for love.''

''Then your parents and mentors cannot be blamed. Was it a woman, then, who rejected you and so soured you on any *affaire de coeur?*''

He snarled at her, baring his teeth in a feral grimace. ''I simply dismissed the girl because she was exercising poor judgment. And this might come as a shock to you, Miss Chloe, but I don't require your permission to do it.''

''Yes, you are the Duke of Strathmere. You answer to no authority other than the king himself, so far above the rest of us are you.''

''Your French idealism is showing. Shall you gather a mob and haul me to a guillotine?''

Chloe's spine went rigid. ''I am not proud of the barbarism of the revolution, but I am most pleased with the result. We are a free country where no man is held prisoner by another because of his station.''

''So you wish to reform me?''

Her hands had curled into fists at her sides, and she jammed them now on her hips. ''You are already being reformed, right out of your humanity. The days spent with your new title bring you closer and closer to this—a thoughtless brute who has given no thought to the consequences of your actions. Servants, your grace, may not count for anything to you, but they are human, equipped with all the emotion and power of thought you yourself possess. Your disregard for them speaks ill of you."

She took a step back, seeming relaxed after her tirade. "I would have thought you already knew that," she added. "But they have been working on you. You are a credit to the aristocracy. But you are becoming a small person—small of heart and small of mind. It is the price you pay for your exalted station." She shook her head. "What a terrible shame."

He was speechless after that, mostly because it was true. It hit him like a blow, stunning him while she made a fabulous whirl and stalked out of the room. It was like a double blow, her words and then that lovely gracefulness.

When she had gone, he paced about the room. He hated himself for allowing her words to gather in his brain. What did it matter what his nieces' governess's opinion of him was? Strange that it annoyed him.

Because Chloe's opinion mattered a great deal to him. That he knew as he went back into the parlor. But he didn't like it.

His mother was waiting, her face lined with tension. "May I be so presumptuous as to inquire what that little scene was about, Strathmere?"

He hated being called that by her. It sounded so formal, so limiting, as if all he was to anyone anymore was the duke. "No, Mother, you may not." He sat down and made no pretense of politeness.

Narrowing her eyes, she said, "I hope you are not

faltering in your station. You allow that woman too much latitude.''

The irony didn't escape him. One woman just berated him for taking his position and title too seriously, and here was another denouncing him for not taking it seriously enough. He sighed.

''Your father or your brother would never have permitted a servant to speak to them in that insolent and forward manner, no matter what the crisis.''

Jareth rubbed his temple. ''I know what is expected of me.''

The duchess looked doubtful. ''You haven't been demonstrating it of late. I tell you, Strathmere, it has not escaped others' notice, as well. Lady Rathford has questioned your intentions toward Helena in light of your delay.''

''They have complaint against me, as well. Devil take it, Mother—why not? Let's bring up the housekeeper and butler and they, too, can regale me of my failings.''

''You are being impertinent to your mother, and even a duke may not do that. Now, you have a duty to the duchy to marry.''

''Yes, my duty.'' It always came down to that.

''When the solicitors return next Monday, you may wish to speak with them about a marriage contract. I believe Lord Rathford is anxious to settle on the matter with you.''

''Will you excuse me?''

''But where are you going? We have many other things to discuss.''

He didn't answer. On his way out of the room, he almost ran into Gerald, who was coming in. The duchess saw him and called, ''Come to me, Gerald.

My son has abandoned me, but your company is amusing. We shall play whist. It will keep me occupied until Strathmere is feeling better. It seems that thief last night got the best of him.''

The tone, more than the words, was scathing. Gerald looked at Jareth and hiked up his brows as if to convey the silent message, *Interesting*.

Jareth left him, filled with disgust at the two of them, both schemers.

He was certain that if either one of them could dispossess him of his title, they just might do it, each for their own reasons.

And then he thought if there was a way to do it— leaving him alive, of course, and more important *free*—he might just allow it.

Chapter Fourteen

Sipping hot chocolate in the small informal parlor after taking the children for a romp in the snow, Chloe sat with her thawing charges. Rebeccah was in a happy mood from their outdoor play and Sarah smiled brightly, her cheeks still wind-stung and her lips just as red.

Chloe was telling them a story, one she had grown up with. The children sat in rapt attention as she explained how the wicked witch kept the poor beauty locked in a tower, using her hair as a rope to climb up to visit her but never allowing her to see another human being. She had just gotten to the point of the prince stumbling upon the girl, when a small knock sounded at the door.

Dr. Esterhaus peeked his head in. "Ah, I was told you were in here." He smiled and stepped inside.

This was the physician who had been attending the children since the accident. Chloe was used to his frequent visits just after the tragedy, but it had been months since he had been summoned.

"A pleasure to see you, Doctor," she said pleasantly. "Is this a social call? We are all in good health, as you see."

"Indeed, everyone is looking fine." He came to sit on a settee, not disguising his interest in the children, who stared back at him with bald trepidation on their faces.

"Rebeccah, Sarah, this is Dr. Esterhaus. You remember him, do you not?"

Rebeccah remembered her manners. "How do you do, sir?"

Dr. Esterhaus was pleased. "I am well, thank you." He looked up at Chloe and beamed. "Such a clever child."

Chloe almost laughed, but kept her counsel. "Oh yes, our Rebeccah is clever."

"And you, little lady," the doctor said, leaning over to peer into Sarah's face. Sarah frowned back and withdrew a bit. "Still not speaking?"

"Non, monsieur," Chloe said, anxious that he was alarming the child.

"Not a sound at all?" He moved in closer.

Chloe came to her feet and knelt before the child, taking her little hand in both of hers. "She is unchanged from your last examination, sir."

He rolled his eyes to Rebeccah. "And…er…the other problem. It has not resolved itself…the one…you know…*at night.*"

He was about as subtle as a bull. Chloe rushed to assure him *all* circumstances were unchanged, lest he blurt out some disturbing information that would make matters worse.

"I would like to examine the girls more closely, Miss Pesserat."

"Certainement," she said reluctantly. It was not

her place to forbid him, though she would have liked to. The children were nervous, and her protective instincts were at full alert.

While she was waiting in the hall with Sarah and the doctor was in with Rebeccah, Chloe pondered the reason for his visit after all this time. There had been no complaint that she was aware of regarding the children, nothing to prompt the visit out of the blue.

When it was Sarah's turn, Rebeccah came to sit next to her on the burgundy upholstered chairs. "Everything all right, *chérie?*"

"Yes, Miss Chloe," Rebeccah answered. Her brow furrowed. "Why did he ask me all those questions?"

"What questions, *ma petite?*"

"About my sleeping and the dreams I have. I don't remember any dreams. He asked about Mama and Papa. If I missed them. That was silly, wasn't it?"

Chloe felt her stomach churn. "*Oui, ma chérie,* it was *très* silly. Pay him no mind."

"It was strange to have someone ask about them," Rebeccah stated with a thoughtful look. "I like talking about Mama and Papa. Sometimes if I don't think about them for a long time, I feel bad. It's nice remembering them."

"Of course, you must always remember them in your heart. That way, they will always be with you."

Rebeccah suddenly smiled. "Do you think Mama and Papa can see us from heaven?"

"I am sure of it," Chloe replied with an answering smile.

Rebeccah's eyes drifted upward. "I think they are with the angels. That is what Mama told us happened to Grandfather when he died. She said he went to live with the angels and I think that is where they are, too.''

''Most assuredly. That is how they can watch over you best, to see you are safe and no harm will ever come to you, and to love you, even from heaven, so that you will never be alone.''

Rebeccah's smile widened. Suddenly, she flung herself at Chloe, wrapping her thin arms about her waist. ''Oh, Miss Chloe, that sounds wonderful! I shall ever be safe, I know I will, with Mama and Papa watching over me, and you here, too. You must never go away.''

The plea struck a bitter chord. ''I shall endeavor never to, *chérie.*''

The door opened and the doctor came out. Sarah hurried toward Chloe and crawled up into her lap without interfering with Rebeccah's embrace.

''Thank you, Miss Pesserat. That will be all,'' the doctor said. Chloe stood, disengaging Rebeccah, but Sarah wouldn't be separated. She ended up carrying her upstairs.

The visit was disturbing for all of them. Sarah stayed curled up on Chloe's lap for the rest of the day and evening, and Rebeccah needed Chloe's attention constantly to look at a drawing or watch her newly learned skills at skipping. Chloe tried to be attentive, but her mind raced.

There was, she had decided, only one reason for Dr. Esterhaus to visit—to answer the question as to whether or not she could be dismissed without detrimental effect on the children.

When the girls were asleep, she entered her room and sat down at the small table. From a drawer, she drew out a clean sheet of paper and a quill.

Mon cher père, she began, writing in French. *I believe I may be coming home soon, perhaps for good.*

What amazed her was that these words, ones that, at times, she had longed to be able to say, filled her with such desolation and loss that she felt the sting of tears in her eyes. She blinked them away and set about to complete the letter.

Jareth passed the doctor a freshly poured whiskey and took the chair opposite him. "How do you find my nieces, sir?" he queried.

"Satisfactory. Certainly no worse. Unfortunately, not much improved, as you know."

"Yes, I had suspected as much."

"Do not be discouraged, your grace. Children are amazingly resilient. I have a good deal of experience with them, and I can tell you their progress is often erratic. One might see no visible sign of improvement for months, and then suddenly the child snaps into normalcy." He chuckled. "I remember one fellow who began walking after a prolonged injury, and when his parents made a huge fuss over him, he behaved as if he were utterly bewildered as to why the adults were amazed. It seemed perfectly natural to him, you see."

"Do you foresee that happening to Sarah? That she will regain her ability to speak in this sudden manner you've described?"

"It may, it may. I can make no promises, you understand."

"Obviously, Doctor. I am not looking for guarantees. Just a general idea of what is in the realm of possibility."

"Then, yes, a recovery of that sort is indeed possible."

"I see. And what of Rebeccah's night terrors? Do you have any insights as to how those can be gotten rid of?"

"The child knows nothing of these in her waking state. This is good. However, when she is in the throes of one of these bouts, it is best to keep her asleep. The conventional wisdom on these things has it that it would be quite detrimental to wake her. The terror of finding themselves face-to-face with their nocturnal fears will be utterly traumatizing and may cause irreparable harm."

"Then what are we to do?"

"Keep up what you are doing. Eventually she will outgrow them." He didn't seem at all confident in his assurance.

There was a short silence, then the doctor broached the subject Jareth had been waiting for. "Er, your mother has asked my opinion on the possibility of dismissing Miss Pesserat."

"Yes. And that opinion is?"

"I realize the woman is a trial to both you and your mother, but the children's attachment makes her a vital part of their lives. I believe it would be quite dire should she be forced away from your nieces, your grace." He smiled apologetically. "I am so sorry if this news disturbs you."

The news did disturb him. Sometimes he believed Chloe was the reason why he was so confused. Yet, in contrast, his most lucid moments were in her company. The trouble was, the things that seemed so clear were not the sort of things he should be thinking. Not as the duke, anyway.

"It is the truth, Doctor, which is what I have asked for. I can hardly hold you accountable if it is less than what I would like."

"Just so. Very sensible, your grace." He paused. "Your mother tells me you have been under a great deal of strain lately. I am pleased to see that if that is so, it has not affected your judgment."

"No strain. Only very busy."

"But you have been a bit short-tempered, would you agree?"

Jareth paused, feeling a subtle shift in the doctor's interest. He replied carefully. "I believe I have voiced my displeasure on several occasions. I would, however, disagree wholeheartedly that I have been at fault."

The doctor seemed thoughtful. "Are you in agreement with your mother's belief that Miss Pesserat should be dismissed as soon as possible?"

Jareth didn't reply. He didn't know what he thought about that particular subject anymore.

The doctor continued. "Tell me, do you suffer from migraines? Are you given to periods of despondency or melancholia? Do you hear any strange noises?"

Jareth's voice was tight. "Noises?"

"Perhaps *voices?*"

Gripping the chair arms, Jareth demanded, "What the devil are you talking about, man? Are you accusing me of being insane?"

"No, your grace. Now, see, you are irate at me, suspicious of my motives. This paranoia is bad for the—"

"Paranoia?"

"Can you control your temper, your grace, or are

you given often to displays of emotionalism such as this?''

Jareth's contempt for the doctor made his tone brittle. ''Did my mother send you to see to me? If so, you may assure her I am of sound mind, and if she has reservations to this fact, she may take the matter up with me personally. I believe this conversation has gone as far as I wish it to go.'' Jareth stood and stalked out the door. He stopped in the cloakroom and wrapped himself in a great wool mantle. As soon as he stepped outside, the cold air hit him like a blow to the face. He headed straight for the lake.

It was frozen, bringing on memories of himself and Charles and some children from the village dashing and sliding across the smooth surface, chasing one another in a game far too rough for good sport. But they were boys, and it was their way. No one had minded the uncivilized behavior back then.

Standing on the bank, he remembered another day when they were much older. It was late in the spring. The lake was overflowing its banks from the rains, and he and Charles had taken the small boat out that they sometimes stole from the little dock. They had been playing rough. It started with Charles slapping him and calling him a name. It wasn't out of meanness that he did it, just the irresponsible horseplay that older brothers often perpetrated against their younger, weaker siblings. Jareth had responded predictably and they had wrestled. The boat capsized and they found themselves in the water. This hadn't alarmed Jareth at first, for they were both of them experienced swimmers. Then he had seen Charles go under. Once. Twice.

The feeling that had gripped him then tightened in his chest even now. Just the memory of those terror-filled moments closed his throat, making it hard to breathe. He had dragged Charles to the shore. They had stood in each other's arms, heedless of the impropriety of it, and wept at what had almost just occurred, and Charles began spouting nonsense. Jarvis, who was old even then, had come upon them like that, and he had heard the things Charles had said.

Jareth closed his eyes against those horrid words. Charles hadn't meant them. Surely he hadn't.

The wind whipped around him, bringing him back to the present, to the cold and the ice and the snow all about him, under his feet.

He hadn't understood it then, or even later. As Charles had matured into the responsibilities of his birthright and Jareth had taken his own path away from the family, the memory had mellowed and he told himself it had meant nothing—a moment's aberration. It had ceased to disturb him.

But he understood now. The despair, the trapped, terrified, empty feeling.

What was worse was that he himself was becoming part of it. Had he not, in full accord with his mother, asked Dr. Esterhaus to come and evaluate the children for the possibility of ridding themselves of Miss Pesserat?

His mother's intentions he understood. She was a snob, appalled at the brazen disregard that Chloe showed for her position. It all came back to that. The *blasted, cursed* title.

Here on these shores, one duke had wept in despair because of that title and all that went with it. Now, another communed with him, knowing at last what had been in his brother's heart all those years ago.

Jareth realized he hadn't been doing this all along for the sake of his mother. Good God, for all he cared at this point, she could go to the devil.

He had been doing it for Charles. For all his beloved brother had sacrificed, for all he had never been allowed to do, and, yes, for all the guilt he himself had felt in his growing years at not being *the one.* Perhaps he thought this was his penance, to follow in Charles's footsteps and bear his pain and die inside and take it just as Charles had had to do.

This realization brought no peace, for his own culpability in the matter remained, but it did bring clarity. The confusion lifted and he knew what it was *he*—Jareth Hunt, a man who no longer existed to the world but was indeed alive and thriving inside him—believed. Not as the duke. As himself.

Jareth Hunt.

He took in a long breath and looked out over the lake. So many memories, good and bad, poured around him. He smiled, and the peace he had sought finally came because he realized there was something he must do.

He had an apology to deliver.

Chapter Fifteen

When Chloe received a message to meet Jareth in the front parlor, she naturally expected the worst. It was with a heavy heart that she pulled her hair into a neat knot on the top of her head, determined to make a good appearance. It was no use, however. The independent mass of rich brown never behaved. Wisps began to curl about her face, turning her countenance into an alluring picture of some Pre-Raphaelite nymph, but she wanted to look serious today. This was a serious matter. She firmly believed she would be asked to leave.

Her eyes, wide and pale gray, stared back at her from the mirror and her cheeks were flushed a delicate pink. Both betrayed the feverish anxiety that gripped her. Bette arrived to see to the children, and Chloe turned away from the looking glass. She drew in a trembling breath and left the nursery.

In the parlor, to her great surprise, a silver tea service had been laid out. The duke was standing by a window, looking out over the front lawn. It didn't seem he had heard her come in. His posture was stiff, his hands clasped behind his back, looking disappointingly, but expectedly, formal. The sun glanced off his chestnut curls and caressed an angular cheek. Chloe swallowed away the rush of pain that surged up at the sight of him.

"You wished to see me, your grace?"

He turned, and to Chloe's surprise, he smiled at her. He said, "Please come in and have a seat."

"Merci." She did as he asked.

He took the seat across from her. "May I offer you tea or coffee?"

"Nothing, please."

He paused, looking at her in a most serious way. Suddenly, Chloe could stand it no longer. "I know what you are going to say," she blurted. "And I wish you to know I think it is deplorable."

His eyebrows shot up. "It is?"

"Oui. All the things I said to you before, well, I meant them and I am not sorry for them, even if they are the reason you are dismissing me. I have my pride, sir, and I shall not forsake it for the likes of this family."

His eyelids drew down into a lazy look. "I had noticed that about you," he drawled. "The pride, I mean."

"I feel a person can only distinguish themselves by their good acts, and although I never claimed to be perfect, I do count honesty as one of the traits of which I am most proud. I will not be intimidated, and if your ordered, perfect world cannot tolerate the truth, then I pity you and your mother for the frightened, cowering beings you are."

"I quite agree."

"And if you intend to separate me from the children, I can tell you that while the very prospect horrifies me, I have reconciled myself to the fact that there is nothing I can do to—what did you say?''

He was trying not to laugh, she noticed, and her consternation grew. He explained, ''I said I agreed with you. About your honesty. It is difficult for others—myself included—to grapple with it at times. It is a heady thing, the truth. Sometimes it is too painful to bear, until we start the lies and realize after a while real suffering is to live a false life.''

Her mouth stayed slightly agape, her brow creased in confusion and she sat perfectly rigid for a good minute or two.

''Will you look at that,'' he said at last. ''I have rendered Chloe Pesserat speechless.''

Chloe snapped her mouth shut. ''I do not understand.''

''That is because I have not explained. In fact, I have not even had an opportunity to say more than a few words.''

She blushed and bit her lip. ''I am sorry.''

He nodded and looked away, thoughtful for a moment. ''Chloe, may I ask you a question?''

''Yes, of course.''

He seemed to change his mind. ''No, let me say it a different way. It may surprise you to learn that I have always admired you, even when I have disagreed with you. I suppose that is what friendship is like—not necessarily thinking the same in all matters but weighing that other opinion because of your high regard for the other person. Do you understand what I am saying?''

''I believe I do.'' She said this, but was as confused by his words as if he had spoken them in Greek.

"With my brother, it was different. Though our love for each other was undoubted, it was typical of us to argue over differences and I don't believe he ever truly accepted the choices that led me into a full life outside of the family." Bowing his head, he lowered his voice as if the next words were difficult for him to say. "I have come to regard you as a friend, Chloe. I value your opinion, even if I think you are daft at times, and I find myself..." He paused, struggling with the next part. "Wishing to have your good will."

She was so touched, she didn't think her voice would serve her. When she could, she said gently, "That you already have."

"Ah, where is your famous honesty now? Did you not just finish reviling me for a shallow, addlepated idiot whom you abhor?"

"I...I didn't mean that I thought you were addlepated." She tried to come to some means with which to convey her jumbled thoughts. His contrite revelation had her undone completely. "I just did not like the things you were doing. They were not you, not the man I had come to know on occasion, when you would allow me to see that side of you. I know you to be caring and try very hard to do the right thing."

He rose and turned toward the window again. "Yes, that is true, but sometimes it becomes very difficult to know what the right thing is."

She came to her feet and took a step toward him. "You know in your heart what the right thing is, do you not?"

He looked over his shoulder at her, and his smile was charming. "I would be willing to wager that you have at times wondered if I possessed that particular organ.''

She pressed her lips together and crossed her arms. ''I believe you have shown little evidence of it on occasion.'' Reconsidering, she amended, ''Although I know you have always striven to do what you thought was best.''

''And at those times you accused me of arrogance?''

''Do you make the argument that your word should be unimpeachable?''

''Chloe, why are you quibbling with me? I have asked you here to apologize to you for my past behavior and find you bristling at me within minutes.''

Chloe was shocked. ''You...wish to apologize?''

''Yes. I was quite unfair to you. I was not always honest, either, and you deserve better than that from me for the fact of your bravery in always facing the truth.''

Shaking her head to clear it, Chloe let out a small laugh and pressed a hand to her forehead. ''I thought I was to be asked to leave.''

''We could never get on without you,'' he murmured, turning to face her.

The words touched something in her, a distant hope, a desire held at bay. It must have shone in her eyes as she raised her gaze to his. ''You could not?''

He seemed to realize his error. His expression sobered. ''I meant for the children, and as we all care deeply about their well-being. All of us need you— for their sake.''

She lowered her gaze, ashamed of what he might have seen in her eyes. The touch of his fingers along her chin made her catch her breath. They were warm and smooth, and tiny shivers of excitement shot forth like sparks from a flint to singe her cheek and sizzle down her neck. "Only for their sake?"

"Sweet Lord, Chloe, are you never satisfied with anything? Do you always need to push me beyond comfort?" His words were harsh but they were spoken in a tone that was almost a caress. "See, I have resolved myself to honesty and already I cannot fulfill it. Do I need you, you wish to know. Yet you already do know, don't you? With your ridiculous philosophies and your brilliant, rebellious spirit— yes, I need you, you little fool. I need you to be my friend." He stopped, then dropped his hand. "Anything more is not acceptable. You must realize that."

"I do," she managed to say, feeling the weight of his words crushing the tender emotions inside her.

"No, you do not. It is not in your nature to accept limitations. But, Chloe, we are not in France. We cannot ignore who we are. This is England. I am an English duke, the Duke of Strathmere, for God's sake, controller of one of the largest and most influential duchies in the kingdom. It is an awesome duty. I am not telling you that I have turned my back on what is expected of me, but rather that I am taking charge of it myself. I want you to know that I acknowledge your worth and service to this family, and will not permit you to be ill treated in the future. As for anything beyond that… Chloe, we are of different worlds, you and I. Desire…it is a mistake we cannot afford to make. I told you that before, in the nursery, the night…the night I lost control momentarily. It was wrong of me."

"You told me it was only a kiss," she corrected. Bravely, she stared at him even in the face of her humiliation. "And I believe there is no such thing, your gr—"

"No! Will you stop calling me that! Not after all this, not after I've told you the things I have. Dear God, cannot one person call me by my given name? If it can't be you, Chloe, then who will it be to restore me to who I was before?"

She was taken aback. "You wish me to call you Jareth?"

"Not in front of others, of course, and God knows what I am unleashing with this request because you ever push beyond whatever confines are given you, but yes, I would like to hear my name from one person in this house."

"It would make me very happy to do it," she said.

"Now, what was I saying?"

"You were about to tell me that the kiss meant nothing."

"No, no, no. That is not it at all. Of course the kiss meant something." Nearly under his breath, he muttered, "God, in some ways it meant everything." He looked at the ceiling as if searching for aid or inspiration. "What I feel for you, Chloe, is real. I shall not lie to you and make it less. If we were two people in different sorts of lives, well, it would be an utterly different matter. But things are what they are. My life, my circumstances must dictate the choices I make. I am not free to choose."

"And if you could choose?"

He closed his eyes and angled his head away as if to shield himself from her question. His lips pressed together in a small, thin smile. "There you go again, always pushing, demanding more." Opening his eyes, he asked, ''Do you truly wish me to answer that?''

She did, oh, indeed she did. But she knew he was right. It would be so sweet to hear him say it, but how could she bear it afterward when he had told her in plain terms that he was not going to forsake his duty or in any way compromise what was expected of him?

''You shall marry Lady Helena,'' she pronounced in a flat voice.

Her heart shattered into a million pieces when he nodded slowly.

''But you wish us to be friends,'' she continued, speaking slowly as if to test the words.

''You have become very important to me, Chloe. I do not wish to lose you completely.''

''I see.'' She met his gaze, as difficult as that was. ''I understand you. You do not love Helena, but you will marry her in accordance with your mother's wishes.''

''Not only hers. They are my wishes, as well.''

''How can you wish this, since you admit you do not love her?''

He expelled a long breath. ''You are a fanciful creature. Love has little to do with marriage. Lady Helena is an excellent choice of wife for her breeding, her accomplishments, her presence and her nature.''

So different from winsome, free-spirited Chloe. She said, ''This is acceptable to you?''

''If you ask me do I like it, then no, I do not. But it is acceptable to me.''

Chloe backed away, disdain coloring her features.

"You English are too in love with your positions and titles to have any room in your lives for real love."

"And you French are in love with love." He raked his hand through his hair, betraying his exasperation. "This meeting is not going as I had planned. Why must you challenge me at every turn?"

"What had you imagined, Jareth? That I would fall to my knees and weep in gratitude for the favors you grant me?"

He gave her a hard look. "You are being unfair." He walked away a few steps then turned to face her again, swiping his hand in the air. "Let us forget this entire conversation."

"By all means, no, I shall not!"

"Chloe, you are trying my temper—again!"

"And you are...are...*impossible!*"

"Why must you always insist on your way?"

"Why can you never see the wisdom in what I say?"

He took a step forward. "I give everything you say the consideration it deserves."

"You give it none, *monsieur,*" she countered with a toss of her head. "I think you are afraid to view it fairly."

"Afraid!" he exclaimed. "Afraid?" Chloe thought that perhaps she had gone too far. His expression was explosive. It was attractive on him, however, with his color up and his hair all awry from raking his hand through it so many times. He was panting, his broad chest heaving from his anger.

He averted his face, bowing his head. Chloe waited while he struggled visibly for control.

A low rumble she couldn't quite place began to sound. It took a moment before she identified it as laughter. He raised his head again. "My God, Chloe Pesserat, you are the most exasperating woman I have ever had the misfortune to meet."

Chloe didn't see why this was so very funny. She crossed her arms in front of her chest and narrowed her eyes.

Jareth spread his hands out in front of him in a conciliatory gesture. "Maybe we should let things go at this—you are not to be dismissed and you are not to worry about that eventuality any longer."

She took a long time to reply. "And we are to be…friends?"

"Indeed, yes."

And never anything more. Oh, yes, that was perfectly clear.

Chloe tilted her head back and said with all the courage she could muster, "I am pleased to have it so. May I go now?"

"Yes, you may." She whirled and walked toward the door, keeping her back straight and her emotions sternly under command. "And, Chloe," he called. She paused and he said, "I am sorry I lost my temper."

"Ce n'est rien," she replied, not breaking stride. She couldn't get out of the room fast enough.

Jareth was not at all certain what had just happened. He walked to his library, carrying with him a cup of tea and setting it on the mahogany desk. Admittedly, he was bemused by the extraordinary conversation. Nearly every conversation with Chloe was extraordinary, however, so he eventually shrugged it off and settled in to look over his master plan for the duchy.

It felt good to have put the weight of his new position in a more comfortable place. He would have more control over his own life, more say in how and when his duties were carried out, and would take charge of the demands that had been tearing at him ever since he arrived home.

Yes, decidedly, he was satisfied. He had studiously applied himself to learning the enterprises that traditionally backed the family fortune. Now he considered it was about time he advanced his other interests. In an effort to tailor his investments to suit his expertise, he began to draw up a plan. He was going to take the duchy in a whole new direction.

He was tired of his mother manipulating his social life, as well. He vowed his passivity in this regard would end. He had no objection to Helena Rathford as his future wife, but no longer would he be moved about like a pawn by the two matrons.

Toward those ends, he suggested a small luncheon party after dinner that evening.

"Whom would you like to invite?" Charlotte Hunt asked, her skirts rustling as she hurried over to her desk in the drawing room and sat down. Pulling out the quill pen, she touched the feather to her lips. "Besides the Rathfords, I think the Bemores...and the Carlesons!" Twisting to her son, she frowned. "Do you remember Herbert Carleson from when you were a boy?"

"I thought him a prig. Do not invite them."

"But they are of good family and it would be—"

"I shall give you the list and you may write the invitations."

The duchess didn't like this, judging by her expression. Surprisingly she kept her counsel.

He pressed on. "And I wish the children to attend. Perhaps Lady Helena could be persuaded to sing. The children should enjoy that."

His mother was instantly on the alert. "Oh, Strathmere, you aren't thinking of having that dreadful Frenchwoman there, as well? She shall disgrace us all."

"Miss Chloe is the children's governess. Make certain to invite her. She is also a relative, and so the family tie must not be overlooked."

Pressing her lips together, the duchess scratched down Chloe's name.

As it happened, Chloe was not at all happy to attend.

In fact, she wished most profoundly to stay as far away from Jareth Hunt, Duke of Strathmere, as she could get—friendship be damned!

When the housekeeper told her of the invitation with a mixture of excitement and envy, Chloe could only think of how she would have to sit in attendance as Jareth paid court to the stunning Helena Rathford.

"No," she told Mrs. Hennicot politely, "please extend my regrets to his grace. While I appreciate his courtesy in remembering me, I do not think it my place."

Mrs. Hennicot was utterly shocked that she would decline such a grand invitation, and left with a bemused expression. No doubt she would simply put it down to the strange things "that odd Frenchwoman" was apt to do. Even though Chloe was well liked among the staff, she knew they found her...well, eccentric, perhaps.

However, the matter of the luncheon would not

stay settled in her brain. She thought about what it would be like to be there. She remembered when he had muttered under his breath that their kiss had meant "everything" to him. What had he meant by that? And he didn't love Helena, he had told her so, and he had intimated that it was she, Chloe, whom he would choose if he were free.

Sitting in the great oak rocker while the children played at her feet, she mulled over the strange conversation. The knowledge of his admitted desire lingered in her heart, spreading an excited heat throughout her body and starting crazy thoughts to whirl about in her head. What if…?

Catching herself up, she shook off the musing. What foolishness was this that she was toying with? He was a duke and nothing would change that fact, and as such he was as far and as unreachable as the stars he so dearly loved to watch and study. There was no place in his world for a woman like her.

She would have to accept it.

But as he himself had noted, Chloe was never any good at limitations. They seemed mere challenges to her. And as much as the sensible part of her cautioned against it—and yes, there was a part, albeit a very small one, that did think sensibly—her mind began to wander once again as marvelous possibilities and fantasies captivated her attention.

It wasn't until much later, in the dead of night after she had been awakened by Rebeccah's cries and was rocking her and soothing her as she did every night, that she decided she would go to the luncheon after all. As terrified as she was to face Lady Helena, to see her rival's perfection and witness the admiration it drew, she knew she must be there.

And she would make her presence known.

Chapter Sixteen

When the afternoon arrived, Chloe sat at the small table in her room and propped a hand mirror upon it. Knowing she would be hopelessly outdone by Lady Helena, she considered what to do. She could hardly go in to a formal luncheon in one of her everyday dresses and with her brown tresses in a simple braid. Having no talent at hair, she struggled to wrap the weighty mass into a twist on top of her head. She used up all her pins and it still wobbled threateningly, so she improvised with a brooch that used to be her mother's. It was simple enough for day wear, and it looked good fastened in the gleaming mass. Not too elegant, but charming, she decided.

Even if she possessed cosmetics, she would, no doubt, be abysmal at applying them, so she contented herself with biting her lips. Her excitement did the rest. Her eyes glowed back at her from the glass and her cheeks were flame-kissed. She sighed to note a few loose tendrils coming out already from the tidy chignon to curl about her face. No matter, it was the best she could do.

The dress she chose was a deep cobalt, a gift from

her cousin. Bethany had given her many dresses, unable to wear them again after each season, lest she become the target of gossip as to her husband's penury. Chloe had a closetful to choose from, but the color of this one made it the best choice. The cut was a modest décolletage with lace trim and very plain otherwise. Although Chloe was not fashion-conscious in the least, she did know when something looked good on her, and this did.

When finished, she felt as if she had been toiling for hours. Her efforts were worth it, she surmised, when she was greeted by a chorus of gasps as she swept into the nursery.

"Oh, Chloe, you look beautiful," Bette declared.

Chloe knew she was not beautiful, but the compliment warmed her just the same.

The girls looked like confections in pink satin and cream lace, matching gowns that suited neither of them. The duchess had ordered them made. The two of them stared at Chloe, looking uncomfortable but excited at the same time.

"Miss Chloe, you look lovely," Rebeccah breathed.

"Thank you," Chloe replied, and took a child in each hand, heading down the stairs with confidence.

Confidence that fizzled as soon as she crossed the threshold of the drawing room.

Across from her, close to Jareth's elbow, Lady Helena looked delicious in a cream gown and perfectly coiffed hair. She was attending to Jareth, her profile noble and so damned…perfect.

"There they are!" the duchess exclaimed. Her smile was a parody. Her eyes darted her disapproval at Chloe's tardiness.

"Hello, *Grand-mère,*" Rebeccah said, dipping a small curtsy. Sarah came up behind her sister and bobbed prettily.

"Oh, Charlotte, I tell you, those children are charming," Lady Rathford purred. Angling a doubtful glance at Chloe, she asked, "And who do we have here?"

Chloe heard the countess introduce her, but her eyes were caught as Jareth turned from where he stood in the corner with Helena and another man. He noticed her and froze, his eyes sweeping over her, and she thought perhaps she needed to sit down because she very much doubted her knees would hold her upright for long.

"Chloe!" the duchess demanded.

"Yes!" Chloe squeaked as she snapped back to attention. The two matrons were glaring at her. Realizing she had just been presented to Lady Rathford, she extended her hand as a man would do. "Pleased to meet you."

Lady Rathford merely stared down at Chloe's extended hand, a look of confusion and horror on her face. One would think she'd never seen a hand before, Chloe mused, then realized what she had done. She snatched her hand back to her side.

"You must excuse Miss Chloe, Lady Rathford." It was Jareth's voice. He had come up behind her, offering an enchanting smile to his nieces. Sarah wiggled her fingers at him, smiling broadly. Rebeccah's greeting was shy.

Returning his attention to the adults, he explained, "Miss Chloe is from the Loire Valley in France. You may have heard of it. It was a favorite region of the novelist, Balzac."

This impressed Lady Rathford, Chloe saw.

Jareth continued, "The traditions from her home may seem strange, but we have learned not only to accept them but appreciate her particular brand of delightful charm."

Turning to Chloe, he smiled a smile to melt her stockings and held out his hand. Dumbfounded, Chloe shook it, bare skin touching.

She stood speared by his dark eyes, those beautiful eyes. She remembered his words, whispering along her spine, chilling her and warming her at the same time. *If we were two people in different sorts of lives, it would be utterly different matter.*

A dulcet voice cut in. "Hello." It was Helena.

The thrilling reaction coursing through her body was doused as quickly as a pinched candle flame. Her hand was still in Jareth's, so she pulled it free. Did she imagine the momentary grasp before he released it, as if he was loath to let it go?

Helena looked at Jareth curiously. Polite, she held out her hand. "We have met before."

Chloe had no choice but to take Helena's outstretched hand. "I remember. It is lovely to see you again, Lady Helena."

She smiled and Chloe's heart plummeted. It was so brilliant a smile, *she* was brilliant, sparkling with beauty and so very poised, with Chloe standing across from her feeling like a mud-covered farmer at a London ball.

"How kind of you," Helena replied, her smile deepening. She looked down at the children. "And I remember these two beautiful ladies, as well."

Rebeccah curtsied again, elbowing Sarah when she was slow to follow her example. The tot bobbed sloppily, but the children were nonetheless the delight of the onlookers.

"May I take them to meet Father?" Helena asked, addressing Jareth. "He adores children."

"Yes, of course," Jareth answered, his eyes straying back to Chloe. When Helena had gone, he spoke in a low tone. "You look very different today, Miss Chloe."

The compliment pleased her. She replied impishly, "I thought I was to call you Jareth and you were to call me just plain Chloe—like friends."

"But we are not alone, are we?"

"No one can hear."

"Nevertheless, I cannot call you plain Chloe, not anymore." His gaze was hot. She felt every inch of his body pulsing with energy, breaching the gap between them, reaching out to her. His eyelids came down, hovering over his eyes so that they looked lazy and languid and altogether too deliriously appealing. Self-consciously, she darted a look about to see if anyone was watching.

Her eyes collided with the searing disapproval blazing in the duchess's stare.

Chloe swallowed hard. "I believe I shall go see to the children."

"I wish to introduce you to—"

"*Non.* They may be frightened among so many strangers. Perhaps later..." The flimsy excuse didn't fool him, she thought as she made her way across the room.

Of course it didn't, but Jareth was grateful for it just the same. She was the wise one today, exercising the restraint he had preached but was finding an enormous amount of difficulty in executing.

How could he be blamed, he argued to himself, when she showed up this afternoon looking like *that*.

It was difficult to say what *that* was. She was no beauty, in the sense of Helena's great gift. Rather she was a pretty girl, always a bit undone, rather sloppy and on the whole appearing a bit mussed. Today, however, she was...what *was* it about her?

She was tidier, that was certain, although her hair was looser than what was the fashion and a few wisps had fought their way free to caress her cheeks and brow. The effect was utterly enchanting, however. And when contrasted with Helena's tight curls, far more interesting. Her gown was stunning, perfectly suited to the occasion, if more elaborate than what he was used to seeing her wear. Perhaps the color changed her, or maybe it was her eyes, which seemed to sparkle today, or her mouth...

A tightening in his loins alerted Jareth that his musings had best be reserved for another time. Another, less public time.

The bell rang for the meal and Jareth ushered his guests into the hallway. A cold, bitter hardness curled in his chest when he saw his cousin had Chloe's arm. He tried to shake off the feeling as he turned to Helena, but his control was nearly shattered when he heard her laughter behind him and Gerald's voice sounding low and confidential.

In the hallway, they proceeded down the corridor. Everyone paired off except for his mother, who trailed along, still chatting with Lady Rathford. Goodness, Jareth thought, those two never ceased. They were as thick as thieves.

''Your grace!'' a voice called from the direction of the front door.

Jareth turned to see his footman trying to restrain a burly man. "What is this?" he demanded.

"A word, your grace, I beg of you," the man replied, looking nervously at the other guests as they filed out of the parlor and gathered in a sort of circle behind Jareth.

By his side, Jareth felt Helena stiffen, heard a sharp, low gasp. He dashed a glance to see her pale as snow, her finely boned hand pressed to bloodless lips.

He looked back to the man, about to demand he leave, when he saw the man's gaze fasten on something behind Jareth. A voice rasped, "Get him out of here!" Footsteps sounded as a quartet of manservants came rushing into the room, and the man broke away from the footman who had been attempting to hold him.

"Get him out!" Jareth ordered. "Gerald, take our guests to the dining room."

Gerald was quick to get himself, and incidentally the others, out of harm's way.

The man gave the footman a mighty shove and bolted through the door, disappearing in a flash. The servants, whose timely arrival had been, Jareth supposed, the reason for the man's flight, paused. "Should we go after him, sir?" one asked.

Jareth shook his head. "Lock the door and check the others. We have guests to see to." He turned to join the others, his brain disturbed by something he hadn't quite been able to put his finger on...something that still disturbed him....

He laid his hand on the knob of the scarred oak door to the dining room and was about to turn it when he stopped and whirled and shouted to the disbanding servants. "No! Go after him!"

They were confused for a moment at this change of orders. Jareth roared, "Get him, now!"

Snapping out of their befuddlement, they charged out of the house in a thunder of footsteps.

Jareth stood in the midst of the hall, his heart banging wildly against his ribs. The ring. It hadn't registered at first. When the man had been struggling with his footman, it had caught the light from the chandelier and flashed for an instant.

The man who attacked him in the garden had a ring.

He gathered his composure quickly, mindful of his houseful of guests. When he entered the dining room moments later, he did so with an easy stride and a reassuring smile.

"Strathmere, what in heavens was that all about?" his mother demanded from her seat. She looked at him as if he were personally responsible for the interruption.

Everyone was just sitting there, waiting for his explanation. His eyes touched Chloe's, noting her concern and her wise stare, which always seemed to see too much.

"Some drunkard who wished to make complaint about his wages. It seemed Garfledger Tavern has raised their prices, and he wants a similar increase to help keep him flush."

This sparked a chorus of knowing grumbles among his guests. Dissatisfied tenants were a familiar nuisance among the wealthy landowners. The conversation took off from there as the first course was served.

Chloe was in the garden, lost in thought.

The luncheon earlier that day had been an abysmal failure as far as she was concerned.

The duchess had been in her element, gloating over her granddaughters in a way that set Chloe's teeth on edge. The woman didn't see or speak to them for weeks, sometimes months on end, yet she played the doting *grand-mère* when others were looking on to applaud the girls' adorableness and excellent manners.

That, at least, had gone well. The girls had behaved beautifully. Even Rebeccah had been charming and polite. The frequent glances to her uncle told Chloe that the girl was interested in his approval, and perhaps it was the desire for his admiration that kept her normally exuberant behavior in check.

Lady and Lord Rathford were particularly taken with the children, insisting that Jareth and his mother bring them with them the next time they visited Rathford Manor.

They had all gaped at Chloe when she interrupted their plans. "I am sorry, that will be impossible. The children do not like travel."

Lady Rathford had looked at her as if she were an insect. A particularly horrible one. "Young lady, I believe the children shall manage nicely. The appointments on the ducal coach are excellent and comfortable in the extreme."

"They mustn't ride in the ducal coach," Chloe stated, looking to Jareth. Surely he understood the significance of this.

"I have a small pony trap that they might find amusing," he said.

"I do not think—"

He had cut her off. "It will be good for the children to have an outing."

"But—"

"Miss Pesserat," the duchess had intervened. Her tone was as brittle as a crusting of ice. "My son and I are perfectly aware of the circumstances under which the children's fears have been formed, but the physician was quite specific upon his last visit. There has been no improvement."

Casting a nervous look at her charges, Chloe had said urgently, "Your grace, please!"

The duchess waved off the plea. Of course, the children's feelings were not to be considered. Her granddaughters barely existed to her, only in a functional way, and then only occasionally.

Chloe saw Rebeccah's sharp eyes taking everything in, her brow creased in worry.

That was when Helena roused herself to contribute. "I shall ride over, and the duke and I can take them with us. It shall be fun. You girls would enjoy that, wouldn't you? We shall sing songs and play similes. Have you ever played? It is a word game, and…" The sentence trailed off. Chloe presumed she had just recollected that Sarah did not speak.

Abruptly, skillfully, Helena had turned to Jareth. "What do you think, your grace?"

He had been distracted throughout the meal—ever since that tenant had appeared at the door—so the question caught him off guard. "What? Yes, yes, certainly, a fine idea. I would appreciate your coming with us. Perhaps a short outing at first."

Helena smiled. "Excellent idea. Then it is settled."

Chloe had lowered her eyes to her plate, deciding to take up the matter with Jareth later, in private.

What a disaster that had been...

A rustle roused her out of her musing, bringing Chloe back to the present. She looked up to see Mary just sitting down beside her.

"What—" she began, squelching the exclamation at Mary's signal. Giving a nervous glance to the windows, she drew Chloe up and dragged her behind a hedge.

"What are you doing here? Oh, it is so good to see you!"

"Chloe, I had to come to tell you, the most wonderful thing has happened," Mary gushed.

"Tell me everything. What is this wonderful news?"

"I am to be married. Oh, Chloe, it was so exciting. I went home, you see, and was terrified of what my da would do to me, but as it happened, he had heard stories of the old dowager, and when I told him I was dismissed for talking to a groom with no improper behavior involved, well, he actually took my side."

"What a happy surprise."

"I'll say, but it still left me in a fix. I worked at Strathmere for three years, and to find another position without a letter from so long an employer is almost impossible."

"Oh," Chloe said, "I never thought about that. But what has all of this to do with your getting married?"

"So, there I was, with no future, although I had my family on my side, when who shows up at my parents' door with a fistful of wild roses but Daniel."

"Oh, Mary! How wonderful!"

"Oh, it was. It is. He and I went for a drive, with my baby sister as chaperon, of course. And when we returned back to the house, he spoke to my father, and the two of them came back in grinning like a pair of mischievous boys, and my da says to my ma, 'Break out the cider, Annie, our daughter's getting married!' and then Daniel got down on his knees, right there in front of everyone, and he asked me to become his wife."

Chloe clasped her friend to her, squealing her excitement.

Mary continued, "I wanted to come back and let you know. You always were so kind to me and I heard how you gave the duke the devil on my behalf. Thank you for that, and for being such a good friend."

"We shall always be friends," Chloe answered. "I am so pleased at your news."

"I am very happy, Chloe. It couldn't have turned out better." Giving Chloe a long look, Mary asked, "And how are things at Strathmere? The duke?"

"The duke is an ass!" Chloe declared. She picked some leaves off a nearby evergreen and began to shred them. "I am out here freezing to death to cool my head. We had another disagreement."

"Come and tell me," Mary said, leading her over to a bench.

"I shall never understand him, never! He says he wishes to be friends, that he values me, and then he dismisses my warnings." Sighing, she started from the beginning. "There was a formal luncheon today and the children and I were invited. It was suggested that Lady Helena and the duke take the children on an outing and I knew at once that it was a disastrous idea. I couldn't argue my case in front of the duchess and all those strangers, so I went in to see him when everyone had gone.''

"What did he say?" Mary gasped. "He didn't sack you, too, did he?"

"*Non, non,* nothing like that. He said…he said some rather unkind things." She wouldn't—couldn't—describe how Jareth had told her he thought she was pressing her advantage, being opportunistic with the admissions he had made to her about his regard for her. His parting words were, ''I will not allow you to interfere with my relationship with Helena.'' Chloe kept those to herself, as well.

What she did tell her friend was that he had chastised her soundly and refused to be dissuaded. Mary was full of sympathy and vehement denouncements of the duke's good sense. "Anyone should realize those children have a mortal fear of horses."

Chloe countered, ''He makes a good argument that the children have made no progress, they have been too sheltered. Perhaps I have been lax in challenging them to confront their fears.''

"But, Chloe, they are babies!"

"*Oui,* my friend, this I know." She bent her head back, working the tensions from her neck. "I cannot allow him to harm them. I must show him that these things must be done gently, slowly. This outing with the Lady Helena must never take place. The duke is wrong, and he must be made to see it.''

Mary gave a short, humorless laugh. "Chloe, haven't you realized by now that the Duke of Strathmere is never wrong?"

Chapter Seventeen

Jareth stood in the midst of disaster and wondered how he could have been so wrong.

Helena was muddied from her knees down trying to get the little brown being huddled in the mire to stand on her own two feet. The dirt-encrusted creature was no fickle gnome or wicked fairy, but Sarah, who had firmly plopped herself down in the mud and refused to stand no matter what he or Helena did.

As for himself, he held a bawling Rebeccah, whose screeches were piercing his eardrums. Helena was saying something to him—this he knew because he saw her mouth moving—but he could hear nothing over the plaintive wailing from the five-year-old.

Unceremoniously shoving her head against his chest to muffle her cries, he shouted, "What did you say?"

"I said here comes Miss Pesserat. Perhaps she could help."

Jareth turned to see Chloe was indeed on her way, striding with that unearthly walk of hers, arms swinging and her legs stretching out in a long, brisk gait. No ladylike minced steps for her. He watched her,

caught in an unwitting moment of admiration until
he took note of her face.

Oh, Lord.

She didn't speak a word, however. Coming up to
him, she yanked Rebeccah out of his arms and into
hers in a single movement. The child stopped her
weeping immediately and wrapped her arms so
tightly about Chloe's neck, Jareth was surprised she
could still breathe. Then they went to Sarah, who
clamored up to her governess's other hip like a mon-
key straight out of the Dark Continent. Thus encum-
bered, Chloe turned and strode up to the house without saying a thing.

Her silence, however, had spoken eloquently of
her feelings.

He and Helena exchanged looks like guilty children. Then she stood upright, as regal and poised as
if she been dressed in silk and surrounded by admir-
ers. "I am sorry, your grace. It was my idea that
started this entire procedure. I should never have suggested it."

Jareth was struck with how extraordinarily sub-
missive she was. It came to him that she was always
like this. He could condemn her for being purple, and
she wouldn't say a word in defense of herself.

Where was the fire? Where was her passion?

She gazed at him with a placid face and he was
filled, all of a sudden, with an enormous sense of
disgust at such subservience.

"It is entirely my fault, Helena. Think no more of
it."

The nursery was quiet when he entered a few
hours later. Quiet and empty. He looked about, but

saw no one in the large playroom. He crept into the children's bedchamber and saw the two clean, peaceful girls asleep. Across the playroom, Chloe's door was ajar, her bedroom empty.

He felt restless. He wanted to speak to her, though he had no idea what he wanted to say.

He knew how she loved to walk in her garden—strange that he thought of it as Chloe's garden—but he doubted even she would brave the chill in the air tonight. She would be coming to bed soon, he reasoned, and he settled down in the great oak rocker.

He looked about him. He liked it up here. The ghostly memories of the past had faded, leaving his mind clear to see the room as it was now, filled with the belongings of two little girls. Two precious little girls to whom he owed a debt after today's debacle.

What had made him dismiss Chloe out of hand when she had protested his taking the children in the pony trap—had it been simply pride? He'd like not to think so. If it were true, then he'd be no better than his mother, and he detested her unfeeling arrogance.

He had been preoccupied, he remembered now. The man with the ring. His men hadn't been able to find him, though they had searched for hours. What had the man wanted, and was he the same man who had cuffed him in the fog?

Those questions had been uppermost in his mind when Chloe had made her argument, and he hadn't listened. He still didn't have his answers about the mysterious man, and he had committed a grave error. He would talk to Chloe, to make it right. He wouldn't rest until he had.

The rocker was comfortable. He crossed his arms

over his chest and tucked in his chin, telling himself he would just close his eyes for a moment. Surely Chloe would be up shortly.

He had no way of knowing how long he slept. He was awakened by agonizing shrieks. Coming out of the chair before his eyelids were fully raised, he looked about wildly, disoriented. Then he saw her, a tiny figure in her nightgown, racing about the nursery and wailing her loudest.

Of course. Rebeccah's night terrors.

Running to the doorway, he leaned out, keeping a watchful eye on his distressed niece. Drawing in a deep, long breath, he roared, "Chloe!"

The cold air should have driven her inside long ago. Indeed, her toes were frozen and her hands and nose had gone numb, but she refused to go indoors.

Indoors where it was warm. But the nursery was making her feel trapped and isolated tonight, and the rest of the house was as foreign to her as this land was, as different and cold as this clime in comparison to the mild winters and carefree summers of her youth. Besides, she had much to occupy her mind, so much so that she barely noticed her discomfort in the deep winter night.

Another letter from Papa had come. In it, he spoke more openly about his affection for Madame Duvier. She was happy for him. Papa was in love, it seemed. She thought of Mary and how gallant Daniel had come to her rescue with his beautiful proposal.

Love was all around her, but love was not for her.

A particularly depressing fate, since she had realized only a few days ago that she was in love with Jareth.

She didn't want to be. She wanted it to be simple attraction, a fleeting infatuation, maybe even full-fledged desire, but love…oh, no. Love was a disaster.

A sound drifted to her, floating on the chill air like a puff of breath. It was faint and indistinct. Chloe listened for a moment. Upon hearing nothing more, she wandered farther into her garden, wrapped up tightly in her thick woolen cloak and her miserable thoughts.

The duke had chosen his course. He admitted his affection for her, his desire. He acknowledged he didn't love the woman he would make his wife. He had looked at her until she thought his blazing dark eyes would singe her flesh, but he would never be hers, never break out of that stifling chrysalis of duty and responsibility. He was a prisoner of his title, a servant of his birth, and he would never again be free to take her in his arms and speak to her of his heart.

Another sound reached her, a lower sound. Like a man's voice. It was very far away. She looked out to the trees beyond the garden wall.

She thought of the drunken tenant who had come to the house during the luncheon party. Could it be him again, come to make some trouble in the night? Perhaps it wasn't wise for her to be so far from the house.

The sounds increased in volume as she neared the mansion. Increased, as well, was her curiosity, and concern as she realized they were actually coming *from the house.* And then the truth dawned on her—Rebeccah!

"Mon Dieu," she swore, wondering how she could have been so thoughtless to have forgotten. She broke into a run, flinging open the door off the

pantry and leaving it swinging in her wake, banging alternately between the door frame and the wall. The sound was like a drumbeat. It faded behind her as she took the back stairs two at a time all the way up to the third floor.

Had she been thinking, she would have realized that the sounds had ceased almost as soon as she entered the house. All had been quiet for the several minutes it took her to get up to the nursery. Therefore, when she burst across the threshold into the playroom, she was utterly shocked by what she found.

Jareth was there. In her chair, the large oak rocker. On his lap lay Rebeccah, curled up nice and tight and looking as content as a cat after a feast. While all of this was positively amazing, what was truly extraordinary was the simple fact that *Rebeccah's eyes were open.*

The child had never been awakened from her night terrors before. The doctor had warned it would produce a trauma so great, she might never recover from it.

Yet here she was, looking at Chloe and smiling. "Hello, Miss Chloe," she said in a sleepy voice.

Chloe looked at Jareth. He was pale, his hair almost standing on end, but he had the most beautifully serene look on his face. "Hello, Chloe."

Inane as it seemed, Chloe replied, "Hello, Jareth. Hello, Rebeccah."

Jareth tilted his head to peer into the face of the little girl. "Are you ready for bed now?"

"Yes, Uncle."

Chloe's mouth hung open as Jareth swung the child up in his arms and carried her to her bed. She was still standing in that same position when he returned a few moments later.

"Come," he said to her, holding out his hands. Dumbly, Chloe stepped forward and allowed him to lead her to the window to stand in the square of moonlight puddling on the wooden floor.

"Where were you? I had the whole staff looking for you." His words were not harsh, but a soft, elegant whisper. His hand still held hers.

"I was in my garden," she answered, not noticing her slip. "I did not hear her cries until just now."

"You went to the garden in this cold?"

"I needed to think. Why is that important? Tell me what happened here. Rebeccah, she awoke?"

He sighed and nodded. "She had a terrible attack. Bette came up to try to help, but she was soon in tears herself. She said it was the worst she'd ever seen. Rebeccah even got out of bed. She was running about."

Chloe's free hand came up over her mouth. "The child needed me and I was not here. She must have been terrified." Then she realized that Rebeccah had not been terrified at all when she had seen her. "What did you do?"

Jareth shrugged. "None of the other servants would come. It was left to me. I had to do something, but I didn't know… I shook her awake."

"Oh, no! You must never do that!"

"Chloe, you saw her when you came in—she was fine."

Somewhat mollified by this incontrovertible fact, Chloe asked, "What did she say? Did she know why she was screaming?"

His face went ashen again. "She said she was having a nightmare…about horses. They were chasing her." He looked away, his expression bitter. "She was terrified, poor thing."

"*Mon Dieu,* I am to blame. I should have been here!"

His hand cupped her chin and brought her face up so his eyes held hers. "Chloe, you are always here when the children need you. The fault is mine."

"The poor child," Chloe said.

"Yes, well, that poor child shaved a few years off my life, I can tell you right now. I thought I was going to go into an apoplexy myself if she hadn't stopped."

Chloe couldn't suppress her giggle. "You seemed to manage."

He looked at her, serious now. "Yes, I did. Now, are you willing to concede that I may have a thing or two to contribute to my nieces' welfare?"

"When this whole incident was caused by your dragging them to the pony trap when they are terrified—I do not think I shall, *monsieur.*"

"You are absolutely right. I should have listened to you."

"You see it is true."

"I shall admit it if you will admit that I did well by the girl."

"Oh, very well, if you must have it, there it is."

"Say it."

She harrumphed. Then, very grudgingly and very quickly, she said, "*Oui,* you did well by the girl."

"Ah, it sounds so sweet when you say it like that." His sarcasm made her giggle again. He took a step closer. She could smell the clean, musky scent of him. It went straight to her head, making her dizzy. She swallowed hard against her flagging strength.

He spoke softly, his breath fanning her forehead. "Do you know what I thought tonight when the servants couldn't find you?"

"No," she answered softly, distracted by the fullness of his lips.

"I thought you might have gone. For good. Run away from us all in this crazy house—the children, my mother. Most of all me."

"I cannot leave." Why was her brain refusing to function properly? The hand that held hers began tugging, drawing her closer.

"Because of the children?"

"Yes, and…"

"Chloe?"

"Yes?" She felt his arm go around her waist, supporting her. She relaxed against it. His body was so close to her—how had he gotten so close?

"I want to kiss you."

She tried to sound flippant. "Go ahead. It is, after all, only a kiss."

"Ah, Chloe, it never was that, and you knew it all along."

His mouth came over hers suddenly, bold and hungry. He pulled her up tight and Chloe cooperated with his intention to move as close as they could, wrapping her arms about his neck and arching her body full against his. He groaned and slanted his mouth over hers, his lips moving, his hands moving, his tongue running along the seam of her lips to tease them open.

It was as before. He had her in his arms, and it was where she wanted so desperately to be. She held back nothing as he poured all of the passion inside of him into that kiss.

With her eyes closed tight, she felt as if she were spiraling away into the heavens, floating or falling— she didn't know which.

He broke away to nuzzle her neck, then her ear, while she gasped in air, trying desperately to clear her head. His breath titillated her prickling flesh and it was hopeless to try to think.

"Chloe, I need you," he said. "I tried not to. It is impossible, the two of us like this. You know it as well as I. But there it is, against all reason. I want you, Chloe. Dear God, I want you so badly, I'm burning for you."

It was as if a bucket of lamp oil had been touched by a match. Her heart was seared by the heat of it. The graze of his roughened cheek against hers, the faint scent of his soap from his morning shave, the feel of his muscles shifting under her palms were like some dream.

Everything she wanted, right in her hands.

He said her name. It was a low, keening sound, born in the depths of his soul. Through a pleasure-hazed fog, she heard his voice. "You don't know what effect you have on me, do you?" She could only issue a small, pathetic sound and shake her head in response. "Do you know the things I want to do to you? Wild, uncivilized things, Chloe."

"Yes!" she gasped as his tongue touched her flesh.

He made a sound, a kind of growl, and crushed her lips with his. Pulling away, still touching, he spoke harshly. "I don't want to do this to you, Chloe. Stop me. I cannot, so you must. It is insanity and it

is forbidden and for that very reason I am helpless.''
He kissed her again until they were both breathless,
his passion belying his rational words. Against her
mouth, he whispered. "Stop this now, for God's
sake."

"I don't want to stop." She panted, letting the
feelings flood her, remove her from the world of
thought and lift her into the realm where sensation
ruled. "Jareth, I love you."

He shook his head, his expression a mingling of
pain and regret. "Don't love me, Chloe."

She grasped his head in her hands, forcing his eyes
to her. "You shall not forbid me this, your grace."
Softer, she said, "I do love you. And you love me."

He bowed his head, as if to demur to argue the
point, but his hands gripped her tighter. When he
looked at her again, his face was lined with leagues
of want, but again his words were a plea for ration-
ality. "Send me away. Do it, Chloe. You know it is
the right thing to do."

Chloe closed her eyes, trying desperately to think.
Why did he leave it to her? She was no more capable
of sensibility than he—less so, perhaps. All she knew
was that her body was on fire, and if they parted now,
never to consummate this exquisite torture that
pulled and twisted her insides, she couldn't bear it.

She could walk with him the few paces to her
bedchamber and give herself to the man who owned
her heart, or she could do what was right and proper,
even required, and quietly tell him to go.

But when had she ever let her head win out over
her heart?

In an instant, she was again in his arms. He em-
braced her, welcoming her back up against him with

a hunger as great as if it had been years since they had last touched. She reached out, tracing her shaking fingers down the clean, angular lines of his cheeks, along his jaw.

"I care nothing of what you say is the right thing to do. I want you to make love to me," she said.

Chapter Eighteen

As desperately as he desired her, Jareth tried to resist. But when had he ever been able to resist Chloe?

He fought nobly not to give in to the mad impulses in control of his will. Every inch of him screamed for him to take command of his runaway senses and leave her now before they had gone too far.

Everything but his heart. That was not his own any longer. It belonged to her. This she had known, speaking with confidence of his love. But, of course, Chloe would know his heart. In so many ways, she knew that part of him better than he knew himself. Could she feel how it soared with her in his arms? Did she sense the brilliant pressure in his chest at her kiss, her scent, her lithe, supple body under his hands?

He felt as if he were drowning in her and still he craved more. Chloe, who had never meant to seduce him but who had, with her subdued loveliness and purity and artless, wondrous spirit, held the balance of all happiness in one slender hand.

Slowly, he disengaged the embrace, taking her hand and leading her to the room off the playroom that was hers, closing the door softly behind him and turning the lock.

She stood in the middle of the room, that unearthly poise holding her body erect with expectation. A touch of apprehension was in her eyes, but it was gone after a moment, replaced by soft, limpid invitation. Its fleeting presence reminded him that she was a virgin, he was sure, and the passion that would have made him rough, frantic, needed to be contained.

He went to her, taking her hands in his, summoning her to come up against him. He wanted to feel her body against his. His lips touched her forehead, gliding across the silken smoothness of her skin.

"I can give you nothing, Chloe. The irony is the world would deem you unworthy to be mine, but it is I who do not deserve you. Even if I were still simply Jareth Hunt, unencumbered and uncommitted by this title I so loath, I would not deserve you. You are…" He lowered his head to study her lips, those full, kiss-reddened lips that fascinated and taunted him to madness. "You are like no other woman I have met." He gave in to the temptation of those lips, brushing soft, feathery kisses at their corners, murmuring, "You are…sunlight…and laughter…and freedom…and dreams. And stars, Chloe. Holding you, loving you like this, it is like dancing on the stars."

Flinging her arms around his neck, she was kissing him feverishly, pressing her body so he could feel her, belly to belly, breasts crushed against his chest, her left leg nearly fully wrapped around his right. He slipped his hand to her bottom and pulled her up tighter, but he was frustrated by the encumbrance of their clothes.

Uninhibited kisses rained upon him, kisses that left him breathless and scorched with need. He pushed her backward, to the bed, breaking away just long enough to lay her down upon it, to stretch out beside her, to gaze down at her face, stained with desire and nearly stopping his heart for just a moment before their mouths came together again.

Was he truly holding her in his arms? It seemed impossible, yet it was exactly where he should be, as if he had waited an eternity to find his way home and now here he was.

Her body was warm under his hands. He had wanted to go slowly, but that particular feat of control seemed beyond him. His fingers moved deftly over the simple fasteners at the back of her dress, greedily slipping inside to glide over the exposed flesh.

She wore no corset, and the knowledge of this sent his poor abused brain into a dizzying spiral. His loins tightened, hardened, pressing urgently against the confines of his clothing. He pulled her dress over her shoulders and down her arms, wrestling it smoothly over her hips, until it was gone. He heard a soft clump as it hit the floor where he had tossed it upon the bare boards.

Wild lightning threaded through his body as his hands slipped under her chemise. It was simple linen, not so fine as the undergarments of the ladies who had graced his bed in the past had worn, but her skin was softer than the most expensive silk. Leaning back on his heels, he wrapped his hands about both of her hips, sliding upward, fingers meeting across her tiny waist, then further to cup her breasts and finally sweep off the flimsy garment over her head.

His breath hissed through his teeth as he gazed at her before him, more glorious than he could have imagined. Slim and lithe, her body was small. Rounded hips flared gently under an absurdly tiny waist to give way to long, long legs finely shaped and lean.

She watched him watch her, her teeth caught on her bottom lip to show her discomfort and reminding him that as much as he could gaze at her in this state forever, she was unused to intimacy. But not unaffected by it, he noted, seeing how her cheeks were flushed crimson. Her chest rose and fell in quick, tremulous pants.

Then she denied all his tender, gentle impulses when she grasped his hands and brought them to her breasts again, arching against the contact. A low groan tore from the back of his throat.

Of course, Chloe would be an uninhibited lover, he thought joyously. He surrendered to the blinding urgency coursing in his blood.

He was on her in a flash, kissing her and ripping open his shirt at the same time.

"Your touch is like flame, *mon amour*," she gasped against his mouth.

He nearly collapsed from the pleasure of those words. Impatient now, he rolled from her and stripped, not bothering to do any more with his clothing than toss them into a heap on the floor.

When he stretched out over her again, he chuckled low and soft against her neck. She stiffened. "What is so funny, *s'il vous plaît?*" she demanded.

"I was thinking how shocked my head valet shall be when he sees my clothes. I hate having a valet."

She grasped his chin and turned him to face her. "You are thinking about your valet at a time such as this? *Incroyable!*"

He slid down her body, an inch at a time. "Shall I show you, *mademoiselle,* of what I have been thinking? Obsessing upon, more likely, until I thought the madness would rip me into shreds."

Cupping her breast, he lowered his mouth over her nipple, smiling against the taut tip when he heard her gasp. Her breasts were small, round and high, perfectly shaped to fit in his hand. The dusty tip strained against his lips, tempting his tongue to venture out and stroke it until she squirmed.

"You are wicked!" she gasped.

Indeed, he was the wickedest man alive to take so freely what he could never repay—this sweet innocence of her trusting heart—but he pushed the flash of shame away and let his hand wander down to play among the soft curls between her thighs.

His mouth covered hers again, alternately kissing her and murmuring words of love against her lips as his fingers touched her. He drank in her response, the movements of her body under his, her short little breaths hitching shakily under his mouth, her hands curling into the muscle of his back. He savored her pleasure, consuming it like a starving man suddenly finding himself seated at a feast.

She pulled back to gaze into his face. "I…" she began, but never finished, for his fingers continued the warm, tantalizing path across her most sensitive part.

"I want to give you pleasure," he murmured into her ear.

She strained against his hand, moving in rhythm with his strokes. His lips wandered, trailing kisses and nibbling at the graceful contours of her shoulders, her throat, her tiny, delicious earlobe.

He felt her stiffen, heard the small, contained cry. Her hand clutched his wrist, squeezing it as she bucked under him until the storm had passed and her movements slowed. His hand stilled, stroking down her thighs.

The expression on her face was one of dazed bewilderment, and it made him smile. "That was…that was…what was that?" she said.

"That was me loving you, darling." The need in his groin was growing painful. He pressed against her hip meaningfully, wanting entrance.

Her lazy eyelids flew open and those stormy eyes settled on him with a degree of uncertainty. "There is more." It wasn't a question.

"Only if you wish it."

"Your body joins with mine." To his utter devastation, her small hand reached down and touched two fingertips against his swollen length. "Here."

He closed his eyes. "Yes," he answered, his voice no more than a harsh rasp.

Seeing the effect of her touch emboldened her and she experimentally ran her hand along his length. "No, Chloe," he managed to say, snatching her hand away.

"Show me how. I want you that way, Jareth."

"*This* is how I want to love you." Shifting his hips, he was at her entrance. Her mouth opened and her head fell back, exposing the tender column of her neck. He hitched his hands under her knees to slide her legs around his thighs.

He paused, his breathing ragged. "Chloe, it may hurt you," he muttered roughly, doubting his ability to refrain from plunging ahead.

"Jareth, I am not a virgin," she answered in a trembling voice, too intent on the feel of him to take note of his shock.

"What?" he said, stopping midstroke.

She blinked. "*Non!* I do not mean that I have been with another man. When I was a little girl, I fell from my pony and bled, and my mama told me that was my virginity. She said it was a good thing, so it will not be painful for me my first time."

He leaned into her, touching his forehead to hers. "Will I never learn to not allow you to shock me?"

Light, taunting touch trailed down his back to the hard muscle of his buttocks. "I do not mean to, you know."

Then he couldn't speak anymore. He pushed her down, sheathing himself fully with her, sealing himself in slick heat. A soft mew escaped from her throat, as gentle as a kitten's cry. The sound inflamed him. Blood pounded in his ears as he withdrew and surged forward again. Blissful sensation left him trembling. As he thrust, she moved under him, matching his movements, her hands running over his shoulders, his arm, down his back. He thought she might climax again, but this first time, when his body was filled with delirious longing, he could not wait.

His release hit him with unprecedented force. Pleasure exploded in his brain in a shower of light. He heard his own voice cry out her name, hardly recognizing the low, guttural cry as his own. Her slim body under his arched to receive his last thrusts as the ecstasy faded into sharp ripples of sensation.

Slowing, stilling his motions, he turned his face into the curve of her neck. Chloe wrapped her arms about him, holding him closely, tightly, until his breathing slowed.

He rolled to his side, wrapping her up tight against his side. Touching her jaw, he said, "That was the worst thing I ever did, but I cannot regret it."

She looked appalled. "The worst?"

"I mean, you lovely creature, that giving in to... I should never have allowed this to happen. But it has, and I am not sorry for it, though any decent man would be."

"Très bien," she asserted with a sniff. "A woman hardly wants to hear that the man who has just made love to her thinks the entire matter a mistake he would rather have not happened."

"Never that," he promised.

"But you said a mere kiss was a mistake, that it was—"

"Yes, yes, 'only a kiss.' Shall you punish me endlessly for that single inane comment?"

She smiled wickedly. "If only one comment had been thus, I certainly would forget it. But after so many..."

"Mademoiselle," he began in playful incredulity, "are you insinuating that I have spoken words that you consider...not of utmost soundness."

She nodded, biting her lips to suppress her giggles. "Most of them, in fact."

He laughed with her, catching her face in his hands and kissing her soundly. "And if anyone had the gall to stand up to me and tell me so, it has been you.

What a sad fellow I am. I make love to a woman, and she proceeds to inform me of my faults.''

She smiled and nestled closer into his side. A perfect fit, he mused with sublime contentment. ''Everyone has faults, Jareth, and I would risk swelling your head to speak of your other…more favorable qualities.''

''There—you admit I do have them!''

''On occasion.''

''Ah,'' he sighed, relaxing into the pillows. ''I shall have to remind you that you said that.''

They lay like that, entwined together, and laughed and whispered and basked in this newfound intimacy. But as the night lengthened, inevitably the world crept back.

He would not have predicted how quickly his conscience would descend upon him. As the sky lightened, desolation took hold, stealing into their warmth like the frigid fingers of a cold fog. Day was here, chasing away the last vestiges of their magical night.

Apparently sensing his mood, he felt Chloe's spirits descend with his.

''Jareth…''

He closed his eyes against the sound of his name spoken with such a mournful tone.

''Nothing has changed, Chloe.''

She sighed. ''No, that is not true, *mon cher amour.* Nothing is the same.'' She paused and asked, ''What shall we do now?''

Jareth opened his eyes and looked into the thinning darkness. ''I haven't the vaguest idea.''

Chapter Nineteen

Those words, *What do we do now?* stayed with Jareth for days.

He thought constantly of Chloe, though he was careful not to speak to her. When he'd glimpse her, leaving the house with the children, stealing into the library on a clandestine mission to borrow one of his mother's novels—a secret he never divulged to anyone—he would feel a wrenching pain in the pit of his stomach.

What do we do now? A week passed and he kept his distance, telling himself he would think of the right thing, he would find the answer to the question and then he would tell it to her.

But as another week slipped behind them, he still had no answer, and then it came to him that *this* was what they were to do—stay away from each other, go on as if nothing had happened, she with the children and he in his hollow, sterile world of nobility.

It was toward the end of the second week he noticed Gerald constantly hanging about the nursery—some business about kittens. Although it made him furious to see his cousin freely enjoying what he had forbidden himself, he rather savored the pain, letting it rip at his insides in clean, bold strokes, heightening his misery. He told himself it was no more than he deserved for what he had done.

Some servants were speaking in the hallway one day and he recognized one as Bette, who had been the only servant to try to help him that night in the nursery with Rebeccah. He overheard her saying that his niece's night fears had eased. The incidents were not as frequent and much milder when they did occur. He heard her breathless voice impart the dramatic secret of the child's cure—it seemed, she reported, that the duke had taken matters into his own hands and woken the child one night against the doctor's strict instructions, and thus the recovery was made.

It should have made him smile, both out of pride for the parts of the story that were true and amusement for the parts that weren't, but not much made him smile of late. He stayed to himself. He even ate alone, working late hours as he poured his energies into fashioning the family's financial empire into his own.

His strategies were aggressive, and it was as a result of these that a visitor arrived one day unannounced, an unthinkably brash move. But rudeness was Philip D'Arc, Marquess of Claremont's particular talent.

Jareth had known him a long time, since their days at Cambridge. He had detested him then, for the man's character was abominable. Charles had particularly disliked him and the three had been cordial enemies since.

And as fate would have it, he was a friend of Gerald's. He introduced him to the duchess.

"I am speechless in the presence of such beauty," Claremont said in his oily way, bowing over her hand and making his mother blush.

Jareth left them and went into his library, but he knew his solace wouldn't last long. Claremont was here to see him, and he knew why. When he had outmaneuvered a competitor for mining rights to an ore-rich field in Cornwall, he hadn't known it was Claremont whom he had edged out in the bidding. He had found out later, through his solicitors, that Claremont was furious. He was here to do business.

Probably going to make an offer to purchase it back, Jareth thought. Looking over his portfolio, he studied his other holdings to see if he would sell it to him. He thought he just might. It depended on how nicely Claremont asked.

This is what he told the marquess when he finally granted him an audience that afternoon. He might have enjoyed making him wait longer, but he realized that the sooner they got the matter settled, the sooner Claremont would leave.

In response to this statement, Claremont merely stared, a wicked smile curling out from behind his crooked forefinger, poised thoughtfully at his lips. "I remember you differently, Strathmere. More of a quiet type. Always so serious about your studies." Both his curled lip and the derision in his tone made it sound like an affliction.

"And I remember you, Claremont. Always looking to do harm."

Claremont chuckled. "Everyone has faults, Jareth."

Jareth started at the familiar form of address. "I am the duke now."

Claremont only shrugged. "That seems a bit of a wicked twist of fate, does it not?"

"I cannot think you shed many tears over Charles's passing."

"Charles was merely one of my enemies," he replied. "I have so many, I cannot become too excited when one goes. No, no, you misunderstand." A cruel smile twisted his lips. "I am given to believe Burke and Hunt Shipping is thriving. An excellent investment. I was about to make an offer for it myself when I heard you were selling your shares, but then your partner—oh, excuse me, *former* partner—pulled in his family connections and, well, it became just another golden opportunity lost to me."

Claremont's reputation barely did him justice, Jareth thought. When he was vicious, he had no peer. Astute of him to bring up the company Jareth had loved nurturing to fruition.

Trying to sound unperturbed, Jareth replied, "Colin is a capable manager. I never had any doubt of it."

"How wise of you." His voice dripped sarcasm like honey, thick and sickeningly sweet. "The irony I was referring to before was the very fact of *your* being duke. I mean, you must admit, Strathmere, you aren't the type. You have no flair. The upper classes thrive on eccentricity and you, my dear fellow, are far too independent. I have watched you all these years. There was all that unsettling business from our Cambridge days, do you remember, so your family held a particular interest for me. After all, your brother was the reason I was sent down."

"Forgive me for reminding you, Claremont, but you were the reason you got sent down. It was you who sneaked that trollop into your rooms."

"Actually, it was a trio of trollops, and it was your brother who informed the prefect."

"He did so only when he was accused himself. He owed you no loyalty."

"And you stood by his side. Do you remember?"

"Of course I do. I stood by my brother because he was in the right."

"Ah, well, it is in the past." His long, elegant hands waved nonchalantly in the air. "I only mention it because it had some bearing on my later years. Missed opportunities and all that."

Seeming pleased with himself all of a sudden, Claremont laughed—a hollow, irritating sound. "I admit I lied before. I was relieved to know of Charles's demise, not for the loss of an old nemesis but for the beauty of the entire matter. Charles gone, never to rear his ugly head and spoil my fun again, and you, the new Duke of Strathmere." He laughed again as if this were the most supremely amusing jest he could imagine.

Jareth's expression must have conveyed his confusion. Claremont roared louder. "But it is all so perfect, do you not see? For you, the dukedom is not to be coveted. By God, man, you were part of one of the premier industries in our nation, and you had to give it all up to come back to the ancestral home and *breed*."

As quickly as it had arisen, his laughter died. Suddenly, he was deadly serious. "For a man like you, Jareth, becoming the duke is like burying you alive."

Jareth's vision contracted, converging on a single

pinpoint. Those eyes, those cold, flat eyes were watching him, waiting with heady anticipation for his response. Drawing in a slow breath, Jareth spoke. "Is that what you have come all this way to tell me?"

If Claremont was disappointed at being robbed of a more satisfying reaction from his prey, he didn't show it. He replied, "No. Your guess was correct, I wish to purchase an investment back from you, but it is not the coal mine. And—" he paused, appearing blithely amused "—I am prepared to ask very nicely."

"What is it you want?"

"There is some property in Herefordshire. Worthless plot of land, nothing but a few cows and a crumbling medieval manor house." He sounded deliberately casual, which raised Jareth's suspicions. "It borders a farm up there that I want to expand, a nice little retreat for me when London gets too much for me. It may surprise you to learn I fancy I would enjoy playing country squire, overseeing the pastoral landscape."

What ridiculousness was this? Jareth wondered. His lies were as thin as gossamer.

He remembered the acquisition of which Claremont spoke. It was a huge parcel of land Charles had bought only months before his death. It was also one of the assets Jareth had already targeted to sell off in order to raise capital for the industries he had chosen to take the duchy in the direction he envisioned.

As much as he despised giving Claremont what he wanted, it would be cutting off his own nose to spite his face to refuse. "What are you offering for the land?"

Claremont grinned, pleased to have piqued the

duke's interest. The bargain he outlined confirmed Jareth's suspicion that the land was no idle request. Country squire, indeed. He made the offer very attractive, too attractive to pass up even if he had been disposed to keep the land for his own uses.

Claremont must want this land very badly, Jareth mused. He must have been extremely put out when he found out his old enemies held it.

Then a thought occurred to him. Claremont had said something about Charles spoiling his fun *again.* Had Charles purchased this land just to vex Claremont?

It wouldn't keep Jareth from striking the bargain if this were the case. Whatever Charles's motivations for buying the Herefordshire lands had been, this was Jareth's duchy now, and part of his self-emancipation from the bindings of the title had been to give up trying to carry on with others' expectations and move ahead with his own agenda. The sale suited his plan, so he informed Claremont that he would agree to the deal provided his solicitor furnished a comprehensive description of the transaction.

Claremont smiled. "Excellent. I shall dispatch myself to London to see it done, posthaste."

"Good journey, Claremont," Jareth said, turning away.

"And good health to you, your grace. Do take special care when out and riding about. It is distressing that even conveyances as grand as the ducal carriage can sometimes be…well, *unreliable.*"

Jareth whirled, but Claremont was already out the door. In his wake, a wicked chuckle echoed in the hall.

* * *

Chloe scooted the kitten aside for what had to be the tenth time that day. This was Sarah's—each girl had insisted on having her own pet—and had been dubbed Harry by Rebeccah. He was a marmalade-and-cream creature with distinctive tortoiseshell markings and a remarkable amount of energy. Rebeccah's gray-striped tabby, named Lady Anne, was, in contrast, quite lazy, but her orange brother more than made up for it.

"See, you have smudged the ink, bad cat!" Chloe scolded. Grabbing the kitten by the scruff of the neck and placing him gently on the floor, she went back to her letter.

What was she to say to Papa? How was she to tell him of the happenings in her life without her unhappiness pouring out on the page?

She sighed and looked out the window. The stubborn kitten leaped on top of the table again and began pouncing about, his little eyes round with an adorable expression that by rights should have amused her. "Sarah, come and get Harry."

The little girl scampered in and carried off her pet, and Chloe stared once again at the empty page. She decided to write about the children and leave herself out of it completely. Papa was no fool, but any suspicions he would have would be far less humiliating than admitting the truth.

What was there for her to be ashamed of? she wondered. Of love? Her mother had raised her better than to hide her feelings like her English aristocrat cousins. Was she ashamed of making love with Jareth? she wondered. Never. She could not regret a moment of that night for all of the admonitions and preachings of sin in the world. If that one night together were the only thing she was to have of him, she would take it with her to her grave and treasure it always.

"Miss Chloe," Rebeccah said, rushing into her bedroom, waving something in her hand. "Look what I have found in a cupboard."

Chloe was more interested in the dust covering the child. "Rebeccah, I have told you not to go crawling about in the closets." Rebeccah ignored her and placed a small leather-bound book on Chloe's desk with a flourish. "What is this?"

"It's a book!" she replied, very proud of herself.

"I can see that. Why do you give this to me?"

"It must have all manner of secrets inside. Perhaps even a map for treasure."

"Oh, really?"

"Miss Chloe, do you not see? The book was *hidden*. So, there must be something wonderful inside. Read it! Go ahead, open it and read it to me."

Chloe picked up the volume. It smelled of mildew. Opening to the first page, she said, "Probably a misplaced picture book that got shoved to the back of a cupboard…"

The page read, "Diary of Charles David Witherspoon Hunt IV, Marquess of Harwether, heir apparent to the Duke of Strathmere."

"What is it, Miss Chloe? What does it say?" Rebeccah was at Chloe's elbow. "Oh! Tell me!"

Chloe closed the book. "It is your father's diary from when he was a boy."

This, apparently, was more wonderful than secret treasure maps, judging by Rebeccah's expression. Chloe waylaid her next, predictable, request. "And I shall not read it to you. When you are older, you may have it and read it on your own. But the things in this volume were a little boy's private thoughts, and I don't think that boy would want a five-year-old and a governess prying into his diary, even if the child is his own.''

''But—''

''*Non, chérie.* When you are older. Now, do not trouble me again.'' Handing her the diary, she instructed, ''Go put this on the shelf.''

Thwarted, Rebeccah looked murderous as she stomped out of the room.

No sooner had she left than Gerald came into the playroom, bellowing, ''What are you ladies doing indoors on such a fine day as this?''

''Hello, Cousin Gerald!'' Rebeccah cried. Chloe laid her quill down and went to the doorway, smiling to herself at how quickly the child recovered from her earth-shattering disappointment of only moments ago.

''How is Lady Anne?'' Gerald asked.

''Come see how she can do a trick,'' Rebeccah said, grabbing Gerald by the hand and pulling him over to where the kitten lay curled on her pillow. However, her attempts to rouse the cat from her sleep were unsuccessful.

Chloe came to intervene because she couldn't bear to see the little thing so harassed. ''Let Lady Anne sleep, Rebeccah. Remember, she is only a baby.''

Lady Anne, however, didn't seem to mind in the least. The moment Rebeccah ceased her proddings, she curled up in a ball and closed her eyes.

''You must be more gentle with Lady Anne,'' Chloe instructed. Rebeccah flounced off, whining something about having a terrible day.

Chloe gave Gerald an exasperated look, and he smiled back. She didn't mind his company, especially on a lonely day like today, although she hardly found his conversation scintillating. The topic he favored was his wicked days in London. She thought perhaps he missed them too much to be as reformed as he was constantly asserting.

"I have come here to invite you all for an outing. It is too glorious a day for staying indoors. What are you doing that is so important?"

"Writing a letter," Chloe answered.

"Put it aside for a day when rain blights the sky. There is a fresh snowfall, and it will probably be the last this season."

The distraction would be welcome, Chloe decided. "Children, would you like to go play in the snow?"

Sarah's lit-up face was her answer. Rebeccah was still in a mood, and when she was like this, her one-shouldered shrug was as good as jumping up and down.

Getting the children dressed for the cold was a substantial task. It took three-quarters of an hour before they were ready to leave. They descended the servants' stairs, their boots making as much racket as an entire regiment of soldiers. Rebeccah's excitement built, and she burst out the pantry door and ran to the walled orchard, Sarah on her heels.

Chloe sighed and followed at a more sedate pace with Gerald at her side. As they rounded the corner, she almost collided with Jareth who was coming from the other direction.

"Jareth!" Gerald exclaimed. "Had the same idea we did, eh?"

"Just a brisk walk." He edged around them, already preparing for a swift exit.

"Care to join us? We are going to build a snow castle or some such thing."

"Castles are for the sand," Chloe said softly. "The snow is for making forts."

"There, you see? Snow forts. We could use the help."

Jareth refused to look at her. He appeared to be studying the treetops. "No. Have work to do."

"No rest for the wicked, eh, cuz?"

One side of his mouth jerked up politely. He gave a nod and turned away, striding purposefully toward the house.

Chloe watched his back, her face as frozen as the tree limbs surrounding her.

Gerald gazed after his cousin and shook his head. "That man takes his office too seriously. If I were duke, I'd make sure to have a little more fun."

"He thinks fun is not allowed."

"Then he is a fool."

And Chloe didn't say anything to that because, after all, she had to agree with him on that account.

Chapter Twenty

Winter grew old, and spring burst in on them with longer, wetter days and plenty of mud. These gloomy conditions gave way to the new greens of spring's first buds as the Easter season approached. When it passed, the skies dried enough to allow an outing, and Chloe had an inspiration.

It was something she had been thinking about for a long time, so she asked a footman to have a table and chairs set up by the paddock and arranged with Daniel for several grooms to exercise the horses. Telling the children to fetch their favorite doll or stuffed toy, she led them outside. They were going to have a very special tea party outside today!

Jareth sat in the parlor with the sheriff.

"Nothing on the man with the ring, your grace. We have reports that he's still in the area, and my men and I are still keeping up every vigilant effort to find him."

"Excellent, sir," Jareth replied. "I thank you for your work." Outside the window, he caught a glimpse of Chloe and the children making their way across the lawn. Gerald was not in attendance, he was glad to note.

Jareth turned back to the man sitting across from him. "I was thinking of another matter, Sheriff, a delicate matter about which I need to speak with you. It concerns my brother's fatal accident."

The sheriff frowned. "The accident? How can I help you there?"

"Was there anything in the carriage that might have given an indication as to the cause of the accident?"

Since Claremont's visit, he had wondered... He hadn't spoken to anyone about the nagging, growing suspicions that dogged him, telling himself it was only one of the marquess's mind games. But that parting comment of his, the fact of his hating Charles, contributed to a growing disquiet.

"There was so much damage, your grace, I would not know how to begin to answer that question. The left door was gone. This was how the children were saved. You see, they were thrown clear early in the carriage's descent. It was, we surmised at the time, after this occurred that the carriage hit a steeper part of the ravine and was shattered on the rocks." He cast Jareth an apologetic look. "I am sorry to be indelicate, your grace."

"I am not concerned with delicacy at this time, sir. I need information. Was there anything on the road that might have indicated how the carriage capsized in the first place?"

"It was a rocky pass. Your brother and sister-in-law had friends on the other side of the woods, up by the river, and they often took the road, I was told at the time."

"Then someone wishing to ambush them would have known they would be coming that way."

The sheriff was silent for a long time. "Is that what you are thinking? That this was no accident?"

That wasn't all Jareth was thinking. Claremont had given him the idea that maybe his brother's death was planned—maybe someone had a reason for wanting Charles dead. Someone like Claremont, for example. He might have been furious at Charles for beating him out in that land deal. Perhaps he had finally had enough from the man who had been instrumental in getting him thrown out of university.

Nor was he the only one Jareth could think of who had a motive. Gerald always coveted the title, and the fortune, of Strathmere. Perhaps he had killed Charles and planned to do Jareth in in due time. It had gotten Jareth to thinking that perhaps the attack in the garden was not a robber at all, but an attempt on his life. Chloe had saved him when she had stumbled—literally—upon him.

The man with the ring was the key. Jareth would be willing to wager someone had hired him. Why had he come to Strathmere that day, and what had frightened him off?

Helena knew something, her reaction was an indication of that. Or perhaps it was merely attributable to a well-bred lady being thrust in the presence of a ruffian exhibiting rude behavior.

"I am merely exploring all the possibilities," he said finally.

The sheriff pursed his lips with sage concentration. "I see. Do keep me informed as these *possibilities* develop, will you?"

"Certainly, sir."

After he took his leave, Jareth went to the window. He had refrained from having anything to do with Chloe for over two months now, but he was not above spying on her. In his mind, he preferred to think of it as keeping an eye on her.

Ever since he had seen her and his nieces cross the lawn earlier, he had wanted to find out where she was going, what she was doing. If he had to stay away from her, he must, but he would not deny himself watching her.

What he saw amazed him, for over by the stables, she was seated with Rebeccah and Sarah and a stuffed bear and a doll at a table and chairs set up directly in front of the paddock. Behind them, a parade of horses pranced by.

The little genius! With the distraction of their play, she was slowly acclimating the children to reestablish their comfort with horses.

So delighted was he at her cleverness that he thought of going out to join them. It had been so long, surely he would be able to maintain his self-control in her presence. And they were out in the open, with an audience of little girls and servants. *And* he missed seeing his nieces. He had been making great progress in winning their trust before he had cut himself off from them.

Eventually, he talked himself into it. It had been only a matter of time before his resolve gave way, and this enchanting picture broke through the last of it.

The air was fresh, moist and sweet and full of the promise of all the freedom of the coming months of summer. He breathed it in deeply as he walked toward the strange tea party, striding with vigor he hadn't felt in...well, two months or more.

When Chloe saw him, she was visibly shocked. "Your grace? Is something the matter?"

"Nothing," he said, drawing up to them. He had to drag his eyes away from her lovely face, kissed by the golden light, and address Rebeccah and Sarah. "I simply thought this an excellent idea for tea and wanted to come and see if I could be invited."

His answer was Sarah's removal of Old Samuel from the chair upon which the bear had been sitting. It was the sweetest invitation he had ever received.

"Thank you, Samuel, for giving up your seat."

Rebeccah giggled, clamping her hand over her mouth. He even saw Chloe smile as she looked down, so obviously awkward with him present.

"What is this young lady's name?" Jareth asked, indicating the doll.

"That is Henrietta," Rebeccah informed him. "Oh, I mean...Cass-e-o-pa. I renamed her."

A shard of guilt shot through him. She had renamed her doll Cassiopeia to honor the constellation, and to honor him. He vowed never to neglect their affections again.

"I just recollected that I never kept my promise to you. For you to come see the stars at night—do you recall? The weather is warming. We shall do it soon."

"That would be lovely," she replied.

Jareth coughed to cover his amusement at her primness. When he sobered, he poured a cup of tea. "So, tell me, does Cassiopeia take tea?"

"Her digestion is bad, so she is not having tea today," Rebeccah replied. Jareth made the mistake of glancing at Chloe. Her eyes were soft and crinkled in the corners and so fathomless he could have stared into those steel-blue depths forever. There was no holding back his smile now, but this one was all for her.

He forced his attention back to his niece. "And does Cassiopeia like horses?"

"Yes," came the child's answer with a definitive nod of her head.

That was certainly a meaningful answer. From the corner of his eye he caught Chloe's eyebrows rising. He made his voice studiously nonchalant. "Then perhaps she will like a canter later. Could you pass me the scones? And I would like some clotted cream, please."

"Let me get it for you," Rebeccah said in a rush, reaching to hurriedly fix him a scone. After slathering a disgusting amount of cream on top—which he took as a sign of her esteem—she shoved the pastry at him in triumph, wincing when a huge dollop flew off and landed in his hair.

Both girls' mouths dropped into tiny O's as they waited for his reaction. Slowly he reached up to his head and pulled off the glob. Then, to their total amazement, he dropped it in his mouth, licking his fingers and saying, "Mmm, delicious!"

They all fell to laughing again. Chloe watched him with wonder, and he was suddenly painfully aware of all the things he wanted to say to her.

"Cassiopeia wants her ride now!" Rebeccah cried, grabbing her doll and waving her in the air with both hands.

"Very well. Come, Cassie. We must pick a mount." He carried the doll to the paddock fence.

The children trailed behind, fascinated at his play. They were probably wondering what had happened to their sour-faced uncle who was wont to brood of late. Probably gone mad, they might assume.

He felt mad, if madness were to be this free and untroubled in the company of two little girls and a fresh-faced young woman with a smile that could dim the sun.

"Now, which horse do you prefer? The gray? The mare? Or did you wish to have the black gelding over there? Hmm. What is that you say?" He leaned into the doll as if she were whispering in his ear.

He turned to Rebeccah with wide eyes. "She says that none suit her. She heard tell of a white mare, and she wants that horse and will have no other."

Rebeccah almost collapsed with giggling. Sarah smiled, that lovely face that was so like the Charles he remembered shining up into his.

"Oh, she is a naughty doll to be so fussy!" Rebeccah declared. "I shall have to speak with her."

"Oh dear, she heard you and now she is quite afraid."

His silliness made the two girls giggle, and he laughed as well, delighted....

He stopped, stunned. Looking to see if he had just imagined it, he turned quickly toward Sarah.

Even Rebeccah turned, silent now, to stare at her sister.

Sarah was laughing.

Chloe ran to them, falling onto her knees before the child.

Sarah laughed and laughed and her audience waited, enraptured until the beautiful sound died away. Then she reached out her hands and laid them on each of Chloe's cheeks. He saw Chloe blink, her eyelashes moist. Sarah said, very soft and very slowly, "Chloe."

Chloe cried out, a wordless sound of joy, and snatched the child to her. "Good, Sarah! Brave, Sarah!" she kept saying.

Jareth swallowed away the emotion in his throat and bent down on one knee beside them. "What a wonderful girl you are, Sarah," he murmured, touching the child's golden hair.

"Oh, ma petite. Que tu es courageuse!" Chloe crooned until the child pulled away, seeming astonished at their making such a fuss. Jareth remembered the doctor's description of how children snap out of maladies of the nerves. Rebeccah had demonstrated a similar reaction when she had awakened to find herself in the midst of the playroom with no one about but her uncle.

He put a hand on Chloe's shoulder and drew her up with him, trying to peel his mind from the way she clung to him. It was a struggle to keep from wrapping his arms about her. "Rebeccah, you must congratulate your sister," he told his other niece.

Rebeccah, who was never pleased with being less than the center of attention, offered a grudging acknowledgment.

Then he realized his silliness had been the catalyst to bring Sarah's voice back, and so wanting to encourage her, he picked Cassie up again and resumed their play.

Sarah spoke no more words, but she laughed until the sound of it filled his heart. Chloe watched her charge, eyes shining, and then she turned that adoring gaze to him and his heart melted all over again.

After a while, the horses were brought inside and the servants came to carry the tea service and furniture back into the house. Rebeccah asked if she and Sarah could go into the fenced meadow and gather some of the early wildflowers dotting the hillside. Chloe said they may.

"But who shall watch Cassie and Old Samuel?" Rebeccah fretted. "I cannot carry her, my arms shall be too full of flowers. I know! We shall take them to visit Lady Anne and Harry's mother and brothers, so then they will not miss us when we're gone."

Chloe agreed this was an excellent idea and brought the children to the deserted corner of the stables where the mother cat had made her home. When the toys were safely nestled among the feline family, the girls raced to the meadow.

"It was a brilliant idea you had," Jareth said from the doorway. Chloe turned with a gasp. She hadn't seen him follow them inside.

She supposed he would flee when the girls went off. She knew he didn't want to be alone with her. Yet he was here now, a soft smile playing on his lips in that way he had that made her want to reach out and touch.

"It was your doing," she said, attempting to remain steady as her heart began to pulse harder. "You said we have to challenge the girls to face their fears, and after I thought on it, I had to admit it seemed a good idea. But *small* challenges first."

He spread his hands out before him. "You know best."

She gave a small laugh. "I do not believe I heard those words from your mouth!"

He laughed, too, and as the sound died, his gaze

remained on her. He wanted to say something, it seemed, but was unsure. They simply stared at each other like that for a moment until Chloe looked away and said, "Maybe I shall go join the girls."

"I missed you," he said.

She closed her eyes, staying very still. "You know where I am to be found."

"And you know that is impossible."

She opened her eyes and glared at him, letting her anger show. "I know what you think is impossible."

"Do not fight with me. Today has been too happy for harsh words."

Her shoulders sagged. "Then what would you have me say to you?" He didn't answer. She went to brush past him, murmuring, "I need to go," but when she passed him, his hand shot out and captured her upper arm.

His mouth was at her ear, saying, "I stayed away because I was too much a coward to face you. If I saw you again, my resolve would have evaporated and the situation would be worse than it is."

She snapped her head around to face him. "If that is true, why did you come today?"

He looked stricken, as if he himself was appalled at his failure. "Because when I saw your absurd, brilliant little tea party, I couldn't resist you any longer. I hoped that with the time apart, it would be different between us. But it's not, is it? Dear Lord, it's worse." His voice lowered into a husky whisper. "I want to touch you so much."

She yanked her arm out of his grasp. "How dare you say that to me. You call yourself a coward, and I quite agree, but for the opposite reason. Not because your self-control is too weak but because it is too strong. You do not know what courage is. You English find virtue in having no emotions, but it takes real courage to *feel!* You play with me like those cats play with mice. First you ignore me, then you come to me—how dare you! *You* may strive to stifle your emotions, but I have no wish for that dry, stoic life. *I* have feelings, and you are trampling them, you clumsy man!''

In a lightning-quick movement, his hands grasped her on either side of her waist and he pulled her toward him. "Everything you say is true. I have said it to myself."

"Then why are you here, Jareth?" Her voice was plaintive, but her hands flattened against his chest, sliding upward as his eyes dropped to her mouth and his head lowered.

He kissed her, long and languid, like a man savoring generations-old scotch. The heady effect was the same—dizzying, intoxicating—and when he broke the kiss to press his lips to the corner of hers, he gave her the answer, "Because I cannot stay away."

"You should not have come," she said. Her hand curled around the back of his neck as she turned her face into his to meet his mouth with hers.

He kissed her again, than moved to brush his lips along the line of her jaw. "My will has run out."

"And what has changed? Is anything altered from what it was?" She was acutely aware of his hand splayed across her waist, moving upward, his fingertips just now grazing the underside of her breast.

His hand stalled. She had heard his labored breathing. "No. Of course, nothing is different."

"Yes. I know." She pulled away enough to look

into his eyes. "Then remove your hands from me and do not touch me again."

She saw the words wound him, and for a moment of madness, she wanted to take them back, tell him she didn't mean it, tell him she would take whatever he could give her, be whatever she needed to be to have him touch her like this again, but she clamped her will down over the impulse and notched her chin up, ignoring the stinging in the back of her eyes.

He sort of laughed and nodded, releasing her and taking a step backward.

"Very well done, Chloe. I applaud you. Next time, add a few epithets and think about the handy slap in the face. You are certainly entitled." He raked his hand through his hair. "Of course, I shall endeavor to respect your request and see to it that there is no next time, but if there is, do not hesitate to put me in my place. But be brutal. For us clod-headed dolts, it is the only way."

He gave her a bracing smile, turned and walked out of the stall.

When the children came in a while later, their fists bulging with wilted flowers, they found her crying. Rebeccah rushed to her, pulling her hands away from her face. Beside her, Sarah's face was solemn alarm.

"Miss Chloe! Miss Chloe! What is it? Why are you weeping?"

Chloe pulled them both closer, a child in each arm. "Do not fret, *mes petites*. These are only tears of joy for Sarah's wonderful recovery. Only tears of joy."

Chapter Twenty-One

Having resolved to himself not to allow his distance from Chloe to interfere with his seeing his nieces, Jareth made it a point to visit them each and every day, usually in the afternoons. At times, Chloe was there. Her manner was always polite and respectful, but she kept her distance and he didn't challenge it.

Her spurning him in the stable had changed everything. There were no longer any possibilities between them. He had lived and breathed on those impossible possibilities, torturing himself with the idea that *perhaps*...

It had always been in the back of his mind that he could have her if he so chose. She was there for him, within reach. It was up to him. He had only to hold out a hand and she would take it, allow him to draw her into his arms....

No longer did he have even those thin fantasies to soothe his yearning heart.

He still thought of her as his, he still cringed when he saw Gerald dogging her steps, he still craned his neck to catch glimpses of her when she passed by, head held high, pretending to ignore him.

Strong, indomitable, lovely Chloe. She was his love, his life. A mere governess, and yet the most noble woman he would ever meet.

And he was the duke. *He was the duke,* and there was nothing more to consider after that single, fatal fact.

Which is why when his mother insisted that he tarry no longer in asking for Lady Helena's hand, he did not argue with the inevitability of the marriage.

Instead, he said, "You know I detest your meddling, Mother. I shall take care of it. I am well aware of my duty."

"Yes, I know you are, Strathmere. However, what you are not aware of is that Lady Rathford has confided in me that she is considering taking Helena to London for the season."

Jareth raised his brows and commented drolly, "Why, that little extortionist."

"Well," the duchess replied with a sniff, "you cannot expect a marriageable girl to wait around forever."

"I will not be rushed," he protested in response to the flitter of panic in his stomach.

"It is time, Strathmere. You are taking too long about it, and the Rathfords will consider that an insult if you wait much more. It will seem as if you do not deem Helena worthy, as if you are delaying entering into a contract with her because you are waiting for someone better."

"That is absurd, the woman is superior in every way."

"Yes, she is, and men in London will vie for her hand. You cannot hesitate. Act now, before she is lost to you.'' Her voice was like a hiss in his ear. ''What is it you are waiting for?''

What *was* he waiting for?

There was nothing in his future to change his circumstance. No one would or could come to divest him of his title or free him from his obligations or elevate Chloe to a titled lady socially worthy of a duke.

His mother's scornful voice came at him again. ''Is it that silly little French girl? Is that what is keeping you from wedding Helena?''

Jareth started. His mother scoffed, ''Oh, I've seen how you look at her. I have known for some time that the chit is in your blood. You men are alike; lust rules you, threatens your good sense. Really, Strathmere, she can never be for you. She is but a servant, you are a duke. More, she is a ridiculous girl with all manner of unsavory ideas. Bed her, if you haven't already, or keep her somewhere as your mistress, only be discreet. And get on with your marriage.''

Jareth finally found his voice. ''You shall not speak to me in this…forward and embarrassing manner.''

''I shall,'' she countered in a regal tone. ''Your father was much the same. He fancied himself a connoisseur of women. I never minded as long as he kept his tarts in a respectable manner. I am a woman of the world, Strathmere, and I know the ways of men. I knew my duty with your father, and I carried it out. So, too, must you do yours.''

He was filled with revulsion at what she was saying. ''I shall not insult Chloe by making her my mistress.'' But he had already, hadn't he? He had taken her virginity when he knew he could never make the promises that she longed for from him, that she deserved.

"Then you must send her away."

No. No! "I shall not," he said calmly.

"It is inevitable. She cannot stay."

"That I will never do. If not for my own selfish reasons, then for the children. They need her, and I, for one, can put my personal feelings aside to give them that."

"Their need for Chloe is passing. It was *you* who took Rebeccah out of her nightmare, and it was you who elicited the first sound from Sarah."

"The doctor informed me that the children would recover in their own time. It was merely coincidence."

The duchess was smug. "All the more reason to dismiss the girl. As you say, they will recover in their own time. The children will miss her at first, of course, but eventually their affections will transfer to their new mother. Helena will be excellent with them, do you not agree? No more cavorting in the dirt, no more screeching and leaping about like wild animals."

How dreadful for them, mother! Helena is a beautiful, talented, but dried-up ghost of a woman!

"And consider this," she continued in her sly, insinuating way. "If Chloe should stay when Helena comes, what will that be like for you? Would you truly want your wife and your mistress in the same house? It is just not done, Strathmere. You would be torn in two."

He already was, he reflected. "Chloe is not my mistress," he said softly. It was a feeble defense because he was beginning to see that what his mother was telling him was true. He had been a deluded fool to ignore it this long.

"If she isn't already, she will be. Desire rules the male animal—another inevitability. You must admit, Strathmere, the girl is a disaster."

"Very well," he murmured. "I shall speak to Lord Rathford this week."

His mother bowed her head into her trembling hands. "Wonderful, Strathmere. I knew you would not disappoint."

She hurried from the room, no doubt to kick up her heels or drink a toast in private or indulge in some other celebration of her victory.

And his utter defeat. He went up to the nursery. Bette was there with the children. "Where is Miss Chloe?" he asked.

"A letter came from her father, your grace, and I told her I would stay with the children if she wanted to take the time to read it. I believe she brought it with her to her garden." She paused, uncertain. "I hope that is all right, your grace."

Her garden. Yes. It was, would ever be Chloe's garden.

He smiled at Bette. "That was very thoughtful of you. If you wish, you may go. I can be with the children since I've come for my visit in any case. I will stay with them until Miss Chloe returns."

"Yes, your grace," she said and left him.

Sarah brought him her bear. "Samuel," she said, or at least it was a reasonable pronunciation of the word. He thanked her and greeted the bear, knowing she liked it when he playfully spoke to their toys as if they were real. "What would you enjoy doing today?"

They decided to paint a bit together. Her pesky kitten, Harry, felt the need to investigate this fascinating activity and tracked watercolors all over the table. Jareth had to stop and clean it up.

"Bad cat," Sarah said with a severe frown.

"Yes, very bad cat," he agreed.

Rebeccah hadn't wanted to be disturbed, having been deep in play when he arrived with a miniature set of dishes, the small table and chairs, and several dolls whom she could boss and would not protest. She came up to him now and asked, "Uncle, will you read to me?"

"Of course. Go choose a book. Sarah, would you like to hear a story, as well?"

The youngest child's tongue stuck out of the corner of her mouth as she swirled a soggy paintbrush on paper. His invitation she ignored. Jareth went to the rocker, and when Rebeccah returned with an old, tattered volume, he pulled her onto his lap.

"What is this?"

"It is Papa's diary from when he was a little boy. Miss Chloe has been reading it to me."

"Well, how wonderful!" he exclaimed, running his hand over the worn leather. He had never known Charles kept a diary. It was something he would very much like to read himself. "Where did she leave off?" he asked, opening the book carefully, not wanting to crumble the brittle pages.

"There," Rebeccah answered, and snuggled in closer against his chest.

Jareth shrugged at the vague answer. There was no marker in the book, so he supposed one place was as good as any.

"May 13, 1826. I spent all day with the tutor, as is my daily habit, one I detest. Jareth is in the garden again. I was supposed to be doing my history lesson, but I watched him from the window. Got three good whacks when Mr. Hampton returned and found me there. For laziness, which is true, I suppose."

Jareth paused, glancing uncomfortably down at his niece. This was certainly not the type of reading he thought appropriate for such a small child.

"He sounds sad," Rebeccah said.

"He must have been having a gloomy day. Let us turn to another entry. Ah, here.

September 11, 1826. Mother is angry at me again. I am forever disappointing her, I think. She is always saying, 'Father would have done this,' or 'Father would have done that.' I can't stand it sometimes. At times I fear…

"Rebeccah, why don't you run and get the storybook we read the other day, the one with all the gay pictures in it."

Rebeccah slid off his lap to obey. "That wasn't exciting at all. It was *boring*," she complained as she went off.

Jareth read on while she was away, caught in a macabre fascination at his brother's spiraling despair.

I hate my life. I sometimes wish I could disappear. Today, I was lying in my bed and Mr. Hampton went to complain to Mother and I wished I could die. Dying would be peaceful. I wish I could have some peace.

Jareth's hands started to tremble.

Rebeccah returned with the book he had asked her to fetch. "Here it is, Uncle. You can read if you wish. I want to go back to my doll party." She skipped over to the table and chairs to resume her play.

He took the picture book dumbly, then let it fall to the floor. The sound made the girls start, and they stared at him.

How had he not known his brother was so unhappy? Hadn't he sensed, even in the smallest way, his despondency?

Of course he had, in that vague, unspecified guilt that had dogged him as a young boy. Everyone else thought Charles the favored one, they even at times felt sorry for Jareth, the second-born. Charles was the heir, the star, the fortunate one, but Jareth had sensed the truth, even back then, in a nagging sense of remorse at his brother's burdens.

Staring off, seeing beyond the playthings assembled on the shelves in front of him, he tried to recall Mr. Hampton. Had he been cruel? To Jareth, the tutor had always seemed rather disinterested, just as his mother had been. They had treated him differently, of course. Mild to the younger son, the two of them had ridden Charles like demons.

That time at the lake, when he and Charles had capsized—it must have been that summer. Yes, he recalled it was the summer before Charles had gone away to school.

He had wanted to die. They had squeezed all the

joy out of his life until all he wanted to do was to die. And he almost had.

Charles had been eleven years old that summer.

He didn't realize Chloe had come in until he heard Rebeccah say, "Miss Chloe, come quick. It's Uncle. He's crying!"

Was he? Touching his fingers to his cheeks, he saw they were wet.

"Why is he crying?" Rebecca asked again, her voice rising.

Chloe came up quickly and snatched the diary out of his hand. "Where did he get this?" she demanded, her voice stern as she whirled on Rebeccah. Jareth looked over, puzzled. Why would Chloe be upset at her for sharing the book with him?

"I told you this was for you when you are older, when you can understand," Chloe scolded. Turning to Jareth, she said for his ears alone, "Oh, Jareth, *je suis désolée.* Come, sit. I see you are upset."

"This…" He waved a finger at the book.

"We found it some time ago. I forbid Rebeccah to read it, or rather refused to read it to her. I shall speak to her severely, I can assure you." She wrung her hands in distress. "I suppose I should have told you about it earlier. I had no idea of what it contained, but I should have been more careful with—"

"Don't," he commanded. "Do not explain. It is not your fault."

She blinked and, thankfully, stopped talking. He stepped past her, not bothering to excuse himself as he fled the room.

Chapter Twenty-Two

Rebeccah was sent to bed without supper and a re-
striction from going out-of-doors for a fortnight. She
cried, she argued, she cajoled, she fell into limp despondency to curry pity, but Chloe was angry, and
she held firm.

Her own guilt followed her into bed and kept her
awake.

It was late when she rose, giving up on sleep. The
midnight hour had struck just moments ago. Slipping
on her wrapper, she crept out of the nursery and
down the stairs.

She thought perhaps Jareth would be in his library.
He sometimes worked until the early hours of morning, she knew. When she looked inside, however, it
was dark and deserted.

Leaning against the door, she nibbled her finger-
nail. He might have gone to bed, in which case she
should simply wait until morning.

But this couldn't wait until morning.

Climbing the stairs, she hesitated on the second-
floor landing, considering the vaulted corridor. There
were things even she found beyond her power to

dare. Visiting the Duke of Strathmere in his bed-chamber was one of the few.

She went all the way upstairs and settled into bed before she muttered, "Damn!" and decided to do it anyway.

Within moments she was in front of the monstrous double doors that guarded the entrance to his masculine retreat. The master's suite at Strathmere did not stint on grandeur, marking it as the private haunt of the man who possessed and governed a vast duchy.

Bending, she checked to see if there was a light coming from underneath the door. There was. She took in a deep, trembling breath. Before she could think how insane this was, she rapped three times.

She almost fled, was about to, when the door opened and Jareth stood on the threshold wearing breeches and no shirt, but with a dressing gown drawn around his naked torso. "Chloe," he said, his voice full of amazement.

"Yes. I—I had to come to see if you were..." The words trailed off as her gaze drifted down to the smooth, swarthy skin that covered the defined musculature of his chest. Did he know his wrap was gaping open like that?

"Chloe? Is something wrong?"

Sheer embarrassment forced her eyes back up to his face, but that was not much better at helping to maintain her control. He looked gorgeous slightly rumpled like this, his dark eyes solemn and steady.

After a brief inner struggle, she remembered why she came. "It is about today. I couldn't sleep for thinking about it. I wanted to explain what happened, why I had the diary."

"You did explain. And as you can see, I haven't flung myself from the ramparts in grief." The brittleness in his voice gave him away.

"It must have been very upsetting."

He turned his head to gaze into a corner, ignoring her comment.

"If I had told you, warned you, you could have been prepared. Perhaps it would not have been so disturbing for you. I cannot forgive myself for being so thoughtless. I can only apologize…"

He didn't seem to be listening.

In fact, Jareth wasn't. Instead, his brain picked at the question—would she be so contrite if she knew the devil's bargain he had made with his mother? Something savage crept out of his pain, making him want to tell her and slam the door shut before he had to witness her reaction.

That was the weak part of him, the part of him that could get angry at her for looking that delicious and arriving at his bedroom door in the middle of the night. Witless fool, she had no idea, even after their lovemaking months before, of what she was doing to him.

She had stopped talking, he surmised, because that gorgeous mouth was no longer moving. He stared hard at it, noticing that she shifted uncomfortably from one foot to the other under the intensity of his perusal.

His soul felt like a hollow husk, ravaged by this forbidden fruit in front of him, needing her after those awful words he had read today. Oh, yes, he had been deeply affected by a glimpse into his brother's innermost thoughts. Since returning to his chamber, he had done nothing but pace, remembering and drinking. The memories scalded him, undulled by the effects of the liquor. Eventually he had abandoned the whiskey since it didn't help and had stood alone and defenseless against the pain.

"Go away, Chloe, unless you want me to make love to you again." He meant it as a threat, but it came out as a seductive promise, an invitation. The little twit didn't even have the sense God gave a kitten, standing there looking bewildered and utterly enchanting.

I wonder if she shall weep when she is made to leave the children? I wonder if she will curse me forever, for I promised her she would never have to fear being sent away.

And damn her anyway, for finding him at his rawest and placing her infinitely attractive self before him to taunt him with all that was precious to him—all he would never have.

Why not? Was it the whiskey or his pain prodding him to question—*why not?* She would hate him soon enough, what was one more night? Just one more time to hold her, feel her strength and her softness and all of her beauty....

Why not? Tomorrow would be soon enough to part. And then he could spend the rest of his life despising himself.

She was saying something. It was his name, he realized as he surfaced out of his thoughts. "Jareth? Jareth? Are you well? Oh, *mon Dieu*, I knew you were disturbed by the diary. You see this is why I could not sleep, I sensed—"

His hand shot out, and in a single instant he had yanked her into his arms and smothered her words with a kiss. A moment's hesitation was all she of-fered, then she melted against him.

"This is what tortures me, Chloe," he murmured against her skin as he trailed kisses down her neck. "You, my love. Only you have the power to wound me."

Her hands made a weak show of pushing him away before grasping the wide lapels of his silk wrapper, holding him as she kissed him back.

He pulled her into the bedroom, kicking the door shut behind them. The bed was a huge monstrosity where generations of Hunts had been conceived and birthed. As he tumbled her onto the thick mattress, he thought briefly that this would be the place where his own children would be born.

Children another woman would bear him.

But before he gave himself over to all of that, like a sacrificial lamb on the altar of social acceptance, this old bed would bear witness to all the tender pas-sion within him. And for the rest of his days, he would look upon it and smile to remember this night, a pair of nights he had spent with a woman beyond measure. With Chloe.

Because that would be all he had.

It was happening again, the sensuous abandon that had claimed her once before and robbed every shred of sanity from her poor wretched brain. She had thought about the last time, the first time, until the memory was a familiar path and every moment was seared into her mind. This, what was happening now—his touch, his kiss, his tug on the tie of her wrapper—this, therefore, was a mere wisp of a dream, elusive and too wondrous to be real. She *wasn't* in his chambers, she *wasn't* in his arms.

He wasn't promising his forever love in an anguished, furtive whisper. He wasn't holding her face in his hands, gazing at her with turmoil in those dark depths. He wasn't promising her that she would always hold the best part of him, no matter what happened in the future.

The future—she didn't wish to think about the future. She wanted to scream this at him, but his mouth closed over hers as his hands worked quickly to divest them of their clothing.

The oil lamps still burned, enough light to see his beautiful male body. The warm silken skin over molded muscle tempted her hand to glide along it, feeling the tensile strength under her fingertips. He bent to her breasts, his mouth awakening unbelievable sensation, and then he was kissing her breathless again. His hand grasped one of hers, drew it down to where he was swollen and ready to take her. "Touch me," he murmured in her ear, his tongue coming out to trace the curve of it and multiply the shivers racking her frame.

She grasped him, holding him for a moment before she remembered the motion that had driven him wild the last time, so she began a clumsy stroking, one he helped along with the thrust of his hips against her thigh.

"Stop, my love," he breathed, catching her hand and pulling it away. "We must go slowly. This night needs to last us forever."

His words washed over her, dismissed by her feverish brain. Sensation filled her, need filled her, and her questing, gentle hands grew more insistent, pulling him closer, signaling her impatience to join.

He made her wait. With extraordinary precision, he petted and teased. Slipping into the secrets of her most intimate parts, he brought her to near release, only to pull away. She asked at first, pleaded next, and then full out demanded that he cease his torture, but he only smiled and began anew, and her voice failed her as the pleasure took over again.

But he dallied at his task, amused when she moaned in frustration. Finally, she pushed him onto his back. He brought her with him, rolling until she was on top of him.

His hands pulled her knees to either side of his waist. And then she saw what he meant and that she would have the power to sate her inflamed desire. He guided her, raising her hips, then lowering them over him until he was fully sheathed inside her.

The feel of him was exquisite. She arched her back, moaning softly as his hands came up over her breasts, teasing them until she writhed. He pulled her down to be kissed, stroking her back until his hands settled at her hips, grasping them tightly as the pleasure built. Their matched strokes allowed him deeper, filling her, bringing her higher until she spilled over into light like a thousand shattered stars. He thrust deeper, deeper, and she felt his body go rigid, bucking powerfully as the hoarse sounds of his climax tore from his throat.

She collapsed on him, spent and exhausted. His arms came around her, nearly crushing her, but she only smiled against the velvety skin of his breast. The feathery ripples of pleasure floated through her limbs, lulling her into contented bliss.

But when she looked up, resting her chin on his breastbone, his face held a disturbed expression.

"What is it?" she asked, touching his cheek.

As if an afterthought, a smile appeared on his lips, but it seemed a sad one despite his effort. "No words yet. There will be words enough later."

Of course, she couldn't allow a comment like that to go unchecked, but something in the way he said it, with a mixture of dread and acceptance, frightened her. She laid her head down again, silent and alone with her thoughts until his hands began to move again.

He took her again, this time with a wild fierceness that surprised her, especially after the lazy, teasing manner that had nearly driven her to insanity before. She gloried in his abandon, knowing this was the man at his most elemental. He was passionate and free and beautifully untamed.

Their bodies came to rest, limbs intertwined, hands caressing lazy circles on heated flesh in the contented silence.

Tenderness faded all too quickly as Chloe felt his body tense next to hers. His hand stilled its meanderings, his face grew dark as he stared at the ceiling. He was slipping away from her and she could do nothing, not understanding but knowing it was inevitable.

Jareth rose from the bed and punched his arms through his dressing-gown sleeves, pulling it over his broad chest and cinching it at his waist.

He spoke, his voice, which only moments ago had been soft and seductive, now rang hard and sharp. "You are to be dismissed. Tomorrow I go to see Lord Rathford and ask for Lady Helena's hand and set the date for the wedding. You must be gone by then. I cannot have you about when my new wife comes to Strathmere. It would be highly...untenable. You may stay on until the wedding day. You should use this time to prepare the children for your departure.''

If he had struck her with his fist, he could not have hurt her more. Breath came in short, strangled gasps as she blinked away the shock and pressed her hands against her forehead, trying desperately to clear her mind.

She wanted to rail against him, remind him of his promise never to part her from the children, appeal to him—something!—but the stony, cold expression on his face told her the matter was final.

Letting the knowledge of his betrayal settle inside her, twist up her insides until they ached, she drew on the pain to feed her anger. She stood, not caring that she was naked. It made her feel powerful, for she could see his eyes flicker over her body. Undisguised was the fact that he still coveted her. Throwing her head back, she said, ''I hate you.''

He nodded, as if he found this reasonable and understood perfectly. ''That is good. Hold on to that hate, Chloe, throughout all your years.''

There were French epithets she knew that she would have liked to fling at him, horrible phrases in English she had come to know, as well, that would wound him as deeply as he had her, but she bit them back. With as much dignity as she could muster, she dressed and went to the door. She faltered a little at the threshold, pausing to look back.

She had to credit him with this much—he didn't flinch. He watched her, every step, as she walked out of his room and his life.

Chapter Twenty-Three

When Jareth asked Lord Rathford for his daughter's hand, the man said simply, "Good God, man, I thought you were going to leave us hanging forever! Take her!" To which they drank a toast of sherry and Rathford spoke with relish to his imminent return to his former life.

"Now that you've come around, I'll have that she-cat of a wife of mine off my back. The woman can drive a fellow batty with her conniving and demands."

Jareth sipped his sherry and made no comment. If he appeared more dulled, less animated than a prospective bridegroom should, it drew no notice from his host. It was decided that the Rathfords should come to Strathmere for dinner that very evening and an opportunity would be availed for Jareth to make the request of Helena.

On the way home, he rode hard, pushing the gelding to his limits. He arrived at the front gate breathless and sweating and uncharacteristically disheveled to find a hired carriage waiting by the front doors.

Since the last thing he wished was company, he

groaned and set himself to avoid whoever it was as he entered the hall. He would have bounded up the stairs to his chamber or perhaps ducked into his library to avoid the unknown guests, when a familiar voice caught his ear.

Colin Burke.

A jolt of delight stirred his deadened heart. Unmindful of his appearance, he swung open the doors to the large parlor to find it was indeed his old partner, and a surprise—Serena Cameron.

She was as breathtakingly beautiful as he had ever seen her. The muted copper of her hair betrayed a feisty nature, but she looked demure just now, with her hands folded on her lap and her gray eyes holding her pleasure to see him again as she watched him enter the room. Jareth's eyes slid to her left. Gerald was seated at her side, no doubt making a fool of himself fawning on her.

His mother looked up. "Ah, Strathmere is returned."

Colin swung toward the door, a wide grin spreading across his face. "There you are. I thought perhaps you saw me coming and sneaked out through the kitchens." He strode toward his old friend, right arm extended.

They shook hands vigorously, Jareth clasping the man's shoulder with fondness. "Good to see you, Colin. To what do we owe this pleasant surprise?"

"I was on a run to York and thought—what's a few more hundred miles?"

"I see. Well, in the face of such extraordinary effort, I insist you stay on as our guests."

"Only for the night, since you have offered."

"Certainly. Mother, have Mrs. Hennicot have two of the guestrooms made up."

"Ah," Colin interrupted. "Just one will be fine. Serena and I have been married."

Jareth should have guessed as much. The man's excitement was palpable and the pleasure on his face was positively insuppressable. He congratulated Colin soundly and turned to Serena. "This is wonderful news. We shall celebrate tonight at dinner," he said as he bent to bestow the customary kiss.

She blushed, her joy apparent in her artless discomfort. Turning back to Colin, Jareth caught him beaming at his bride.

Tonight, he was to ask Helena to be his wife, but he would never gaze at her like that.

Jareth was immediately aware of a desperate need to get out of the room. "Come, Colin, let me show you what I am doing with my investments." They adjourned to the library.

Dinner was an ordeal. It might have been in any event, with the duty that awaited him at the meal's conclusion to ponder through six onerous courses, but their guests' presence made it much, much worse. Not that Colin or Serena did anything to make anyone uncomfortable, but one would have had to be blind and deaf not to notice their happiness. The scintillating tension between them was something one could *feel* in the air.

He tried to eat, if only not to draw comment, but it was difficult with his stomach clenched tight.

The faces around him were like a travesty. Lady Rathford, flushed with triumph, for tonight would bring the fulfillment of her dream. Lady Helena looking composed. Looking, in fact, the same as she had every day he had known her. Lord Rathford eating with relish, no doubt thinking of his freedom ahead now that the pesky business of marrying off his only child was behind him.

His mother, serene and catlike as she surveyed the scene, and Gerald, whose only amusement tonight was to stare openly at the beautiful Serena.

And then there were the Burkes, seeming as foreign and attractively exotic in this assemblage as a sheikh and his veiled concubine would have been.

After the meal, the ladies adjourned, leaving the males to their masculine traditions. Jareth could read Colin's concern, but the presence of the other men prevented him from pursuing it.

When they joined the ladies, Jareth requested that Helena take a brief stroll with him. The entire room fell quiet as she inclined her head in acquiescence. They left amid this expectant silence.

In the garden, he did it as it was to be done. Down on one knee, he proffered the family betrothal ring and asked if she would do him the honor, and so on.

She accepted and he rose, slipping the ring on narrow finger. The murky blackness held no stars tonight, so the large sapphire did not dance or show off any of its brilliance.

When they returned to the others, he announced the engagement and stood stiffly to receive their congratulations. Colin came up, questions in his eyes that Jareth had to ignore.

It was done.

Chloe took the reticule containing her wages from the past year and spilled its contents out onto the counterpane. It was a great deal of money, for she had spent little since coming to Strathmere. Just presents for Rebeccah and Sarah on their birthdays and Christmas.

Plenty of funds with which to return to France.

There was no time to write to Papa. She would see him soon enough to explain.

She would leave in the morning. Suppressing the urge to look in on the children one last time, she gathered up her savings and deposited them back into the old reticule, then placed that with her bags and the letter to the duke.

That was how she would think of him from now on. Only as the duke.

At breakfast the following morning, the duchess was in an unprecedented mood, all but purring in contentment. Gerald, still intent on the fantastic reality of Serena's gorgeousness, had offered a curt congratulations and went back to his gawking and fawning. Serena suffered this nobly, helped along by her husband's solicitous touches. These unconscious movements were subtly protective, as if part of Colin's brain was always trained on his new wife even as his sharp eyes never strayed from Jareth.

Frederick came in to stand behind his master and quietly whispered in Jareth's ear. Jareth knew Colin's gaze didn't miss the way his shoulders slumped slightly or the resigned nod he gave the servant in dismissal.

His friend and his new bride were set to depart directly after the meal, but when they were finished eating, Colin begged Serena's pardon and asked Jareth if he would help him oversee the loading of their bags into the carriage.

It was a flimsy enough excuse that Jareth was braced for the challenge when they stood alone outside.

"We've been friends for a long time," Colin began.

Jareth nodded, squinting at the clustering clouds. God, they reminded him of Chloe's eyes—steel gray against sapphire blue. "It's going to storm. You might want to think about delaying your departure," he said.

"You might want to think about this marriage, Jareth. Anyone can see you are miserable."

Jareth looked at him then. "Things have changed from when we were friends, Colin." His voice surprised him in its coldness. "This marriage is the right one for me."

"The devil it is."

Jareth said, "Helena is…perfect."

"She's admirable, certainly. You just don't want her. Is there someone else? Is that what has you as distant and stony as a statue?"

"There can be no one else for me."

Colin waited a moment, then nodded. "I see. I shouldn't have brought it up. Things aren't the same as they used to be. You are…well, things are different. I should have remembered that."

Jareth felt a moment of panic pierce his numbed state. Since the news this morning that Frederick had whispered in his ear, *Miss Pesserat is gone,* he had felt a curious and blessed detachment from all feeling. It was merely the culmination of what he knew would come, and strangely, it hadn't hurt. Yet.

But his friend's reaction did. Losing Colin's partnership had been difficult enough, but to allow the duchy to come between them and forbid the continuation of their friendship, that he couldn't bear.

"Please, Colin, forgive me. I…just cannot discuss this, not with anyone. Suffice to say you are correct. However, those facts change nothing. It is done."

Colin looked as if there were many things he would like to say in response to that, but instead heaved a sigh. "I'll wish you luck, then. And happiness. One day."

Jareth almost winced. He held out his hand and they shook. He said, "The same to you, friend. Never take for granted what you have. Never. Serena is…she's splendid, and I know…"

He didn't finish. He couldn't.

Colin swallowed and nodded before going back into the house to collect his wife.

Chapter Twenty-Four

Jareth's mother got started immediately on the wedding plans, holed up with Lady Rathford to discuss all the details. He didn't expect to be involved. It was not the sort of project he would find interesting, even under different circumstances. However, the two matrons made no pretext of consulting Helena, and this Jareth considered an insult. He told his mother this, and Helena was grudgingly included.

He heard that Chloe was still at the inn in the village, waiting for a ship that was due in a week's time and would take her directly to France. Jareth tried not to think of her, of how she was close enough to get to within an hour's hard ride if he so chose.

He still saw the children at least once every day. He had them brought down to tea or took them for strolls, to the lake, to the stables, into the woods, and tried to pretend he was still whole. They missed Chloe, too. Their somber faces pierced his heart like a thousand bayonet blades, but this he considered his just penance.

When he entered the drawing room one evening, Lady Rathford and his mother were sitting with material swatches spread over their laps. Helena sat in a corner, face turned to the dark window. He went to join her, looking out. It was a brilliant night, a night ripe for stargazing, but he felt no such inclination.

He wanted to make conversation, but found he had nothing to say to Helena. The elder women's conversation reached him.

"No, no, Charlotte. Helena looks awful in peach. Jewel tones are her best colors."

"But a wedding gown of jewel tones—you cannot be serious. It would be so gauche. Softer colors would suit the occasion best. Concentrate on a pastel palette."

His foul mood churned in disgust. "I have a novel idea, ladies," he said, advancing on the pair of them as stealthily as a tiger. "Maybe Helena would like to have a say in what gown she wears for her wedding. Helena? Would you like to tell us what your preference is?"

She seemed startled and mildly alarmed at his outburst. "I defer to the wishes—"

"You must cease deferring, Helena," he said curtly.

She bowed her head. "Yes, your grace."

"No! Damn you, do you have no spirit? Look at me and defy me at once for my rudeness. Speak your mind, woman. And I demand you stop calling me your grace. Nevermore, understood?"

"Yes, of course, sir," she said immediately, her face registering a modicum of alarm.

"How unnatural to address me so when I am your affianced. You will call me by my given name and no other."

"Strathmere," his mother gasped, "sit down at once!"

"I am not Strathmere!" he shouted. "My name is Jareth. It was less than a year ago that you all called me that, in this very house, this room, in fact. We sat here all together, and I was simply Jareth. Have you forgotten it so soon?"

Gerald tried to appear helpful. "I had not forgotten."

Jareth stuck out his arms, palms up. "*This* is Strathmere. It is a place, a building. It is also my title. It is not *me. I* am a man. Not a building, not a title—a man. My name is Jareth Hunt."

His mother's eyes flickered wildly to touch on the others. "Hush! Have you gone mad?"

He swung on her and bared his teeth. "Yes, Mother, I believe I have." At her blank expression, he exhaled, his sudden rage deflating. In a calmer voice, he said, "Look, Frederick is here to announce dinner. Would you like to go in?" He crooked his arm at Helena and led her into the dining room as if his outburst had never happened.

But once seated, he still felt like shouting, stomping, smashing. He loosened his cravat and picked up his spoon, trying to concentrate on the bowl of soup before him. The walls seemed to be closing on him, stifling him. Dear God, he felt on fire! "Is it warm in here? Frederick, open the French doors."

The footman did as he was bidden. The ladies wrapped themselves in their shawls, not daring to voice any discomfort. They cast him wary looks. His mother shot glares that were as sharp as daggers; the others seemed merely afraid. Helena sat stiffly erect, spoon poised as she took tiny increments of the soup to her mouth. Her eyes touched him, skittered away.

He looked down at his place setting, replete with cut crystal that shimmered brilliantly in the candle-light, beautifully pressed fine linens and bone china of the most delicate sort, rimmed in halos of gold.

I wish I were dead.

He jerked his head, hearing the words from Charles's diary.

The soup was eaten in silence. Lord Rathford, who appeared to care little for the peevish fits of a duke, commented that it was delicious, and the dowager duchess, grateful for his bravery in speaking up, agreed with enthusiasm. Gerald joined in the halting flow of conversation, always his aunt's best and brightest sycophant.

Sometimes I hate her.

Jareth closed his eyes and bowed his head, willing his brain under control. A vivid thought burst into his brain—that Chloe was still near. He could see her if he chose.

If he chose.

How I wish I were not to be duke.

"Your grace, you are not eating," Lady Rathford said.

His head snapped up, looking around at their faces, all turned toward him in expectation.

Jareth stood. Behind him, the expensive Chippendale chair crashed into the Hepplewhite buffet and then to the floor.

Tossing his napkin down beside his untouched soup, he said, "Please carry on without me."

"Strathmere? What are you doing? Sit down and eat at once."

He didn't answer. Striding to the door, he almost knocked a servant out of his way. "Where are you going?" his mother demanded in a voice perilously close to *emotional*.

Whirling on her, he faced them all. All of his demons, neatly assembled in one room. "To Chloe. I am going to Chloe. If she'll have me. I have no right to ask her to forgive me. I have behaved abominably. God knows I have so much to make up to her, I don't know where to begin. But I shall start this very night, and I shall not stop until she tells me it is enough, and even then I shall not let up because I love her. I love her to madness, do you hear me, and I cannot marry you, Helena."

To Helena, he said, "You deserve better than life with a man who wants someone else. We both do, Helena."

Lady Rathford stood, her face alarmingly red. "No! How dare you! I shall see you thrown in jail, you lying, duplicitous fiend. You cannot renege—the betrothal is sealed."

Lord Rathford appeared annoyed, as well, but his expression was more a mingling of exasperation and resignation. He gazed at Jareth as if to say, *See what you've done! Now she'll never shut up.*

What an inconvenience this would be for everyone.

Gerald was excited, his ruddy face ruddier. As for the duchess—Jareth did not even dare venture a glance at his mother.

But she made herself known.

"If you do this, Strathmere," she said, her voice as sharp as a razor, "you will be attesting before

these witnesses that you are out of your head. I can
have the title removed and Gerald shall inherit—''

''Do that, Mother. Do it. I beg of you. Do you
think I would dread such a thing? I can tell you I do
not. But you know as well as I that Gerald will prove
no easier to control. And I am a good duke, as
Charles was, if I am left to myself to govern this
duchy as I see fit and make my own way. But I
cannot do it alone. I need Chloe—to live, to breathe.
And I will have her.'' He gave the duchess a cold,
cold stare brimming with his determination. ''I *will*
have her.''

She visibly faltered, seeming to deflate as she
choked, ''How dare you put that little tramp above
me.''

''Mother, she is worlds above all of us. That is the
point.'' His mother groped for the arms of her chair,
sitting down with a plop.

Jareth lifted his gaze to the others. He caught Lady
Rathford's furious eye.

''You shall pay for this,'' the woman growled at
him.

Inclining his head, he said, ''I deserve your loath-
ing, madam, for not being honest with you and your
daughter sooner. But I shall not relent. The marriage
shall not take place.'' To the room in general, he
said, ''Now, if you will excuse me, I will take my
leave of you. And please accept my apologies on my
unforgivable behavior.''

And as he walked out the door, he passed Frederick. The man smiled meaningfully and said, ''Good
luck, your grace.''

Strangely, that small message—from a servant, no
less—buoyed him.

The momentousness of what he had just done was not lost on him. The future was uncertain—his and that of the Strathmere title. His mother's threats, he knew, were not idle. If there were a way for her to punish him, she would do it. But not at the expense of the duchy. Gerald would be a disaster. He hoped she realized that fact.

Yet he was not afraid. For the first time since his brother's death, he was not afraid.

He was filled with the euphoria of his emancipation. Not knowing what to do first, he went into his study and shut the door, prowled about for a moment or two like a caged beast before flinging open the glass doors and stepping onto the terrace. He strode out onto the lawn, breathing in deeply of the thick, sweet air, ripe with moisture from the mists rolling in from the direction of the sea.

Circling, he remembered. This was where she had romped that first time he had seen her, dress muddied, making ridiculous sounds and bounding about with that unnatural grace so that her gamine movements had seemed like art in motion.

He headed around to the back. There was her garden. He looked at it for a moment, recalling how she had danced to Helena's song.

Turning back to the house, he studied Strathmere, stretching wide and tall amid the wisps of cloudlike fingers snaking through the air. His home, his prison. Strathmere. It was really only a pile of stone, after all.

Like Charles, he would rather die than belong to this place and all it represented, but unlike Charles, he would never mature, grow into acceptance of his lot.

No.

He gazed at it all, a single word in his mind, final, definitive, unambiguous. *No.*

He went to the stables, his heart thundering in his chest. Dragging the gelding out of its stall, he saddled it himself, too impatient to rouse Daniel and have him do it. Swinging astride, he kicked in hard and pulled the reins to the right.

In the direction of the village.

Chapter Twenty-Five

Chloe did not think about Jareth while she waited for the ship to take her to France. She didn't owe him that. He had made it perfectly clear that he did not want her affections, that they were *inconvenient* at best, abhorrent at worst.

She decided he had been playing the oldest game known to man, the game of seduction. It didn't really sit well with her. And a large part of her knew better, but it consoled her to think this rather than the possibility that he had truly loved her, that he wanted her as much as she did him, but was simply too weak. Or perhaps too strong.

Instead, she worried over the children, thinking of that last time, when she had told them she must leave. She had resolved to be positive—no tears, no recriminations. She had sat them in their little chairs in the playroom and knelt before them, a forced smile on her face and a cheery note in her voice.

"I have some exciting news, *mes chéries*. I am to return to France." Immediately, tiny frowns appeared on their faces. Chloe had rushed to continue. "I am so happy, for I have missed my sister, Gigi, and my brother, Renaud, and my papa. I shall meet my tiny niece at last.''

Predictably, Rebeccah's response was sour. "I don't want you to go."

"But you must think of how lonely I have been, and how much I have missed my family."

"Don't you love us?"

That almost choked her. "Of course, *mes amours.* Never doubt it."

"But who will take care of us?"

Oh, mon Dieu! "Everything will be all right, you will see. Another nursemaid will come and she will love you. You will love her, too, and soon you shall not miss me at all."

Sarah shook her head. "No."

Rebeccah said, "I don't want another nursemaid." The familiar intractable look came over the elder child's face.

Chloe swallowed, treading carefully. "You must give her a chance, *chérie.*"

"I want you to stay!"

Sarah's blond hair flew as she shook her head more violently. "No!"

"There is other news, good news. Y-your uncle is to marry. Lady Helena is kind—you liked her, remember? You will be like a family again, *n'est-ce pas?*"

"No!" Rebeccah said, louder this time. "No, no, no! I don't want anyone else. I want you, Miss Chloe!"

Helpless, Chloe had let her facade crumble. She was never good at deception, what made her think she could fool this precocious child? "I must go," she said in a soft voice filled with her own sadness.

Rebeccah exploded into action, hurling herself off the chair, fists flailing as she charged Chloe. "I hate you for leaving me! Why do they always leave! I hate you!"

Chloe tried to catch the girl to her, to try to calm her, but Rebeccah flew out of the room, racing into her bedroom. From where she sat, Chloe saw her on her bed, kicking and pummeling, heard her muffled cries of frustration against her pillows.

But for the solemn little face still before her, Chloe would have retreated to her own bedroom and followed suit. She looked at the tiny child, touching the rounded cheek, watching it blur as tears filled her own eyes.

Sarah had simply said, "No, Chloe. Stay."

With Rebeccah's tormented cries echoing around them, Sarah had turned calmly and walked into the bedroom, climbed up into her bed and curled up with Samuel.

Chloe had stood in the doorway, clutching the frame for support. "I shall always love you, *mes petites*. Remember that." She had stayed thus until Rebeccah's wailing subsided and Sarah's breathing deepened, lengthened, and Chloe was certain they were both asleep. Then she had found Harry and tucked him under Sarah's arm. The cat, with its unerring instincts, had forgone his usual mischief and curled contentedly against his tiny mistress. Lady Anne proved as content in Rebeccah's bed as on her own pillow.

It was a small deviation from the rules, but under the circumstances...

The following morning she had left, with only a curt note to apprise the duke of her departure. She walked all the way to the village to await her passage home.

When the news of Jareth's engagement reached her, she became almost frantic to flee England. Only a few more days, she told herself, settling down to bear the last of her ordeal.

It was a few evenings later when she was seated in her small room, lost in her thoughts, that the door was pounded upon mightily. Startled, she stood up and backed against the wall, wondering who would come to her here.

Then she heard his voice. "Chloe! Chloe, open this door, please. It is Jareth. I wish to speak to you."

She looked frantically about her, as if another means of exiting the room would suddenly materialize in the solid wood paneling.

"Chloe," he said, softer now. "I know you are in there, the owner told me."

Still she didn't answer. Sidling silently to the window, she looked at the warped sash.

What was she thinking? She would leap from a window to avoid him—why was she suddenly so afraid?

She was, in fact, terrified.

"Chloe. If you do not answer me or unlock this door, I shall break it down."

She couldn't move. Questions screamed in her mind, deafening her to the pounding when it started up again.

Why had he come?

What did he want from her when there was nothing she could give him but her heart, something for which he had no use?

The wood began to splinter, and somehow the sound of this destruction broke her out of her shock.

"Go away! I do not wish to see you."

There was a moment of silence, then the whole room shook as he flung himself against the failing portal again.

"*Non!* You will not do this. Go away."

"Chloe, get away from the door."

Her mouth snapped closed and her eyes flared wide at his curt command. A second later, the door—what was left of it—gave way and he came stumbling into the room.

He stood there, looking wildly about him until his dark eyes found her. His coat was torn and there was blood, just smudges of it, up his arm where he had used his shoulder to decimate the wooden planks.

"Chloe," he said, and his face lost its terrible aspect. He came toward her, covering the distance in two long strides, and then he was on his knees, his hands capturing both of hers, his forehead pressed against her thigh.

"Chloe, forgive me."

She waited, stunned and unmoving.

Had he come all this way, burst in on her like a ravenous Hun, broken through a solid wood door, just to ask her forgiveness? Well, she wouldn't. Damn him if his conscience pricked him. Let him go to a priest for absolution—she would not ease his tarnished conscience with those words he wished for.

But her hand stole into his curls, feeling the soft texture, stroking the hair away from his sweat-soaked forehead.

"No, do not forgive me. Not today." Abruptly, he stood, her hands still in his. These he brought up to be kissed, each in turn. "I shall spend a lifetime asking you to forgive me every day, and when we are old and ready to sleep, you shall at last grant it, but not a moment before. Do you understand?"

She shook her head slowly.

"Of course you do not. Look at you, staring at me as if I were demented. I am, you know. I even admitted it to my mother when she asked me at dinner if I were mad. I have to be, do I not, to allow you to leave me?"

He threw his head back and laughed. "Oh, what a dinner it was. I am sorry you missed it. I swear it, we shall never take another meal apart again."

Chloe tried to pull her hands out of his. He held firm. "No, I shall not let you go—ever. Do you hear me? Ever! Chloe, marry me."

She grew truly angry now. "Have you grown lonesome for your cruel sport so that you had to seek me out here to play again?"

"What—sport? No, no. Listen to me, you little fool. I love you. I adore you. You are my life, you sweet idiot, and I cannot live without you."

"You love me," she repeated flatly.

"Oh, Chloe, if it were only love, I might have made it through all of this without having to toss everything else aside, but you have more than my heart. I am soulless without you, nothing without you. Just these last days, seeing all of my life stretch out before me without that spectacular smile of yours or the way you walk into a room like a prima ballerina entering center stage, or the ridiculous mess your hair is always in, or the storm caught in your eyes when you are angry—if none of those things I can ever see again, then I don't want anything else.

Chloe, I told them I wasn't going to do it—marry Helena, I mean. I told my mother that I was bringing you back and we are going to be wed—if you will allow it after all the ill I've done you—and that *you* were the one to whom I belonged, not the title, not the house, but to myself, and so I give all of it gladly to you.''

She was speechless, breathless, confused.

"Please, Chloe," he said, coming closer, cradling her face in his hands. "Take me back into your heart. I've come on a terrible journey, from far, far away, and I have finally made it to your side. Take me as your husband, I am begging you."

A single sob escaped her before his lips closed over hers. And then, like a miracle, he was kissing her, holding her, and she flung her arms around his neck and held on as tight as she could.

To her dismay, he cut the kiss short and shoved her away. "Oh, blast!" he exclaimed, patting his thighs and his chest as if searching his pockets for something. He suddenly looked apoplectic. "Oh, no."

"What?" Chloe demanded.

"The ring. My family's betrothal ring. Helena still has it."

"Does it matter?"

He grinned. "Does it matter to you?"

"Of course not, you dolt. What would I want with a ring?"

"Well, you shall be a duchess, you know."

She gave him a haughty look. "I have not accepted your rather *unconventional* proposal."

He sobered. "No, you have not. Will you, Chloe? Will you give me the chance to make it up to you?"

"No, I shall not. I wish our marriage to be done with all of the past. None of this nonsense of forgiveness and such—"

"Is that a yes?"

She was exasperated. "Of course. Why is it you never understand what I am saying?"

He chuckled, throwing his head back. "I shall learn, love, I surely shall."

"And I do not know what sort of duchess you expect me to be, but I shall certainly not emulate your mother."

His lips jerked as he fought a smile. "Of course not."

"And I am not going to dress in heavy brocades and prance about with my hair piled up so high that I cannot turn my head for fear of tipping over."

"I should not think so."

"And how will I ever get used to everyone bowing and scraping to me, and calling me your grace and laughing at my jokes when they are not at all funny, and—"

"And lying beside me every night, making love with me and bearing my children and looking upon a face each and every day that adores you," he whispered. "I do not know how you will bear it."

His words had been successful in melting her. "Oh, Jareth," she sighed, and reached up to kiss him.

In the instant before his lips touched hers, a thunderous explosion shattered their joyous calm.

"Jareth—what was that?" she cried.

He only looked at her, all traces of their earlier amusement gone.

"Jareth?"

Slowly, he slumped forward, landing heavily in her arms. She staggered under his weight as the acrid smell of gunpowder filled her nostrils.

Slick stickiness met her right hand where it grasped his back. He sank to the floor and Chloe went with him, not understanding until she looked up to see Lady Rathford standing in the doorway.

In her hand was a pistol pointed straight ahead, a slow curl of smoke drifting lazily from the muzzle.

"And now for you," she said, raising a pistol in her other hand.

"Mother!" another voice shrieked. "Mother!"

The gun went off. The roar of it seemed to Chloe to come from a long way off. More immediate was the brittle pop of the window frame inches from her head as the ball burrowed harmlessly in the wood.

"Blast!" Lady Rathford shouted.

Helena ran into the room, breathless and wild, her eyes wide as she cast her frantic gaze about the room. She saw Jareth on the floor, Chloe hunkered down over him as if she could stop the deadly balls from ripping into his flesh. The blood. The blood was everywhere.

She looked at her mother, dazed. "Mother?"

"Helena! Get out of here. How did you follow me?"

"I thought… Oh God, I hoped I was wrong." She looked back at Jareth, horrified as the full weight of what she had found descended on her brain. "Oh, dear Lord, dear sweet Lord, what have you done to the duke?"

Chloe stayed crouched, frozen, aware of nothing more than Jareth collapsed before her. She could feel his blood on her hands.

Lady Rathford snarled, "I killed him, and I'm going to kill his whore." Shoving one of the empty guns at her daughter, she barked, "Load this in case he is not dead. I may have to shoot him again."

"Mama, no!" Helena declared, recoiling from the weapon held out to her.

Lady Rathford shook the empty pistol at her. "I have already done it. I only need to finish it."

Helena looked about her with a frenzied expression on her normally placid face. "They will hear you downstairs. They must be coming now. We must leave."

Jareth lay unmoving, pale. Chloe felt frantically for a pulse. Nothing.

Lady Rathford scoffed, "Do you think this is the first time a gun has been discharged in this establishment, because I can assure you it is a frequent occurrence. No one will pay any mind. Besides, I know this place, I used to meet that idiot, Henken, here sometimes. I can get us out of here unseen. Now load that gun, Helena. Watch me. Take the powder…that's right. Now the ball. Shove it in good, make it nice and tight…good."

The world had ceased making sense to Chloe. While Helena followed her mother's instruction—blind obedience born out of years of subservience—Chloe could only think of the way Jareth's chest seemed so still.…

Fumbling for a pulse, Chloe found it at last. It seemed strong. There was no time to examine his wound. She simply pressed her hands, one over the other, on it to stem the blood flow. To her relief, she heard him grunt softly. It was a response, at least, and her heart filled with tremulous hope.

The Rathford women completed their task. ''Give that to me and wait downstairs,'' Lady Rathford ordered Helena.

Chloe looked up, her mind focusing on the twin threat of those primed pistols.

Lady Rathford held out her hand. Helena pulled back. Her expression was strange, washed clean of the careful composure Chloe had always seen. There was passion in her eye.

Helena said, ''So, then, I was correct when I recognized that man at Strathmere the day of the luncheon party. He came to the house once, didn't he? I remember how agitated you were. Secretive.''

Lady Rathford waved her loaded gun at Chloe. ''It was *her* I sent Henken to kill. He got confused in the fog and ran off without doing a thing. Well! I refused to pay him, of course, and he threatened to go to the duke and tell him everything. I didn't believe him until I actually saw him there that day. What luck! But not to worry, darling. I am ever favored by the fates. He is silenced.''

Helena's face collapsed and she moaned, ''No, mama. Oh, no. Why? Why would you do this?''

Chloe looked about desperately. Even if she could get clear of the woman's aim, she could never leave Jareth at their mercy. She had to think of something—something!

''Do you think you will not yet be duchess? Did you imagine I would allow this—'' she gestured again to Chloe ''—this *nobody* to take that away from you—from us! After all I had done to bring Jareth home? I saw how he was falling in love with her, and I had to stop it. Oh, darling child, you shall know only with your own children how deep a mother's love runs for her offspring. It was *I* who got rid of Charles. I saw after Jareth's visit last year how to make you the duchess. With Charles gone, Jareth inherited, and he needed a bride. You. I did it for you.''

This time, it was Chloe's breathless voice that spoke. ''You killed Bethany and Charles? *Mon Dieu!*''

Barely sparing her prey a glance, Lady Rathford continued to speak to her daughter. ''You shall reign at Strathmere, and our families will be, together, the most powerful in all England!''

''Helena—'' Chloe began, then stopped when Lady Rathford swung on her, arm raised. The gun was pointed straight at her heart.

Lady Rathford closed one eye and took aim.

Chloe looked to Helena, knowing this woman was her and Jareth's only hope. ''Helena, she is deranged. You can see that! You must stop her.''

Helena's face was wild with the horror of her mother's crimes. ''You killed them! And now you have shot him! You have shot the duke, Mother!''

Lady Rathford paused, the gun dipping as she turned to defend herself to her daughter.

Chloe half rose, seeing her opening. ''Yes, she shot him, Helena. The duke. And she has killed before. If not for chance, the children, too, would be dead at her hands. Think about it. She is a murderer many times over. Stop her—''

''Shut up, you little tramp,'' Lady Rathford snapped. The gun came up. ''You were the one to die all along. See what comes from forgetting your place?''

''All is lost,'' Chloe goaded, coming to her feet.

Desperation made her reckless. "Helena shall never marry the duke now."

Lady Rathford smiled. "She shall. Gerald shall become the new duke, and she, my darling daughter, the seventh Duchess of Strathmere!"

Jareth roused, groaning as his head rolled from side to side. Lady Rathford swung the pistol down at him, then up at Chloe again. "Give me the gun, Helena. Now. He is rising and we must finish this quickly."

"Helena," Chloe called. "It is up to you—you can save him."

"Shut up!"

No more delays. No more hope. Chloe crouched before the madwoman, watching as her index finger flexed on the trigger. She tensed, knowing the only possibility now was to leap at her and try to knock the gun aside.

She saw the knuckle turn white, and she knew there was no chance. And then she heard the shot.

She waited for the pain. It never came.

Through a dull haze, she heard a sound. She saw Lady Rathford was on the floor. Helena was weeping. The smell of gunpowder smoke was acrid and sharp, stinging Chloe's eyes.

It came from the gun dangling in Helena's hand, lifting in a sultry dance of pale light twining about her head like a perverse halo.

Under Lady Rathford's body, a slow, lazy puddle of crimson began to form.

Jareth stirred again. Chloe snapped her attention back to him, anxious to see the extent of the damage from the wound. She quickly undid his clothing, ripping apart the expensive material with strength that surprised even her. The ball had entered just under his shoulder on his left side. She was no physician, but it looked as if it was embedded in muscle, too far from the lungs or heart to have done any fatal damage, and the bleeding seemed to be stopping already. She bowed her head, offering a silent prayer of thanks.

He began to awaken. "Where—what happened?" He looked about him, then down at his blood-soaked shirt. "Am I shot?"

"Hush, *mon cher amour.* It is over. Helena has saved our lives."

His eyes flickered to the woman standing and the woman felled. "My God," he murmured, his gaze returning to Chloe. "Did they hurt you?"

She smiled reassuringly. "I am unharmed."

He closed his eyes as he relaxed back in her arms, too weak to ask more. Chloe settled him comfortably after tying a tight bandage around his torso, improvised from his shredded shirt.

"Go to Helena," he murmured. "I can hear her crying."

Chloe nodded, disengaging herself to move cautiously toward the other woman. Slowly, she unhooked the gun from Helena's limp fingers and threw it on the floor.

Pointing back to Jareth, Chloe said, "He is hurt. I need to go for the doctor."

"No," Helena said, wiping the back of her hand against her cheeks. "Stay with him. Comfort him. I will go."

As Helena turned to leave, Chloe reached out, touching her on the shoulder. Helena looked back.

"Thank you," said Chloe.

Chapter Twenty-Six

Jareth's recovery was slow. Although he balked at the meager rations of his meals and the forced inactivity—his boots had to be hidden from him after he was spotted attempting to sneak out-of-doors—the time spent healing was not so bad. After all, Chloe attended him. This was exquisite torture, having her so close at all times, yet with the vigilant chaperonage of Lisette. The portly maid sat in her chair by the hearth and seemed ever to be dozing, yet Jareth's hand had but to move one inch closer to Chloe's and the woman never failed to waken and glare, lest propriety be breached on her watch.

The enforced platonic relationship with the woman he was mad for was by far the most troublesome burden in his recuperation.

To Chloe, Jareth muttered, "How much longer do I have to endure the presence of that damnable woman?"

Chloe's smile held more than a hint of agreement. "Until you are released from bed by the doctor, or upon the event of our marriage, whichever comes first."

"Can't we just have the ceremony in here and get rid of her? I cannot even touch you, Chloe. It is driving me to distraction."

"For a man who was so despairingly bound by convention, you are making enormous progress into impulsivity in a short amount of time," she observed.

"Is that a complaint?"

She laughed. "When have I ever made complaint?"

It was his turn to laugh.

So, they contented themselves to talking. They spoke of Helena, who was closeted at Rathford Manor and refused to see or speak to anyone. Everyone was certain the inquest would be a mere formality and she would be cleared, but it was apparent she was finding it difficult to forgive herself.

"I feel some culpability in the matter," Jareth confided. "After all, it was caused by my actions. I couldn't say I would think ill of her if she blamed me."

"Nonsense," Chloe replied strongly, reaching for his hand to give it a reassuring squeeze. Lisette's chair creaked, an ominous warning to desist. Chloe twisted her mouth in disappointment and dropped Jareth's hand.

They talked of his mother. She had come only once to visit her son. It wasn't an errand so much to see to his recuperative progress as to inform him she was taking herself to the London town house—permanently. She would return for the wedding, and that only to avoid more gossip.

When Jareth told Chloe this news, she did her best to look serious. "Oh," she said, "does she really have to go?"

Jareth chuckled and did something in response to her mischief that sent Lisette into a full rise out of her chair.

They talked of the children and their joy at being reunited with Miss Chloe and Rebeccah's reservations about having Chloe become her aunt. With so much change in their lives in the last year—and none of it good—Chloe understood the child's fears. She did her best to reassure the both of them, as did Jareth when they came to visit, laden with drawings. They picked wildflowers and any other treasures they could scavenge to express their love for their uncle.

They talked about the wedding and the fact that Papa was to come with Gigi and her baby, and that Lord Rathford accepted the invitation Chloe had insisted be sent. This signaled there were to be no hostilities between the families, despite the fact that Helena understandably declined.

Jareth tried to be sensitive to Chloe's wishes as the plans for the wedding took on enormous proportion, but as he gained strength and began to assume more of his duties once again, it was clear that the wedding of the Duke of Strathmere could be no modest affair. Just his business obligations alone tallied up more than one hundred guests.

But on the day, when it finally arrived, even with the small orchestra playing and people packed into the pews of the village cathedral, and elaborate arrangements of flowers crowding the church and Rebeccah and Sarah tossing rose petals on a red velvet carpet, the simple woman who had captured his heart shone through.

In an exquisite gown of yellow silk, she glided down the aisle of the cathedral with that preternatural grace that had always bewitched him, her face so radiant he felt his heart ache. Even on this day, her hair escaped in willful tendrils, framing her face with an enchantingly mussed look that Jareth guessed the young women would be copying back in London.

She progressed slowly down the aisle, head held high as curious eyes followed her. She knew as well as he did that they had been the topic of countless conversations and speculations since the moment their engagement was announced. He had to admit he was more than a bit concerned about how she would hold up, but here she was with the same quiet dignity and self-possession that had delighted—albeit at times infuriated—him from the start.

And that smile, so true and bright and full of joy. Only Chloe could look like that, with her heart open for all to see, and melt the most sour looks of disapproval from some of his mother's friends, transforming each one into a wistful smile as she passed.

She was his. Forever. And for that he would face down every raised brow, every snide look from those small-minded folk who had once—almost—counted him as their own.

As he waited at the altar, he turned to the man who stood with him and exchanged a look. Colin nodded, as if he understood. Jareth supposed if anyone did, it was he.

Then Chloe was before him. Her father placed her hand in Jareth's.

He promised her his heart, mind, body and soul and listened as her faintly accented voice vowed the same. Then he kissed her, frustrated by the eyes that watched them.

But that night, after the reception at Strathmere,

he held her in his arms and loved her with all of the passion in his soul. No frowning Lisette between them now, not the bitter regret of all they wouldn't share as when they had last lain together, no obligations tearing him apart—just the two of them for the first time.

When they quieted, he held her for a long time.

"Ah, I do love you, Chloe," he whispered into the darkness.

She smiled and ran her cheek over the angular line of his jaw. "And I you, Jareth. Even if you are a duke."

His arms tightened, pulling her closer. "Come, love me again."

"Yes, your grace," she said softly, moving closer to comply. "I am, after all, your obedient wife. It shall be as you wish."

It was the first and last time he heard those words, but throughout the years, he could not say he missed them.

* * * * *

This season, make your
destination Great Britain with
four exciting stories from

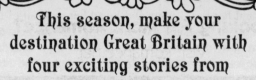

In October 1999, look for

LADY SARAH'S SON #483 by **Gayle Wilson**
(England, 1814)

and

THE HIDDEN HEART #484 by **Sharon Schulze**
(Wales, 1213)

In November 1999, look for

ONE CHRISTMAS NIGHT #487
by **Ruth Langan, Jacqueline Navin and Lyn Stone**
(Scottish Highlands 1540, England 1193
and Scotland 1320)

and

A GENTLEMAN OF SUBSTANCE #488 by **Deborah Hale**
(England, 1814)

Harlequin Historicals
Where reading is truly a vacation!

Visit us at www.romance.net   HHMED9

Looking For More Romance?

Visit Romance.net

Look us up on-line at: http://www.romance.net

Check in daily for these and other exciting features:

Hot off the press

View all current titles, and purchase them on-line.

What do the stars have in store for you?

Horoscope

Hot deals

Exclusive offers available only at Romance.net

Plus, don't miss our interactive quizzes, contests and bonus gifts.

PWEB

"This book is DYNAMITE!"
—Kristine Rolofson

"A riveting page turner…"
—Joan Elliott Pickart

"Enough twists and turns to keep everyone guessing… What a ride!"
—Jule McBride

See what all your favorite authors are talking about.

Coming October 1999 to a retail store near you.

HARLEQUIN®
Makes any time special ™

WIN A DREAM

In celebration of Harlequin®'s golden anniversary

Enter to win a *dream!* You could win:

- A luxurious trip for two to *The Renaissance Cottonwoods Resort* in Scottsdale, Arizona, or

- A bouquet of flowers once a week for a year from **FTD**, or

- A $500 shopping spree, or

- A fabulous bath & body gift basket, including **K-tel**'s *Candlelight and Romance* 5-CD set.

Look for **WIN A DREAM** flash on specially marked Harlequin® titles by Penny Jordan, Dallas Schulze, Anne Stuart and Kristine Rolofson in October 1999*.

RENAISSANCE. COTTONWOODS RESORT
SCOTTSDALE, ARIZONA

FTD

K·TEL

*No purchase necessary—for contest details send a self-addressed envelope to Harlequin Makes Any Time Special Contest, P.O. Box 9069, Buffalo, NY, 14269-9069 (include contest name on self-addressed envelope). Contest ends December 31, 1999. Open to U.S. and Canadian residents who are 18 or over. Void where prohibited.

PHMATS-GR

From bestselling author

Ruth Langan

comes a new Medieval miniseries

The O'Neil Saga

RORY
March 1999

CONOR
June 1999

BRIANA
October 1999

Siblings and warriors all, who must defend the family legacy—even if it means loving the enemy....

Harlequin® Historical

Available at your favorite retail outlet.

HARLEQUIN®
Makes any time special™

Look us up on-line at: http://www.romance.net   HHRL

This season,

**Harlequin®
Historical**

is proud to introduce four very
different Western romances that will
warm your heart....

In October 1999, look for

COOPER'S WIFE #485
by Jillian Hart

and

THE DREAMMAKER #486
by Judith Stacy

In November 1999, look for

JAKE WALKER'S WIFE #489
by Loree Lough

and

HEART AND HOME #490
by Cassandra Austin

**Harlequin Historicals
The way the past *should* have been.**

Available at your favorite retail outlet.

HARLEQUIN®
Makes any time special ™

Visit us at www.romance.net

HHWEST4

COMING NEXT MONTH FROM

HARLEQUIN HISTORICALS

- **LADY SARAH'S SON**
  by **Gayle Wilson**, author of HONOR'S BRIDE
  Desperate to protect the child she has raised as her son,
  Lady Sarah must seek protection from the very man she jilted
  four years previously.
  HH #483 ISBN# 29083-7 $4.99 U.S./$5.99 CAN.

- **THE HIDDEN HEART**
  by **Sharon Schulze**, author of THE SHIELDED HEART
  A nobleman on a secret mission for his country is reunited with
  a beautiful heiress whom he had loved as a young man, in the
  fourth book of The l'Eau Clair Chronicles.
  HH #484 ISBN# 29084-5 $4.99 U.S./$5.99 CAN.

- **COOPER'S WIFE**
  by **Jillian Hart**, author of LAST CHANCE BRIDE
  Sheriff Cooper Braddock saves a widow and her daughter from
  dangerous outlaws, then proposes a marriage of convenience that
  brings joy to their lonely hearts.
  HH #485 ISBN# 29085-3 $4.99 U.S./$5.99 CAN.

- **THE DREAMMAKER**
  by **Judith Stacy**, author of THE HEART OF A HERO
  A fiery young woman and a handsome farmer, who were
  swindled by the same man, find their dreams fulfilled when they
  team up as business partners.
  HH #486 ISBN# 29086-1 $4.99 U.S./$5.99 CAN.

DON'T MISS THESE FOUR GREAT TITLES AVAILABLE NOW!

HH #479 STRATHMERE'S BRIDE
Jacqueline Navin

HH #480 BRIANA
Ruth Langan

HH #481 THE DOCTOR'S WIFE
Cheryl St.John

HH #482 BRANDED HEARTS
Diana Hall